WALKER

LIGHTHOUSE SECURITY INVESTIGATIONS

MARYANN JORDAN

Walker (Lighthouse Security Investigations) Copyright 2019

All rights reserved. No part of this book may be reproduced or transmitted in any form or by any means, electronic or mechanical, including photocopying, recording, or by any information storage and retrieval system without the written permission of the author, except where permitted by law.

If you are reading this book and did not purchase it, then you are reading an illegal pirated copy. If you would be concerned about working for no pay, then please respect the author's work! Make sure that you are only reading a copy that has been officially released by the author.

This book is a work of fiction. Names, characters, places, and incidents either are products of the author's imagination or are used fictitiously. Any resemblance to actual persons, living or dead, events, or locales is entirely coincidental.

Cover Design by: Becky McGraw

ISBN ebook: 978-1-947214-38-5

ISBN print: 978-1-947214-39-2

❦ Created with Vellum

AUTHOR'S NOTE

I have lived in numerous states as well as overseas, but for the last twenty years have called Virginia my home. All of my stories take place in this wonderful commonwealth, but I choose to use fictional city names with some geographical accuracies.

These fictionally named cities allow me to use my creativity and not feel constricted by attempting to accurately portray the areas.

It is my hope that my readers will allow me this creative license and understand my fictional world.

I also do quite a bit of research on my books and try to write on subjects with accuracy. There will always be points where creative license will be used in order to create scenes or plots.

Four years ago, my husband and I discovered the Eastern Shore of Virginia and fell in love with the area. The mostly rural strip of land forming the peninsula originating from Maryland, has managed to stay non-commercialized. The quiet, private area full of quaint towns captured our hearts and we rushed to buy a little place there.

It has become our retreat when we need to leave the hustle and bustle of our lives. I gather ideas, create characters, and spend time writing when not walking on the beach collecting sea glass.

This is dedicated to my daughters who were able to travel to Italy and Greece when they were in high school. I am glad they did not have these misadventures, but their trips were an inspiration for this story.

1

Breathtaking. It was the only word Julie Baxter could think of at the moment. *Breathtaking.* And she should know, considering she had spent the last ten days looking at one incredible site after the other. With the sun shining in the brilliant blue sky and the lush green forests in the distance, she felt as though she could see forever into the past, peeking into ancient civilizations.

She had started her journey in Villahermosa, Mexico, on a two-week private tour of the Mayan ruins. In the past ten days, she had experienced the splendor of Mexico and learned more about the Mayan culture than she could have possibly imagined. Cities that lay in ruin. Buildings where the jungle threatened to overtake the stones. Temples to ancient deities. Architecture. Daily life. Royal life. Pyramids that reached to the sky affording a view unlike any she had ever seen.

And now, the city of Chichén Itzá was the stop for the day. The breeze blew her dark hair, whipping it about her face. Reaching inside her large, cross-body bag, she pulled out a hair clip and with a practiced hand twisted her hair up and clipped it into place. Reaching back into her bag for her phone, she began taking what seemed like the millionth picture since the tour had begun.

She wanted to capture every image possible considering this was the trip of a lifetime. On a teacher's salary, she would rarely be able to afford a two-week private tour that included luxury accommodations with all meals provided.

"Ms. Baxter! Ms. Baxter!"

Turning, she smiled at her charges. Tiffany Daniels, Andrea Tucker, and Jackie Dumont scrambled up the stone steps toward her. All wearing capris and t-shirts, comfortable sneakers, and ball caps to shade their eyes from the strong sunlight, they looked every bit the American teenager tourist.

"I don't suppose you'd have an extra granola bar in your Mary Poppins bag, would you?" Andrea asked, coming to a stop a few steps below her.

Responding to Andrea's pleading expression, Julie shook her head. "I told you to eat more breakfast at the resort this morning." As she spoke, she began digging in her bag.

"I know. I know," Andrea agreed, tossing her blond braid over her shoulder. "I just don't feel hungry first thing in the morning."

"That's not my problem," Jackie said, her hands on her hips. "I think I could eat anytime, anywhere!" She took off her cap and ran her hand over her hair before pulling the dark curls back into a sloppy bun, flyaway tendrils around her face already wet with sweat.

Tiffany plopped down on one of the stone steps and looked at her arms. She began digging in her small backpack, pulling out sunscreen. "I wish I tanned like you do, Jackie. All I seem to do is burn." With her pale skin and strawberry blonde hair, she was ripe for burning.

Julie's sharp eyes ran over Tiffany's complexion and immediately squatted in front of the young woman. "Let me see." Ascertaining that Tiffany was just turning a little pink but not a serious burn, she brought out more sunscreen. "You and me, sweetie. We both burn."

After a moment, the four moved to a section of the pyramids that did not have the direct sun beaming down on it. The girls shared granola bars and bottled water while Julie reapplied her own sunscreen. Pulling out her ever-present planner, she made notes of what they had seen this morning.

"Oh, it looks like Hernando is looking for us again," she commented, seeing their friendly, ever-smiling tour guide climbing the steps.

"What did you think?" Hernando asked, wiping his brow with a large, white handkerchief. Dressed in khaki pants and a khaki shirt he looked every bit the efficient tour guide. "Did you make sure to clap at each different side of the pyramid to hear the different sounds?"

The girls nodded, their enthusiasm never waning, and Julie was proud of them. A two-week tour of Mexico during the summer had been fun and educational but also hot and tiring. The girls were troopers and began chatting with Hernando, alternating between listening to his lectures and asking questions.

"Why does Chichén Itzá have less jungle around it?" Amanda asked, staring at the wide lawn of grass. "It's beautiful here, but Palenque looked more primitive."

Hernando rubbed his hands together and exclaimed, "Excellent question! The jungle around Palenque covers almost ninety percent of the beautiful site near the main temple. And of course, that's what gave it the beautiful, lush atmosphere. Because the Chichén Itzá is closer to the tourism of Cancún, the lands around it have been graded to push the jungle back. From what the archaeologists tell us, this is more like what it would've looked like when the Mayans lived here. With Palenque, the jungle has naturally grown closer and closer, overtaking many of the buildings."

Julie listened to Hernando's explanations to the girls' questions and soaked in all the history that she could, thrilled to be on this journey. Moving from the shade, the group made their way to the Great Ball Court where Hernando demonstrated the acoustically perfect walls. Sending the girls to different locations, he said, "Miss Daniels, turn and speak to the northern wall, and Miss Tucker will be able to hear you as she stands at the southern wall."

They all began to try his experiment, laughing as they realized he was correct. Using her phone, Julie videotaped the girls, deciding to send it to Senator and Mrs. Daniels that evening.

Hernando continued, "We know from the carvings along the walls that this area was used for some games."

"Like the Olympics in Greece?" Jackie asked, moving closer to the wall so that she could view the intricate carvings.

"I would like to say yes," Hernando admitted, "but we are not exactly sure. The walls are eight meters high, about twenty feet, and the entire length of the main playing area is over three hundred feet long."

"How does that compare to our football fields, girls?" Julie asked. She watched as they quickly calculated and determined that it was almost the same size.

"But why is the wall so high?" Tiffany asked, her gaze roving upward. "Where would the spectators stand?"

"It is supposed that the spectators would've stood at the top of the walls looking down. The sport has several variations that have been discovered through many carvings throughout the centuries. Generally, it is thought that the players would keep a rubber ball continually bouncing between these two walls."

Julie stood at the end and tried to imagine the shouts from those above as the players below engaged in an epic battle of sport. Just as she was wondering what accolades the victors would win, Hernando continued his lecture.

"They may have worn a belt of some kind, used to hit the ball." He moved his hips, demonstrating the movement, eliciting peals of laughter from the girls.

Moving closer to the wall, he captured their attention when he pointed to a particular group of carvings. "Here, we can see the depiction of a beheaded player, so we can assume that some of them paid the ultimate price when they lost the game."

"Eew," Tiffany shuddered, taking a step back. Julie moved closer and placed her arm around Tiffany.

"That's horrible," Andrea said, turning toward Hernando with a scowl on her face.

As the athletic one of the group, Jackie declared, "That's sports."

Nodding, he agreed. "If there's anything you've learned from me in the last week or so, it's that the Mayans were not to be trifled with. If you recall, when we were discussing Mayan culture, blood was considered to be a source of nourishment for their gods. They did not just sacrifice anyone. It was usually high-status prisoners of war that were sacrificed. So perhaps, whoever was forced to play in the Ball Court were prisoners. The lower status captives would have been kept for slaves. It is suggested that one of the reasons their culture did not survive was that they did not subjugate when they captured another kingdom. But rather, they would eliminate everyone."

"We've seen the pyramid and temple. Can we now take a look at the observatory ruins?" Julie prodded.

"Of course, of course! Follow me," Hernando said, his ever-present, wide, white-toothed smile beaming at them.

Julie gave Tiffany a one-armed hug and whispered, "Are you okay?"

"Yeah. I feel silly when I get upset about those kinds of stories." Giving a rueful chuckle, Tiffany added, "I've always been a scaredy-cat."

"I'm surprised that you wanted to take this trip."

"Dad really wanted me to do something different this summer since I'm getting ready to start my senior year. He and Mom researched the area and decided that this part of Mexico was the safest." Shrugging, she added, "And I really do like ancient history."

Seeing Hernando walk away at a brisk pace, she said, "We'd better catch up. We don't want to miss anything."

They jogged ahead, quickly pulling alongside the others as Hernando began pointing out the ruins of the observatory.

"Of all the ancient cultures, the Mayan's calendar system is the most complex and accurate. They used shadow casting devices and observations to trace the pattern of the sun. They used these alignments in the placing of pyramids and buildings in their cities."

As Hernando continued to lecture, Julie walked around, impressed with the ancient people's ability to study and learn. *Beats playing a ball game where only the winner gets the right to live!*

Not particularly athletic, she understood the desire to study the heavens much more than appreciating an ancient sport.

2

Walker paid no attention to the gorgeous Maine coastline nor the shouts coming from the grassy knoll next to the rocky shore. As a former SEAL, James Walker knew how to focus entirely on the matter at hand. And right now, the matter at hand was trying to get the ball into the net at the other end of the watery field of play while kayaking.

The two teams were evenly divided, five men each. Captain of his team, Walker claimed Rank, Tate, Cobb, and Bray. The other team, led by their boss, Mace, sported Josh, Blake, Clay, and Drew.

Mace Hanover had created Lighthouse Security Investigations, determined to hire the best. Each of his nine employees was recruited from former SEALS, Rangers, Special Forces, Deltas, and Air Force Special Ops, but they had also been trained as CIA Special Ops. Nicknamed Keepers from the Lighthouse Keepers of old as the original rescuers.

Mace believed in teambuilding, camaraderie, and staying fit, and none of them were opposed to healthy competition. *Or any kind of competition*, Walker thought as he came up behind Drew and used his kayak as a weapon, snagging the ball away. The waves made for an unpredictable playing field.

"Fuckin' hell," Drew cursed, righting his kayak and turning around.

It was too late since Walker had the ball, and his team was providing perfect coverage as he paddled toward the nets. Looking over, he saw Mace paddling from the left, fast enough to come between him and the goal.

"Walker…clear!" Tate called from the side.

Hating to miss his shot, he nonetheless fired the ball toward Tate who snagged it easily but was almost tipped over by Clay, whose paddle knocked the ball out of Tate's hand.

"Fuck," he grunted as Mace came at him from the side. Maneuvering around quickly, he paddled closer to Clay as Cobb captured Clay's attention on the other side. Even in August the water off the coast of Maine was cold, but as it sprayed over his body, the cool felt refreshing.

Clay tipped, and Walker snagged the ball, tucking it between his knees as he dodged the others on his way toward the goal. Seeing Mace coming at him again, he faked a toss, and Mace hesitated just enough for Walker to plow through the sliver of open water. With only a few seconds left before Josh came at him, he threw the ball into the net.

Hands in the air, a war cry was emitted while a cacophony of laughing and cursing ensued. No matter who won, the competition was good-natured, and the ten men began paddling toward the small strip of pebbled beach. Now, on the ocean field of victory, he was able to appreciate the blue, choppy water and full sunshine with only a few white clouds dotting the sky. Careful of the waves that were crashing against the shore, he easily maneuvered his kayak closer.

Beyond the rocks stood the tall, glistening white lighthouse. The main house was connected, white-washed as well, with a red roof. Even in August the grass was lush and green and the surrounding forest thick with trees. He had traveled all over the world but had to admit that Mace had found a slice of paradise to start his business.

Nearing the shore, the men jumped into the chilly water, lifting their kayaks over their heads, scaling the rocky hill toward the spectators.

Setting his kayak on the ground, he grabbed one of the towels laid out for them and scrubbed it over his hair and body. Forgoing a T-shirt, he enjoyed letting the sun offer its warmth straight to his skin. Tall, muscular, his dark hair and blue eyes gave evidence to his Irish heritage.

Mace's adopted son, David, ran over to give his dad a high-five. Walker watched as Mace's hard face softened into a smile as he thanked David for his exuberant cheering. Mace then walked over to his wife, Sylvie, planting a kiss on her lips as she beamed adoringly into his face.

Walker had seen that scene unfold before him numerous times, but it never failed to move him. He and Mace had connected once they were both assigned to CIA Special Operations. Mace was as hard, tough, dedicated, and as driven as any man he had ever met. Being with him during the process of building his business had been inspiring. Mace had never lost his edge but now managed to combine a loving family into the whole package.

David ran over to Walker and looked up with a huge smile on his face. "That was amazing, Walker. I didn't think you had a chance to get that last shot!"

Ruffling David's hair, he chuckled. "Your dad may have been Special Forces, but don't ever doubt the prowess of a SEAL in the water."

"I can't wait till I can play with you all," David exuded. "I'm going to be the best at kayabaskepolorestling!"

Walker and the others laughed at the name given to the LSI's mashup game of kayaking, basketball, water polo, and wrestling.

His closest friend, Rank, made his way over to his wife, Helena. Picking her up with his wet body, he twirled her in a circle as she screamed and laughed. Walker shook his head at their display as well. Rank was another meticulous planner of missions, but from the moment Helena dropped into his world, he had not been the same. Still meticulous...but with less hard edge.

"Let's eat!" Marge called out before swatting at her husband, Horace, who was first in line at the food table.

The others laughed and grabbed the heavy paper

plates as they moved to the food. Marge and Horace Tiddle had been hired by Mace, but Walker could not imagine what all their job description would entail. Horace, a retired SEAL, tended the grounds around the compound, kept the vehicles in running condition, and their equipment and weapons in top shape.

Marge, a former CIA Op, retired from the field years ago but had developed a special relationship with Mace. She took care of the LSI building, cooked for the men, and was all around den mother.

Babs, another CIA Operative and badass that Mace had met, had no problem keeping up with the guys, but she chose not to work in the field. Mace understood and respected her reasons, and the others accepted her, grateful for what she brought to the team. She, along with Sylvie, managed the business end of Lighthouse Security Investigations. Petite, her hair was cut shoulder length, black with purple tips. Walking by her, Walker pretended to bump her out of the food line, earning a laugh and a shoulder punch. Stepping back to let her go first, he observed her eyes constantly drifting over to Drew and wondered when the fellow Keeper was ever going to realize Babs was sweet on him, no matter how hard she tried to keep her feelings from showing.

Shaking his head, he was glad romance was not a bug that had bitten him and did not plan on it happening. He loved the freedom of choosing any mission that Mace needed him to go on, not worrying about the quick planning needed or being encumbered by a relationship back home.

With Rank and Helena making eyes at each other in the line in front of him, he gave Rank a slight shove, saying, "Move the fuck on. You're holding up the food."

Before he had a chance to say anything, Mace cleared his throat loudly, reminding them that David was present.

"Dad," David groaned. "Just because I hear curse words doesn't mean I'm going to say them."

"Sorry," he grumbled, the tips of his ears burning hot. Another reason to not have a relationship or become a dad...*I can't say what I want when I want.*

Soon the group had settled into lawn chairs scattered about the lush grass overlooking the ocean crashing on the rocks below. Behind them sat the white, red-roofed house next to the lighthouse. The lighthouse was no longer in use, and Mace had bought the entire acreage of land all around to ensure their privacy. Appearing as just a group of friends gathered for a meal, the outside world had no idea the hub of their compound had been built into the caves below.

With his belly full, he stretched his legs out in front of him, crossing his ankles. Leaning back, he closed his eyes and let the August sun warm his body.

Bolting awake, Walker sat up in bed, his attention sharp as he searched for the reason why he awoke. There were no sounds to be heard, and his Spidey senses were not going off. Laying back down, he punched his pillow, willing sleep to come again.

As a SEAL, Walker learned to sleep in any environment. The cold, hard ground. The hot, desert sand. On a boat rocking wildly in the waves. An airplane during turbulence. And now that he was a civilian, he sometimes found the soft mattress on his king-sized bed to be a difficult place to sleep.

A strange uneasiness had filled him during the evening hours, and sleep had finally come after fitfully tossing from one side to the other. Some nights the dull ache in his lower back kept him from finding sleep. He had chafed at his forced retirement when his back could no longer handle the physical demands required by a SEAL. Medical retirement was much more prevalent than most people would ever imagine for SEALs, whose bodies had been pushed to their limits.

Now, he wondered if he would be able to go back to sleep. Eventually, he did but remained fitful during the night.

3

To beat the heat of the day, Julie and the girls spent the late afternoon at the hotel swimming pool. The water was clear, and the surrounding area, filled with palm trees and the sound of birds, was a bit of paradise. The thatched roofs of the bungalows and the terra-cotta tile roofs of the main hotel, lush green grass, and thick trees around continued the realization that they were in the tropics.

They were traveling at a less-crowded time of the year, but August made for a hot trip. Occasionally dipping into the water herself, Julie spent most of her time stretched out on a lawn chair, hoping her pale skin did not burn while keeping an eagle eye on the girls in the pool. The trip had been a dream come true, one that she never expected.

The Ancient History teacher at Belford Academy, the private high school in Florida where she worked, had made arrangements with Senator Daniels' daughter and two of her friends to chaperone the two-week Mayan private tour. The week before departure, the teacher had to have an emergency appendectomy, and the entire trip was in peril.

When Senator Daniels appeared in Julie's office, she was shocked when he proposed that she become the chaperone.

"But I don't know anything about ancient history," she protested. "I would be no better than the average tourist."

"That's perfectly fine," he insisted. "It's a private tour, so you won't have to worry about being around a lot of other people. You will have the same tour guide for the entire two weeks, and I have vetted him and his company, assured that they are the best. My daughter adores you, and my wife and I feel that you would be the perfect chaperone."

Before she had a chance to protest more, even though the idea of going on the trip was already sending excitement through her veins, the Senator continued his persuasion. She looked down at her planner, already knowing the summertime was not filled with places she had to be or things she had to do.

"The accommodations will be at the best resorts. All meals are included. Airfare is already arranged. And you know my daughter, Tiffany, and her friends, Andrea and Jackie. They're mature, well behaved, and won't give you any problems. We just need a responsible adult, someone we can trust explicitly, to accompany them."

Her teeth nibbled on her bottom lip for just a

moment, but she could not come up with a plausible reason for why she could not take the trip. Her lips begin to curve into a smile, and she burst out laughing as the Senator was already grinning while rubbing his hands together with enthusiasm.

"Wonderful!" he said. "Of course, you will be compensated for your time."

Blinking with surprise, she protested, "That's not necessary. Just being able to take this trip is payment enough!"

"Nonsense. For the two weeks that you will be on this trip, Mrs. Daniels and I will offer you a full month's salary. We know it's an imposition to ask this of you so close to the time of the trip. We want you to be able to purchase anything that you might need for the trip and to take care of anything you might need to here at home before you go."

She had accepted his offer, and now, baking in the sun under the shade of a palm tree, she was so glad that she had. Never impulsive, she was stunned at how perfectly the trip was going. All three girls had finished their junior year of high school. Tiffany and Jackie were seventeen and Andrea was only a few months shy of her seventeenth birthday. They had proven to be the perfect traveling companions to chaperone. Mature, inquisitive, and extremely well behaved.

Glancing to the side, she observed several men with their eyes pinned to the three girls in the pool. She watched carefully, ready to pounce if any of them approached the teenagers, but she was pleased when they finally turned and went back to drinking at the bar.

"Girls," she called out. Gaining their attention, she said, "It's almost time for dinner." The girls dutifully climbed out of the pool, their youthful, bikinied bodies once again capturing the attention of several of the men, but thankfully the girls were oblivious. Once more glad to not be in charge of flirtatious, oversexed teenagers always trying to slip out at night, she stood and sent a scathing glare toward the men as the girls dried off with their beach towels and slid on their coverups and flip-flops.

If Julie was hoping to cease the men's attention, she only managed to have their gaze now slide over to her. Rolling her eyes behind her sunglasses, she turned and wrapped her towel around herself and walked with the girls toward their suite.

Dinner in the red-tiled dining room was not too crowded, and they were quickly served. The girls had grown used to drinking bottled water with every meal and had not complained about the cuisine during the entire trip. This particular restaurant included pizza and hamburgers on the menu besides their delicious Mexican food. She was glad the accommodations were such that she did not have to worry about any of the girls becoming sick.

Wandering musicians playing violins and guitars strolled amongst the tables. Glancing around, she saw several families and couples dining. One couple in particular, sitting at a corner table, stared into each other's eyes. They could not have declared themselves honeymooners anymore if they had had a neon sign plastered over their heads.

For a moment she allowed herself the memory of her own honeymoon right after college. Not in a beautiful resort in a tropical country, but rather a weekend at a ski lodge in Pennsylvania. She had been young, in love, and determined that they would be together forever.

"Ms. Baxter?"

Hearing her name jerked her from wandering down memory lane, and she swung her gaze back to her own table companions. "Yes?"

"We were just finished and ready to head back to the room," Tiffany said.

Embarrassed to have been caught with her mind wandering, she said, "Absolutely. It's getting late, and we have a lot to do tomorrow."

After dinner, Julie sat with the three girls in their large suite. Their accommodations throughout the tour had been wonderful, the private tour espousing the best hotels along the way. Pulling out her planner, she reviewed the notes she had made, inwardly glowing at the ruins they had visited so far. They had flown into Villahermosa, Mexico, and had toured Kolem Jaa, Palenque, Chicanná, Becán, Xpuhil, Calakmul, Uxmal, Kabáh, Mérida, and now Chichén Itzá. They had another day at Chichén Itzá before leaving for Tulum, and then on to a resort in Cancún, where they planned on a few restful days at the resort beach before flying back to Florida.

As with each evening, she asked, "What is your favorite so far?"

"I still like Palenque the best," Jackie said emphatically. Sitting on the bed with her back against the pillows, she explained, "While everything has been beautiful, the jungles around those ruins were just... I don't know, special, I guess."

"It looked like something out of a movie," Andrea added. "Today there were so many tourists around that I didn't get the chance to just imagine that I was in a different time and place."

Nodding, Julie said, "I think that's one of the things we have learned about each other on this trip. We like to look at ancient ruins and try to imagine what it must've looked like when they were in their prime."

"I thought the ones in the jungle looked more like something Lara Croft would have been discovering," Tiffany said with a grin, sitting on the bed, rubbing lotion onto her legs and arms.

"Well, the day after tomorrow will be a little bit different," Julie said, pulling the itinerary from her planner. She said, "We will head to Tulum and then spend the afternoon at the Akumal Ecological Center, where we will have a lecture on Sea Turtle conservation. "

Sitting up quickly, Jackie said, "Oh, that's where we get to go out on a turtle rescue team, right?"

Nodding, Julie continued to read from the itinerary. "Tour members will be part of the night search, patrol, and rescue team."

The three girls exuded excitement, and placing the itinerary back in the planner, Julie stood. "I'm heading to my room, so I'll say goodnight. See you guys in the morning."

With goodnights ringing in her ear, she moved into

the next bedroom of their large suite. An hour later, sitting on the balcony, she sipped a glass of wine. The quiet from the other bedroom indicated the girls had finally gone to sleep. She could see the light show in the distance taking place at Chichén Itzá, something they had enjoyed the night before.

Her eyelids became heavy, and she slipped into her pajamas before sliding into bed. Sleep came easily as the overhead fan helped cool the room.

Julie's eyes jerked open, uncertain what had woken her. She sat up quickly, cocking her head to the side as she listened. She could have sworn she heard a rumble in the distance, but as she sat there, all was quiet.

Wondering what she had dreamed, she climbed from the bed and walked to the small refrigerator in the room. Pulling out a bottle of water, she drank thirstily.

A strange uneasiness moved through her, but unable to discern the cause, she crawled back into bed she and pulled the sheet over her, willing sleep to come again.

4

Walker never set an alarm, relying on his internal alarm clock to always wake him at the right time. Climbing from bed, he headed to the shower, already anticipating the first cup of coffee of the day.

His apartment was old but comfortable. He did not like the large, open, industrial look of many of the newer apartments, preferring the wooden floors and exposed brick walls of his two-bedroom, third-floor apartment.

Padding into the updated kitchen that he enjoyed cooking in, he had barely poured his caffeine-hit when his phone rang. Looking at the caller ID, he answered, "Sarah. Why the hell are you up so early?"

"Mommy! Uncle Jimmy said a bad word!"

Dropping his chin to his chest, he shook his head. "Susie, why are you calling me this early in the morning? Put your mom on the phone." He heard the jostling of the phone before his sister answered.

"Jimmy! Why are you saying a bad word to Susie?"

"I didn't know it was Susie, now did I? My phone rings this early in the morning and the caller ID says it's you, so pardon me for assuming it was you."

Sarah huffed, "So you'd be cussing at me? And that makes it okay?"

Pinching the top of his nose with his thumb and forefinger, he stared down at his cup of coffee, wondering if it was going to be enough for today. "Sorry, Sis. Let's start over." Clearing his throat, he grunted, "Good morning, Sarah. What can I do for you?"

She laughed, saying, "The words sound better, but you still sound like a big grump. You never were much of a morning person. Anyway, I wanted to remind you that today is Mom and Dad's wedding anniversary. I know they'd love to get a call from you."

As much as his older sister could be a thorn in his side, he appreciated that she kept him apprised of family dates that he would undoubtedly forget. She never made him feel guilty, understanding that his job sometimes made it difficult to remember those occasions. "Thanks, Sarah. You're the best. I'll make sure to give them a call later on today." Getting ready to disconnect, he added, "Sorry about what I said to Susie. I'll try to answer the phone a little nicer now that I know she's old enough to place a call."

His sister cackled then said she loved him before disconnecting. Taking a grateful sip of coffee, he added calling his parents to his mental list of things he needed to get done today. With a quick look at the clock on the stove, he poured his coffee into a travel mug and headed off to the compound.

Driving to the LSI compound, he reveled in the fact that he did not have to work in a corporate office. Nodding to Horace and Marge as he walked through the kitchen of the house, he hustled down a back hall toward the lighthouse. Turning to the wall, he opened a hidden panel, tapped in a security code, then stood for the retina scan. Next, he placed his finger on a finger scanner and waited while his digital prints were taken. A door swung open, and he moved through quickly, shutting it behind him.

He tapped another security code into the elevator panel and began the descent downward. At the bottom, the door opened, and he walked down a hallway with a single door at the end. Repeating the security systems again, the final door swung open. The main room of the Lighthouse Security Investigations was a cavernous space, the walls and ceilings reinforced with steel beams and panels. Underneath his feet was a concrete floor, smooth and solid while retaining the original look of the cave. Mace had had the room sealed and environmentally protected, and it was filled with computer equipment, stations where several of the men were already manning the keyboards while staring at screens.

Specialized printers, processors with high-speed connections, servers, and other computer equipment filled the back wall. Another wall contained large screens, multiple images flashing upon them. Software tools, specific to each employee, enhanced their ability to organize, access, and analyze information.

Hurrying by two of the desks near the entrance, he offered chin lifts to Babs and Sylvie on his way toward the conference table. Glad to see he was not the last one there, he snagged a loaded breakfast biscuit from a basket sitting in the center.

Chewing gratefully, he said, "Thank God for Marge's breakfast biscuits!"

The others chuckled knowing that Marge, who could take down a much bigger man, use a weapon with deadly accuracy, and was incredibly intelligent with a sharp, analytical mind, could also cook like a southern grandma.

The last few Keepers came into the room, and the group quickly settled as Mace brought the morning meeting to order. "Blake? Updates on the Honduras situation?"

"I'm still working with the CIA agent and thought I was going to have to travel down there this week, but the CIA's person of interest has already been brought back to the States," Blake began.

"When were you going to tell me you wanted me to cancel the travel arrangements?" Babs asked, piping up from the corner, a scowl on her face.

Ducking his head, Blake mumbled, "Sorry…uh…I guess I won't need those travel arrangements."

The group grinned as Babs muttered her own curses from her desk as her fingers began flying over the keyboard.

Continuing, Blake added, "I'll get my report in after I have another meeting with the agent."

With a short nod, Mace looked at Tate. "Identity changes?"

"We're working on one right now, with another possible two coming up. I get the feeling from the FBI director, Jerry Dalton, that he would like to use us exclusively for their identity changes."

Walker looked between Tate and Mace, seeing a dark eyebrow lift on his boss' sardonic face.

Tate quickly said, "Don't worry. I made no promises and reminded him he would have to talk to you about that." Shrugging, he continued, "But, for now, it's just a couple that I'm finishing up."

"Chatter?" Mace asked.

One of the things that Mace had emphasized was that he felt strongly about using LSI's resources for local and national assistance when necessary. He had the Keepers routinely monitor police reports, reading and dismissing most taglines until they came across one that snagged their attention. Then, with a little research, they could determine if it was a case that they felt needed their assistance. It was on a mission like this that Mace met Sylvie when David witnessed a murder and the local police did not believe it occurred.

Drew leaned back in his chair and shook his head. "I came in early and checked but didn't come across anything that looked like it needed us."

Several more Keepers gave reports on the missions they were working on, and Mace brought the meeting to a close as he gave out a few new assignments.

Walker headed over to his computer station, having

agreed to work with Tate on one of the identity changes. He never minded any of the work that Mace assigned to him, but he nonetheless felt the itch to get back out into the field. As he thought on the strange feeling he had in the middle of the night, he wondered what it could mean. *Maybe something interesting will come in today.*

5

The morning was spent continuing their tour of Chichén Itzá, following Hernando around as he lectured on the various buildings and history. Julie had read that they were no longer able to climb to the top of El Castillo, listed as one of the new seven wonders of the world, because years before a woman had fallen to her death.

"Wouldn't it be amazing if we could go to the top?" Tiffany said, her head leaned back as her gaze reached the top of the temple.

Smiling benevolently, Julie said, "Just pretend that you're one of the common Mayan people. They would have never been allowed to enter many of the structures and certainly not climb to the top."

Turning around in a circle with her arms spread wide, Andrea said with awe, "It's so hard to imagine that these buildings have been here for over a thousand years and are so well-preserved!"

Smiling widely, Hernando beamed. "You ladies are an absolute dream for a humble guide like myself. To be able to show our beautiful sites and historical architecture to someone so young and so appreciative makes me truly happy."

Julie could not help but meet his smile, pride moving through her. They finished their tour and began walking back to the parking lot. Their resort was right next to Chichén Itzá, but in the hot sun, the walk would have been unbearable.

Snapping a few last pictures, she tucked her phone into her bag, pulled out water bottles for the girls, and climbed into Hernando's small van.

He dropped them off at the front of the resort and said, "You have time to eat lunch here and then you will need to have everything packed and ready to load up by one o'clock this afternoon. Then we will travel to Balam Caverns for a tour and lecture before traveling to our next destination."

Leading the girls through the lobby, Julie said, "Let's go back to the room and freshen up and get our bags packed. Then we can meet down at the restaurant for lunch."

Glad for the two bathrooms in their large suite, Amanda and Tiffany took showers first, and then Jackie and Julie did the same. As she was getting dressed, there was a knock on the bathroom door.

"Ms. Baxter? Is it okay if we go on down and get a table?" Tiffany asked.

Ever cautious, Julie had made sure to accompany the girls everywhere, but she was almost ready, so she agreed. "Grab a table, and I'll be there in just a moment." She heard the door close, and she pulled her hair back into a ponytail. With a swipe of lip balm, she stepped out of the bathroom, grabbed her purse, and made sure to lock the door as she left.

Since they were only on the second floor, she decided to skip the elevator and take the open-air steps that were close to their room. Pausing on the landing for just a moment, she cast her gaze out over the palm trees and lush grass surrounding the blue swimming pool. This, by far, was the nicest resort they had stayed in, and she almost hated leaving it. But in another two days, they would be in Cancún, at a huge resort with multiple swimming pools, pristine white sand beaches, and a chance to simply lie in the sun.

She placed her hand on the rail as she turned to go down the last steps when a loud, rumbling boom sounded out and the world began to shake. She fell forward, bouncing on the last few concrete steps, crying out in pain. A large crack appeared in the wall next to her and bricks began to shatter, falling from the ceiling, crashing all around.

Scrambling to her feet, she threw her hands over her head and tried to run into the cafeteria, her steps as wobbly as a drunk. The screams of others met her ears, and her gaze darted around the room. Part of the ceiling had crashed to the floor, chairs overturned, dishes shattered next to upended tables.

Desperate to find the girls, she screamed for them, grateful when Jackie screamed her name in return. Their wide-eyed, frightened expressions locked on hers and they rushed to her, their steps as drunken as hers. They clung to each other, tears streaming down Tiffany's cheeks while Andrea's and Jackie's expressions registered shock. The shaking of the building had slowly subsided, but as she looked above to a precariously swinging light fixture, she cried, "We've got to get out of here!"

She herded them through the large doors, the glass now shattered about the floor. Rushing over the grass along with other resort visitors and staff, they stood near a tree.

"Oh my God, oh my God," Andrea cried, pale and shaking.

Tucking Andrea close to her, she felt the girl's body quivering, and with her hands on her shoulders pushed slightly, encouraging her knees to buckle so she could sit on the grass.

"Ms. Baxter, what are we going to do?" Tiffany asked, her lips trembling and her chest heaving.

"Our stuff. All our stuff is in the room," Jackie moaned, kneeling next Andrea. She jerked her face up toward Julie's and continued, "I left my purse up there. I shouldn't have, but I left my purse up there and it's got my passport!"

Standing, Julie looked around, her mind racing. People were still pouring out of the resort, some being held by others, some with injuries. *Hernando? Where's Hernando? He'd know what to do.*

Not seeing their intrepid tour guide, she tried to reason out the best thing to do. Squatting, she said, "Girls, listen to me. I need you to focus and listen carefully to me." Assured that she had their full attention, she said, "I'm going to run up the steps and grab what I can. I won't be able to get everything, but I'll grab what I can, especially your purses and passports. But do not leave from this spot! I don't care what anyone says to you or who comes by…you must stay here! When I get back out here in a few minutes, I can't wander around wondering where you are. Promise me!"

The promises from the girls came quickly, and she squeezed their hands. Uncertain if she was making the right decision, she refused to waste any more time thinking about it and ran toward the building.

The crack in the wall running by the stairwell was even wider, but she refused to focus on the danger. Several more people were hurrying down the stairs, and she pushed against them, going against the flow. Rounding the top of the concrete steps, she rushed to their room, pulling out the room key with shaking hands. Fumbling, she prayed that the earthquake had not disarmed all of the automatic doors. "Come on, come on," she grunted in frustration. Finally hearing the click, her breath left her lungs in a rush as she pushed open the door.

Their room was a mess, more cracks in the walls exposed, tables toppled over, and the glass windows were shattered. Stopping for a second, she closed her eyes and centered her focus, forcing her tangled thoughts to what she needed. *Purses. Passports. Change of clothes. Water bottles!*

She ran to the girls' bedroom, finding Jackie's purse, glad that Andrea and Tiffany had theirs. Throwing open their suitcases, she grabbed a few clothes from each one, shoving them into their small travel backpacks, heedless of which clothes went into which case. Remembering that the girls were wearing flip-flops, she saw their sneakers near the beds and grabbed those as well.

The building began to shake again, and her heart halted its beat for a second until the shaking stopped. *Aftershocks. That must've been an aftershock.* A few more pieces of ceiling tile fell, and her sense of urgency heightened even more.

Running into the next bedroom, she grabbed her larger backpack, shoved some clothes in it, glad she was wearing her sneakers. Racing to the small refrigerator, she filled another bag with water bottles and all the snacks they had accumulated.

Arms now full with four backpacks filled to capacity, another bag equally heavy with food and water, and her ever-present large purse stuffed with more things she could grab, she fled the room.

The building shook with another aftershock, this one slightly stronger than the last, just as she got to the stairs. Shock and adrenaline had kept her from noticing the pain in her wrist and knees, but she instinctively clutched the railing as she went back down. Continually glancing above, praying no pieces of the building were going to fall on her, she rushed out onto the lawn.

Hearing her name screamed, she looked up, grateful to see all three girls where she left them, now running toward her. They collapsed to the ground, and she fought to catch her breath.

"When we get somewhere safe, we'll repack everything so that you know what's in your own bag. I was just grabbing and shoving things in any bag open, so I'm sure all your stuff is everywhere. Double check to make sure you've got your passports, phones, and billfolds."

"You're hurt!" Jackie exclaimed, looking down at her shins.

"It's just some scrapes," she said, glancing down at the abraded skin. "I'm fine."

"Ms. Baxter, we haven't seen Hernando yet," Tiffany said, her eyes watery.

Reaching over to grab her hand, Julie squeezed. "I'm sure he's running around looking for us." The lawn was filled with other vacationers and staff, some nursing injuries, many crying. Standing, she spied a tall palm tree off to the side and said, "Let's go over there. We can go through our belongings, and I think Hernando will be able to find us more easily if we're out of the main crowd."

"What's gonna happen to us?" Jackie asked.

Shaking her head, she replied, "I know we'll be fine, and I don't know exactly how the resort management and local police are going to handle this, but I'm sure we'll be fine. If the van is okay, then Hernando can find us and get us out of here."

She herded the girls over to the bare ground near the tall palm tree, and they set their bags down, kneeling next to them. Wanting to give them an occupation to focus on, she said, "Dump everything out and carefully go through it. Take your things and put them in your own bag."

While the girls divided the belongings that she had

managed to grab, she stood guard over them as she tried to ascertain if there was any rhyme or reason to what the resort management was doing. Her wrist was beginning to throb, and she was grateful when a man walked over to them and asked if they needed any medical assistance.

"I think we're okay, except I fell when leaving the building, and my wrist may be sprained."

He gave it a cursory glance, dug into his bag, and pulled out an elastic bandage. "This is all I have." He handed it to her before hustling over to the next group.

She wrapped her wrist as best she could, then turned to see how the girls were doing. Pleased to see they were finished, they stood, each slinging their own backpack over their shoulders. Turning back around, her gaze continued to scan the madness of the scene before her, searching desperately for any sign of Hernando.

"Where can he be? He must be looking for us."

"Can you call him?" Jackie asked.

Swinging her head around, she realized that Jackie had come up with a solution she had never thought of. *Jesus, I'm the one who supposed to be taking care of them!* Nodding, she said, "You're right." Pulling her phone out of her bag, she dialed the number he had given them on the first day. The phone rang several times, but there was no answer.

Finally turning back to the girls, their wide eyes staring at her, she recognized trust. *Shit. They're looking at me to make this all better, and I've got no frigging clue what I'm doing!* Giving a quick mental shake, she said, "I think we need to walk around and see if we can find

Hernando. I want us to stick together, though. Under no circumstances do I want us to separate at all."

The girls immediately nodded, none appearing to desire separation either. Making sure they had all their belongings, they began walking through the throngs of people, searching for any sign of their guide.

The earthquake had only struck forty-five minutes earlier, but evidence of humanity was all around. People were assisting each other. Hotel staff was passing out water bottles. And the few harried medical personnel helped those they could.

Turning to the girls as they continued to scan the area for Hernando, she assured, "We'll be fine. There'll be food and drink here, and I'm sure rescue officials will come and let us know what to do." As the words left her mouth, she realized she had no certainty that she was speaking the truth but could not imagine that help would not come.

The sound of a phone ringing met her ears, and she turned to look at Tiffany as she was digging in her bag. Tiffany pulled out her phone, looked at the caller ID, and connected. "Dad? Dad, can you hear me?" She paused for only a few seconds, and then burst into tears, saying, "Dad, there was an earthquake!"

6

The morning had continued to be slow, each of the Keepers working on their assignments. Walker considered what he wanted to do for lunch. It would take almost thirty minutes to drive to the nearest restaurant, but Marge kept a well-stocked refrigerator and pantry in the house upstairs. *At least I can fix a sandwich. And maybe Marge will have some of her homemade soup as well.*

Disgusted with himself for spending so much time thinking about food, he recognized the restlessness as needing to get out into the field. Deciding on a workout in the gym, he stood, stretching his back, wincing at the pain that always hit him after he had been sitting for too long. Before he had a chance to see if anyone else wanted to hit the gym, Babs called out, "Mace! Senator Daniels from Florida is on the line. Says it's an emergency."

"Put him on speaker," Mace ordered.

Walker turned and faced his boss, and like all the other Keepers was immediately on alert.

"Senator Daniels. Mason Hanover here, what can I do for you, sir?"

"Mr. Hanover, I need you and I need you now." The Senator's words were rushed, and his voice was shaking with obvious emotion. "My teenage daughter is on a trip in Mexico, and they just had an earthquake."

Mace nodded toward Tate, who, with a few clicks of his keyboard, pulled up the news and a map of Mexico on the big screen. According to the seismologists, an 8.2 earthquake had occurred in the Yucatán between Mérida and Chichén Itzá.

"Have you had contact with your daughter?"

"Yes, I just managed to get hold of her, but we could only talk for a moment. She and two friends are with a chaperone on a two-week tour of the Mayan ruins. According to their itinerary, they were at a resort next to the Chichén Itzá ruins. She said the resort is destroyed, but they're okay. I tried to make some calls, but it's chaos down there. I even tried to book a private jet to get me there, but I'm afraid I won't be able to get to her in time by the time I get a clearance to travel there. My wife is hysterical, and I confess that I'm not much better."

Walker heard Senator Daniels voice crack, and he thought of how terrified his sister would be if anything happened to his niece. He swung his head around, making eye contact with Mace, and with a nod indicated that he was in.

Mace gave Senator Daniels a moment to pull himself

together, then said, "Sir, I'm going to need you to send me everything you've got. I need their names, passport information, itinerary, phone numbers, everything. I'll hand you back over to my administrative assistant who will get the information from you and give you a secure email to use."

"So…" the Senator began, then cleared his throat. "So you'll take this? You'll go get my daughter and her friends?"

"Absolutely, sir. We'll start initial planning right now, and as soon as we get the information from you, we can move forward."

With a nod, Sylvie took the call off speaker and began to talk calmly to the Senator, getting the information from him. Hanging up, she looked over at Mace and said, "He'll get it to us in a few minutes, and I'll send it to the screen."

Mace turned toward Walker and said, "You want this?"

Nodding, he replied, "Absolutely. I know some of the others have missions they're working on currently, but my slate is almost clean." Looking toward Drew, he asked, "What about you? Can you get us in and out?"

Drew had been an Air Force pilot with their Special Ops and could fly planes as well as helicopters with ease. Walker noted the spark in Drew's eyes as he grinned and nodded.

"I'll start lining up flights and birds," Drew said, immediately plopping back down into his chair with his fingers on his keyboard. Looking over his shoulder, he called out, "Babs? Come on over here and help me get these things lined up."

"You just want me sitting next to you, big boy," Babs quipped, standing and moving over to a chair next to him anyway. Casting him a narrow-eyed glare, she said, "Just make sure you keep your big mitts on the keyboard and off my leg or you won't be able to use your fingers for anything since they'll be in little miniature casts."

"Damn, you're a hard woman," Drew replied as he winked at her before turning his attention back to the screen.

Mason and Walker walked over to another computer, watching as Sylvie forwarded the information to them. Tiffany Daniels, age seventeen. Jackie Dumont, age seventeen. Andrea Tucker, age sixteen. Julie Baxter, chaperone...who looked barely out of her teens. *Shit, three teenage girls and a young female chaperone.* Checking her age, he was stunned to discover that she was thirty years old. Her passport photograph was not flattering, but he could still admire her beauty. Dark hair, pale complexion, dark eyes, and lips that held a slight smile as though she had a secret and could not wait to spill it.

Blinking, he pushed her appearance to the back of his mind and continued to read. Counselor at the small, private high school in Florida. *Still, she must be completely out of her element.* Hoping they would be smart enough to stay with the group and out of trouble, he, Mace, and several of the others began planning the mission.

"The resort they were staying at is a four-star resort,

so they should have plenty of food and bottled water to last until we can get there."

Blake, working at his station, called out, "I'm working intel on the area. No way would the Senator need to be heading into this mess. There are at least four drug cartels that are working the area in the Yucatán, from Cancún westward, including the area where the girls are. For vacationers coming in and staying at resorts, there haven't been a lot of incidents, but I'm already seeing chatter of movement. With the instability of villages, cities, and resorts due to an earthquake, they would be quick to move in, ready to take advantage of the lessened police protection."

"I'd feel a fuck of a lot better if the girls were already in Cancún," Walker said. "According to their itinerary, they would've been there in two more days."

"I got a plane that can get us down to Florida where we can refuel, and then we can make it to Mérida," Drew said. "Once we get there, I've got a contact that can get a bird for us to get to the resort to pick up the girls and get us back to our plane."

Printing off the information that he would need, Walker said, "We can pack from here, get what we need, and head straight to the airport."

With a curt nod from Mace, Walker grabbed the papers off the printer, called over his shoulder for Sylvie to send the rest to him, and headed down the hall to their equipment room. Drew followed, and they grabbed duffel bags and began to pack weapons, Kevlar, food, water, and some clothes.

Standing, they faced each other, both with slight

grins on their faces. The smiles were not for a lack of understanding of the seriousness of the situation, but the itch to be in the middle of a mission, knowing success was at the end, was a high that they understood well.

Walking back through the large room of the compound, they accepted the back slaps and well wishes from the other Keepers. Shaking hands with Mace, Walker headed straight to the elevator. Turning, he caught Drew stopping by Babs' desk. Her expression warred between defiance and concern.

"Be safe," she said, her voice low.

Drew's ever-present cocky response did not come forward, much to Walker's surprise. Instead, Drew held Babs' gaze for a few seconds before he winked and said, "Don't worry. I'll be back before you have a chance to miss me."

The elevator door opened, and as Walker stepped through, Drew was right behind him. An hour later, they were airborne, heading to their first stop in Florida.

7

Julie had tried to keep the fear her out of her voice when talking to Senator Daniels, hoping to instill confidence in both him and the girls that were standing there looking at her. The adrenaline had passed, and she felt shaky but hoped that they would be able to find Hernando soon. Senator Daniels had assured her that he was hiring the best security company to get them out of Mexico and that as soon he had the information, he would call her back and let her know who was coming to their rescue.

Looking at the girls, she said, "Okay, our plan is still the same. Let's keep walking around and see if we can find Hernando. Tiffany's father is hiring a private company to come down here and escort us safely back home."

They had circled the entire area at the back of the resort where the two swimming pools were but decided to look down a palm-lined path that led to a parking lot toward the side. There they found more staff and tourists who were resting in the shade, and over against the trunk of a tall tree, Hernando sat propped up.

"Oh, my God, there he is!" she cried out, hustling toward him with the girls in tow. Dropping to her knees next to him, her gaze immediately dropped to his bandaged leg and ripped, bloodstained pants.

Before she had a chance to ask him what had happened, he grabbed her arm and cried, "Praise God! I was so worried and could not get around to find you."

Andrea burst into tears, and Jackie wrapped her arms around her. Julie knew the girls were suffering from the same shock and adrenaline rush that she had, and their emotions were bubbling to the surface. Sending a quick smile toward the others, she turned her attention back to Hernando.

"What happened? How bad is it? Do you need a doctor or hospital?"

Shaking his head, he said, "No, no. I had come in from the parking lot and was headed to my room when part of the ceiling fell. It cut my leg, but someone came around with bandages and wrapped it up."

"We'll stay with you, but let's see if we can get you somewhere more comfortable."

Handing her backpack and bag to Tiffany, she assisted him to stand but was concerned when he leaned over to whisper.

"I don't want to leave you and the girls until you have been rescued, but I will soon need to go home. I talked to my son and I'm needed. My daughter will soon have a child, and my wife is concerned about the roads."

She did not want to say anything out loud for the girls to hear, but she stammered, "Oh," terrified for them to not have him with them.

He held her gaze, a pleading expression on his face, and she gave an imperceptible nod. As they made their way slowly to a grassy area, still away from the others but where they could be seen if someone was assisting, she tried to comfort everyone.

"I'm sure the hotel will be able to provide some food and more water for us all, so if we sit here, we'll be able to get some when it comes around. And since Tiffany's father is sending someone to pick us up, I'm sure they can be here tomorrow, and we'll just wait for them."

She hoped her voice carried more assurance than she felt looking around at the scattered staff, no one seeming to be in charge.

Keeping in the shade from the afternoon sun, she closed her eyes as she leaned back against the trunk the palm tree. Andrea had curled up on the grass, her head resting on her backpack, and appeared to have fallen asleep. Tiffany and Jackie had done the same, but their eyes were still open, sleep having not yet claimed them. Twisting her head around, she saw that Hernando's face was pale, sweat beading on his forehead.

Leaning closer, she whispered, "Is there anything I can do for you?"

His dark eyes opened, and he smiled, although it appeared forced. "No, no, Ms. Baxter. I confess that my leg gives me pain, but tomorrow it will be better. After I see you and the girls safely away, I'll go to my home where I have a neighbor who is a doctor."

"If I could get you there myself, I would," she said.

"Oh, Ms. Baxter. I have to say that you and the young ladies here have been one of my most favorite tour groups of all time. At first, when I heard that I was going to be spending almost two weeks with three American teenagers, I was sure that it would test my patience. I apologize for having such uncharitable thoughts before even meeting all of you. But their interest, questions, and decorum, along with having you as their companion, has made this tour memorable."

Her heart warm, she said, "That's lovely of you to say, Hernando. It's been a wonderful trip for us as well." Unable to keep the snort from slipping out, she added, "Well, at least until an earthquake rocked our world."

He chuckled also before closing his eyes once more. Hearing voices in the distance, she looked over and saw some of the staff pushing carts with what looked to be sandwiches piled onto platters. Speaking to Tiffany and Jackie, she said, "Stay here. I'm going to get us some food."

She stood and quickly moved to one of the lines, impressed that the tourists were queuing up in a civilized manner. She recognized one of the restaurant servers when she approached the cart, and asked, "May I get enough for my group?" Gaining his approval, she was given a tray on which she placed five sandwiches, several bags of chips, and a platter of fruit. One of the other workers also gave her five bottles of water, for which she offered her grateful thanks. Walking back to the corner of the yard, she wished she had more coins to be able to give to the workers but was afraid she might need them later. Determined to send money back as soon as she returned to the States, she hurried toward her charges.

They devoured the sandwiches, chips, and fruit, and drank thirstily. Hernando thanked her, but she waved her hand, and said, "You've taken good care of us for the past two weeks, we can certainly repay you by helping take care of you now."

She looked at the three girls and could see fatigue and stress pulling at them. "Girls, when I was in the food line, I heard others say that the bungalows were not so damaged, and the bathrooms there still work. How about we go check them out?"

"Oh, God, yes!" Tiffany enthused.

Amanda added, "I thought I was going to have to go to the bathroom in the bushes!"

"I desperately want to wash my face!" Jackie said as she jumped to her feet.

Not wanting to burden Hernando with keeping an eye on all their bags, they loaded up and walked down the path toward the bungalows. Finding an empty one, they went inside and took turns using the toilet. With clean towels and washcloths there, they washed their faces before reapplying sunscreen.

When she left the bathroom, she noticed Jackie staring toward the bed. "What are you thinking?" she asked.

Jackie looked at her, and said, "I was thinking that Hernando would be more comfortable if he was in here than out in the yard." Her face scrunched in thought, and she added, "But maybe that's selfish. I know there are other people that would like to be indoors as well."

Uncertain what to do, Julie looked outside and recognized one of the hotel managers walking along the path. Calling to him, she asked, "Would it be all right if we brought our tour guide in here to rest? He's injured his leg, and it appears this bungalow isn't being used by anyone else."

Nodding emphatically, he replied, "Of course, Ms. Baxter. We are in the process of letting some people back into parts of the hotel that appear to be fine and assigning bungalows to some others. I am more than happy for your group to use this room for the night. We hope to have buses here tomorrow to transport people out as soon as we find out if the roads are passable."

Smiling, she said, "Thank you so much. We're expecting someone to come for us tomorrow."

Leaving Andrea and Tiffany behind in the bungalow, Jackie and Julie hurried across the yard to Hernando. Explaining what they had for him, they assisted him to stand, helping him back. Once inside, he protested loudly that they should have the bed, but they insisted.

He lay down to rest, and she grabbed blankets and pillows from a closet, creating makeshift beds on the floor. The sun had gone down behind the tall trees nearby, casting the room in shadows. The girls quickly fell asleep, but Julie was restless.

Her gaze roved around the inside of the bungalow, thinking it would have been perfect for a honeymoon. Small and intimate. The dark rattan furniture and colorful pillows giving it a casual, comfortable feel. She stood and walked over to the window, barely able to see the yard, but it looked as though most people had found a place to go for the evening. Looking up into the night sky, she wondered who might be coming for them and hoped they were already on their way. Fearful for the girls, she prayed, *Please God, let our rescuers come tomorrow.* She had read enough romance novels to imagine the rescuers being tough, ex-military types. Snorting, she thought, *Yeah, right. Probably an older man will show up and do nothing more than fly us somewhere.*

Fatigue finally pulling on her eyelids, she walked over to the beds on the floor and slid under the blanket. It seemed as though sleep had barely pulled her under before shouts in the distance caused her to jerk awake, heart pounding once more.

8

Walker, belted into the copilot seat in the Cessna Turbo Stationair airplane, listened through the headsets as Drew received landing instructions from his contact in Mexico. Easy-going Drew appeared agitated which heightened Walker's curiosity and added a small bit of concern. Keeping quiet, letting Drew do his job, he waited until the communication stopped.

"What's up?"

"We took extra time to make sure we had the Mexican manifest ready for Immigration, but the airport in Mérida is chaos. Cancún is no better. There was some minor damage to the airstrips, flights were canceled, and their infrastructure can't handle that many people trying to leave all at one time," Drew said.

"This large of an earthquake had repercussions for hundreds and hundreds of miles in every direction," Walker surmised. "And it's right in the biggest vacation area of Mexico. The tourists are all looking to leave."

Nodding, Drew said, "I've secured a place to land on a small, out-of-the-way, private strip. It'll actually be good for our purposes, only it's going to be harder to get the bird I wanted to have once we arrived."

Walker acknowledged Drew's irritation, but they were masters at changing plans in an instant. They had originally secured a large helicopter, capable of carrying six passengers, planning on taking it from the Mérida airport to the resort where the girls would be waiting for them.

"ETA?" he asked.

"Calculating the changes to our destination, ETA is about twenty minutes."

Looking at the map, he said, "It's a hundred and twenty miles from the resort to the Cancún airport. Can we divert to the Mérida airport after we get the girls?"

Shaking his head, Drew said, "Mérida may be closer, but it was also closer to the epicenter of the earthquake. They shut it down completely. The landing strip we're going to is between Cancún and Mérida. My contact is working on securing a bird and having it there when we arrive. That'll still be the fastest way."

Drew began the descent, and Walker stared out into the dark night, watching as the lights from the small, private airstrip came into sight. In the dark, the ground was indiscernible except for the lights guiding them in on the sides. With anyone other than a Special Ops pilot he would have been concerned, but he trusted Drew explicitly and relaxed as they landed with a few bumps and jolts and taxied to the single building at the end.

"Is this a cartel airstrip?" he asked, staring at the thick forests barely illuminated by the lights around the building.

Chuckling, Drew commented, "Beggars can't be choosers." Sobering, he added, "Actually, this is run by a private company whose owner was former Mexican military. Who he allows to fly in and out of here, I don't know, and I didn't ask."

Shaking his head, Walker agreed. "Let's just hope he got us a bird that'll handle the mission."

Continuing to taxi into the hangar, they watched as a stocky man approached, his salt and pepper hair in a military buzz, his dark eyes pinned to them, and an automatic rifle slung about his shoulder.

"Friend or foe?" Walker asked sardonically.

"That's Joseph," Drew replied. "Can't say he's a friend, but he's all we've got."

Climbing from the plane, Walker watched as Drew and Joseph approached each other, handshakes offered and given. Making his way around the front of the plane toward them, he felt Joseph's appraising gaze rake over him.

"Joseph, meet my friend Walker. Walker, this is Joseph Martinez."

Extending his hand, it was clasped in Joseph's firm shake. Walker was impressed…the handshake was not a grip with threatening intent nor was it weak. "Good to meet you, Joseph. Thanks for your help."

"You may need to save your thanks until after you see what I was able to get," Joseph said with a shrug.

He led them around to the back of the metal hanger

to where another man was standing next to an old, small, four-seat R44 Raven helicopter. "Four seats?" He turned to Drew who was already protesting.

"Joseph, fuckin' hell. We've got to get four people out."

Joseph's dark eyes snapped, and he barked to the man near the helicopter, speaking in rapid Spanish. The conversation did not last long, although the flurry of words and gesticulations between the two would have been amusing to watch if Walker was not sure that another recalculation in their mission was getting ready to take place.

Throwing his hands up to the side, Joseph said, "My apologies. The word given to me was that you would need four seats, not a total of six. Although, to be honest, I'm not sure I could've gotten a six-seater anyway. As you can imagine, the police and military are grabbing every resource they can."

Walker and Drew eyed each other, unspoken words between them plotting out what needed to change. It would now involve two helicopter trips to get everyone out. Turning to grab his bag from the airplane, Joseph's words halted him.

"Unfortunately, in an area as poor as we are, there are people who will take advantage of any situation. I have reports that roving gangs are moving into resort areas, looking to loot and steal anything they can from vacationers who are fleeing the area."

Turning, Walker pinned him with a hard stare, waiting to see if there was more, but he did not have to wait long.

Joseph continued, "And of course, the ever-present cartels are immediately looking to take advantage of the country's unfortunate situation. The Gulf Cartel has recently been pushed out by the upstart CJNG...the Jalisco New Generation Cartel. They've even managed to rival the Sinaloa Federation and have made their moves in this area."

"Do you suspect that we're going to have trouble with them?" he asked.

Shrugging, Joseph replied, "It's my understanding they're already setting up roadblocks and moving into some of the resort areas. I would suggest, my friends, that at first light you're in the air."

Looking at his watch, he knew that dawn was only a few hours away. Shaking his head, he ground his teeth in frustration as Drew cursed under his breath. "We'll have to make two trips," he said unnecessarily.

"Two and two?" Drew asked.

"No, no way. We'll get the three girls. You get them back here and make sure they're safe with Joseph and his firepower and then you can come back for me and the chaperone."

Nodding, Drew agreed. "I'll check out the bird and make sure we're ready."

He sighed and finished getting their bags from the plane. Their easy mission just became significantly more challenging, and he just hoped this was the last surprise they were handed.

9

Julie peered out into the dark night after rushing to the window. Unable to determine what was going on, she nonetheless could hear men yelling in the distance. Hernando rose unsteadily from the bed, and she turned to offer him assistance, but he waved her away.

Moving beside her, he cocked his head and listened to the sounds coming from the main resort hotel.

"What is it? What are they saying—"

His hand on her arm halted her questions, and his eyes bore into hers as he said, "We must leave. Immediately."

The ludicrousness of his words would have made her laugh if not for the concern in his voice. "Why? Please tell me."

He jerked his head to the side, peering down at the three sleeping girls on the floor before lifting his gaze back to hers. "I do not know who is out there," he said, "but they are not good people. My guess would be that looters have decided that a resort is a good place to steal from vacationers who have been frightened out of their rooms."

"Looters?" She may have posed the word as a question, but she knew exactly what he was talking about. She remembered stories of looters in the United States after hurricanes had devastated an area and many people fled their homes. Television cameras caught people robbing and mugging others in an effort to steal from unoccupied homes and shops. Her mind raced with fear and she asked, "I think the men coming for us will be here tomorrow…I mean today…in a few hours."

He was already shaking his head. "We cannot wait and take that chance. I cannot bear the thought of something befalling you or the girls." Turning to her, he grimaced. "Ms. Baxter, I need to get you to safety."

Jerking her head up and down, she said, "Yes, okay. Okay, fine." Her mouth may have been agreeing, but she had no clue what to do.

"We might can get to the van. It's parked on the side of the building away from the main road. But I don't know what the main roads will be like. They may be filled with looters…or worse."

Eyes huge at his dire implications, she repeated, "Worse?"

"There is an element of our society, Ms. Baxter, that does not just reside in the underworld, but in everyday life. There are Cartels, who in many ways rule parts of our country. Here in the Yucatán, our lives are much better and safer than in other places in Mexico. But I have no doubt, as opportunistic as they are, they will find a way to take advantage of the situation." He lifted his hands and placed them on her shoulders, his fingers digging in almost painfully. "We must go. We must go and hide from the evil that is creeping toward us until your rescuers can come."

As though his final words crept past the fog of denial, she jolted into action. Hurrying over to the other side of the room, she dropped to her knees and began shaking the girls awake as quietly as she could, shushing their sleepy protestations.

Tiffany, as usual, awoke quickly. Placing her fingers over the teenager's lips, Julie gave her head a sharp shake. Jackie was next, and she quieted her the same way. The sleepy-head of the group, Andrea, was sitting up grumpily, but with Tiffany and Jackie sensing something was wrong they hushed her as well.

Whispering, Julie said, "There are looters at the main hotel. It's only a matter of time before they make it down the path and come this way. We've got to get out of here now in order to protect ourselves."

She hated the look of fear that replaced the sleepy confusion in the eyes of all three girls. She tried to steady her voice, shaky to her own ears, and said, "Put everything in your bags. Go to the bathroom, but don't flush the toilet. We don't want to make any noise at all. I'll get everything else, and then we'll slip out the back, and Hernando can get us to the van."

Tears shimmered in Tiffany's eyes, but she obeyed, scrambling up with Andrea and Jackie. While they used the bathroom, Julie put the pillows and blankets back in the closet and ran her hand over the bed, smoothing where Hernando had lain. Catching his gaze, she said, "In case they come in here it won't look like there was anyone using this bungalow."

He nodded, a slight smile curving his lips as he said, "You are very smart, Ms. Baxter."

"Not really," she admitted, "I just read a lot of suspense novels." Not wanting to speak aloud any more than necessary, she raced to her bags to finish pushing everything into them. The small refrigerator in the bungalow held more bottles of water, and she took all that she could carry in her backpack. The girls came out of the bathroom, and she rushed in after them, quickly using the toilet.

As they finished gathering their bags, Hernando also made a trip to the bathroom. As he came out, they moved to the back door and slipped out into the night.

"Ms. Baxter?" Tiffany barely breathed, "How will the rescuers know where to find us?"

Moving through the thick jungle of trees around the back of the resort toward the employee parking lot where Hernando had left their van, she had no answer for Tiffany. And that thought terrified her.

An hour later, hiding in the ruins of the Chichén Itzá temple, Julie knew exactly what terror truly was.

They had easily slipped through the dark jungle, following Hernando's lead, and made it to the employee parking lot on the side of the resort. That parking lot was quiet, and Hernando whispered that the looters probably figured the workers had nothing but poor automobiles and no valuables. He unlocked the van, grimacing as he put more weight on his leg. Julie sent him a questioning look, he shook his head, and she assumed he was indicating that he did not want her assistance.

Turning to the girls, she made sure they climbed into the van, stowed their backpacks, and she added the instructions for them to lean over, keeping their heads down. She had no idea why that suggestion sounded good other than she had seen it in movies, so she made it nonetheless.

Once they were all settled, Hernando started the van, and suddenly, her heart pounded out of her chest at the thought that others would hear the sound.

He must have understood her concern, because he said, "They are making so much noise, I do not think that they will hear us. But I'm going to drive with our headlights off. I've been over these roads giving tours for twenty years. I have no doubt that I can get us over to the ruins."

"Can't we go farther?" she asked. "Can't we go all the way to your village? Or Mérida? Or...I don't know...somewhere?"

As he gently pressed on the accelerator and they slowly moved out of the parking lot and onto the short road leading to the ruins, he said, "I don't trust what may be on the roads right now. Until we know that the police or the military will be coming to deal with the looters and gangs, I don't want to take a chance with your safety."

"Will we be safe at the ruins?"

"We will be able to hide there because they will not expect anyone."

It only took a few minutes for him to make his way to the ruins, driving around to the side and parking the van in the jungle nearby. Carrying their bags, she and the girls followed him to El Caracol, the observatory temple. Visitors were not allowed to climb the steps, but without any preamble, Hernando began the painful ascent, motioning for the girls to follow.

Tiffany moved up behind Julie, and said, "Give me your bags, Ms. Baxter. We can carry those, while you help Hernando."

Heart warmed at the girls' caring suggestion, she divested herself of her backpack and bag, handing them to the others before turning to Hernando. Pushing aside his protestations, she shoved her shoulder under his armpit, wrapped her arm around his waist, and assisted him upward.

When they were halfway up, he signaled for her to stop. "I'm going to stay here so that I can keep an eye out for anything untoward. I'm not expecting any trouble, but I'd like to be sure. You take the girls and go on up to the top level, into the observatory. We will stay here until daylight. I can call my cousin who lives in a nearby village to see what the roads are like at that time. If they are passable, then I'll leave once you know your rescuers are on their way."

With a short nod, she helped him to settle against the stone steps before moving with the girls up to the top. The climb was arduous, the steps steep, and when they reached the top she stood and stared at the small door leading into the arched, stone building. The idea of being in the dark in an ancient structure that could topple on top of them at any moment was terrifying.

"Maybe we should stay out here," Andrea whispered, her eyes staring widely ahead as well.

"Maybe you're right," she replied. "But let's move around to the backside." Leading them around to the side closest to the jungle, they settled on the ancient stones, the sounds of the jungle all around and the black of the night encasing them.

Tate looked up from his computer screen and twisted his head around, catching Mace's eyes. "They may have a problem, boss. I'm keeping track of what's going on in the Chichén Itzá area, and the police are reporting widespread looting. There's also chatter of cartel movement in the areas affected by the earthquake."

Mace stood and walked over to where Tate was once again looking at his computer screen. He stared silently for a moment then calmly ordered, "Get this to Walker and stay on it. I want a lock on the chaperone's phone as well as each of the girls. We're round-the-clock until we know they got everybody out safe."

He walked back toward his desk and saw Sylvie's wide eyes pinned on him. He changed directions and headed straight to her. She stood as he neared, and he placed his hand on the back of her neck, his thumb sweeping over the apple of her cheek. "Don't worry, sweetheart. Drew knows how to land a plane or a bird anywhere, and Walker is one of the best I've ever seen at being able to recalculate the plan of a mission."

She offered him a small smile and lifted her face for a light kiss before sitting back down at her desk.

"Mace?" Babs called out softly from the desk next to Sylvie's. Gaining his attention, she said, "I know Drew's got the mission covered, but with the changes…do you need me?"

He cocked his head slightly to the side, listening as she continued, "Three girls. Three teenage girls and one chaperone." Shaking her head as though to clear her thoughts, she added, "Drew may need assistance from another female if the girls are separated from their chaperone. If things get hairy…if I can be of use…I'm here."

Mace considered her for a long moment, but her gaze never wavered.

"This…I could handle," she added, her gaze hardening as though challenging him to deny it.

Dipping his chin, he acknowledged her offer, knowing the struggle she must be feeling. "I'll let you know. Thanks."

With that he walked back over to his desk, overseeing the call between Tate and Walker, the satisfaction of knowing he had truly hired the best for his LSI Keepers moving through him.

10

Getting off the phone with Tate, Walker growled as he headed toward Drew readying the bird. "Got more problems," he said, gaining Drew's attention. "Tate just called. Looters are in the area of the resort near Chichén Itzá, so we may have a more difficult time landing and getting to the girls."

Drew turned and faced him, a scowl on his face that Walker knew matched his own. "Fuckin' hell," he cursed. "Lawless men scouring tourist areas are not just going to be looking for loot, and those four young women are sittin' ducks."

Pulling out his phone, he said, "Tate is getting a lock on their phones. I hadn't planned on calling the chaperone until we arrived at the resort. I'm going to give her a call now to see exactly where they are before we take off."

Drew grabbed their bags and tossed them into the bird before continuing his preflight checks as Walker headed off to the side, noticing that Joseph and his workers were no longer around. Glad for the privacy, he placed his call.

"He...Hello?"

The soft voice that so hesitantly answered his call shot his brain straight from the mission directly to the photograph he had memorized of Julie Baxter. Not one to give into imagination, he could hear the fear mixed with hope in that single word.

"Hello. Is...is anyone there?"

Blinking, inwardly cursing that his silence had caused her more concern, he quickly replied. "Ms. Baxter?"

"Um...yes."

"My name is Walker, from Lighthouse Security Investigations. Tiffany Daniels' father hired our company to escort you safely back to the United States."

An audible sigh accompanied by, "Oh, thank God," met his ears.

"Ms. Baxter, I don't want to alarm you, but we received intelligence that there may be—"

"Looters!" She was still whispering, but her voice was clearly alarmed, surprising him with her words. "Our guide heard them in the resort, and we snuck out. We're not there!"

"Our company is getting a lock on your phones, Ms. Baxter, so we'll know exactly where you are—"

"I know where we are," she said softly. "We snuck away from the resort, and Hernando was able to get us to our van. He didn't want to take a chance on the roads, so we went back over to the ruins. We're hiding in the El Caracol temple of Chichén Itzá."

"The where?" he growled, mentally recalculating again. "Can you be more specific? We want to be able to land the helicopter as close as possible." Looking up, he caught Drew's lowered brow, questioning gaze, and mouthed, 'They left the resort and are in the ruins. Get Tate.'

"Do you know where the ruins of Chichén Itzá are?" she asked.

"Yes. I'm getting a map of the ruins as we speak," he said, his finger moving over the tablet that Drew was holding out for him. "What was the name of the temple again?"

"It's the observatory. It's the only building that has a domed top to it."

Seeing the barest hint of blue in the east against the rest of the dark night sky, he knew it was almost dawn. "Ms. Baxter, we're leaving now. We'll be there shortly. We'll land as close as we can to you, but I want you and the others to stay hidden until we're there."

"How will I know that it's really you and not looters or drug gangs?" she asked.

Surprised at her question, he answered, "I'm not sure anyone else will be arriving at dawn in a small helicopter, Ms. Baxter, but the pilot and I both have matching lighthouse tattoos."

"Oh, of course. How stupid of me…of course, local looters won't be in a helicopter."

Her voice, calm and soft, made an impression, and he immediately wanted to place her at ease. "Keep your phone with you and call this number back if anything changes. Make sure everyone is ready, but stay hidden until we land."

Gaining her assurance that she understood his orders, he disconnected. Turning to Drew, he asked, "I don't know if I admire her for getting the girls to safety or irritated that she didn't stay at the resort."

"Sounds like she made the right choice. There may be more to the little chaperone than we thought."

Fastened in, he asked, "Ready to fly?"

"Fuck, yeah," Drew said with a grin. "Let's get this mission going! Damsels in distress...here we come."

Chuckling, he shook his head at Drew's antics, knowing Drew was all in for making the mission a success. Failure was not an option...for either of them. As soon as they were airborne, he gave the new directions to Drew and reported to Tate.

Slipping back around the side of the stone observatory, Julie moved in the early morning light toward Hernando. He was awake and lifted his gaze to her as she approached.

"How are you?" she asked, placing her hand on his arm.

"I'm fine, Ms. Baxter," he replied, grimacing only slightly as he shifted on the hard surface. "How are you and the young ladies?"

"I don't think they slept any, but they're resting. I

wanted to let you know that the men coming to rescue us will soon be here. "

His wide eyes registered his surprise, and he asked, "Are they able to get through on the roads?"

Shaking her head, she shrugged. "I don't know anything about the roads, but he said that they were coming by helicopter." Seeing his furrowed brow, she asked, "Why? Are you concerned?"

"We will not stay hidden with a helicopter nearby, but perhaps the miscreants will think it's the military or the police and stay away." Nodding more enthusiastically, he continued, "Yes, yes. I'm sure that's what they'll think."

She pulled a bottle of water from her bag and handed it to him along with a granola bar. "I'm going to go back and make sure the girls have something to eat and drink before the men arrive. We were told to stay hidden until they land."

He accepted the water and granola bar with gratitude and nodded his acquiescence. "I think that's very wise, Ms. Baxter. I'll stay quietly here until you determine that it's safe for us to go down. As soon as you have gone, I'll head to my home."

With another pat on his arm, she climbed back up the last steps, moving to the back of the stone walls. She had not slept, her mind racing with not only the situation they were in but the realization that she was sitting on stones in a building that was over a thousand years old. If she were not in such a bizarre predicament she would have been enthralled.

Three pairs of very tired, very frightened eyes met hers as she rounded the back of the observatory. Plastering a smile on her face, she said, "Girls, I've talked to the rescuers. They're on their way and will be here shortly. Hernando is fine, and I've given him something to eat and drink." Pulling more water bottles and granola bars from her ever-abundant bag, she passed them out. "Please do the same so that your stomachs won't be too empty."

"How are we getting out of here, Ms. Baxter?" Tiffany asked, a sheen of sweat on her brow despite the early morning chill.

"A helicopter," she replied. Seeing their eyes widen with worry, she added, "I'm sure it will be a nice big one. What an adventure we'll have to tell!"

"I don't do well with heights," Andrea moaned.

"Oh...well, I'm sure the flight will be quick and then we can get back down on the ground." She hoped she was telling the girls the truth, when in fact, she had no idea what a helicopter ride would be like. Tiffany turned her pale face up toward her, and she reached out to touch her warm forehead. Biting her lip, she was concerned about the young woman, but overwhelmed, she just smiled in encouragement.

Just then, the faint sound of the whirling blades of a helicopter could be heard. Grinning widely, she said, "Ladies, I think our chariot is arriving." Stomach rolling with nerves, she added, "I want you all to stay here until I make sure it's okay for us to come down."

"Can we stay with Hernando?" Jackie asked.

Shaking her head, she replied, "No, I'd rather you stay hidden. I'll come get you when it's safe."

In the distance, she could see a small helicopter land on the flat, grassy lawn next to the temple. The circling blades slowed, and the passenger door opened. A dark-haired man climbed down from the helicopter, and, ducking low, he moved away from the aircraft. Looking straight up toward her as though his eyes were on a tractor-beam directly to her, her breath halted in her lungs.

Stalking toward the bottom of the temple, he came closer, taking the tall, stone steps easily. Scrambling down, she stopped when she was about ten feet away from him.

The closer she came, the more she had an unobstructed view to the power in his body. Tall. Muscular. Dark hair. Aviator sunglasses hiding his eyes. Cargo pants, boots, and a T-shirt stretched over his torso. And incredibly handsome. Uncertainty filled her, not knowing what she should do.

"Ms. Baxter, I presume," he said, his voice deep and smooth. He slid off his aviator sunglasses, and his blue eyes held her attention.

"Um..." she stammered, torn between wanting to jump into his arms for coming for them and terror at not knowing if he was who she was supposed to trust.

She watched as he pulled up the arm of his T-shirt and turned, exposing his shoulder. An intricate tattoo of a lighthouse, all in black and white with the exception of the yellow beams coming from the light, was on his upper arm. He pulled his shirt back down and handed her an ID badge, saying, "I'm Walker. From Lighthouse Security Investigations."

She scrambled down the next few steps, and his hand reached out to assist her when she grew nearer. Her hand tingled where he touched her, and she sucked in a quick breath. Fatigue and nerves had her on edge. "Hello. I'm Julie Baxter."

His gaze shot to her wrapped wrist, and his brows snapped downward. "You're injured."

"Not bad. It's more like a sprain," she said, attempting to tug her hand from his.

He continued to hold onto her, his grip firm but light. "Let me see," he commanded, and she nodded without argument. He unwrapped the elastic bandage and said, "It's not wrapped correctly."

"I did it myself, but didn't know the proper way," she mumbled. He gently moved her hand and wrist in several directions. Letting him know when it hurt, he rewrapped her wrist before pinning her with another stare. Unable to discern his thoughts, she looked over his shoulder toward the helicopter. Narrowing her eyes, she stared before cocking her head to the side as she looked back at him. "Um…it doesn't look very big. Can it carry all of us?"

He held her gaze, his eyes peering deeply into hers, and said, "No, ma'am. It can't."

11

Walker would have recognized Julie from her passport photo but had to admit it did not do her justice. The slightly rumpled, exhausted woman standing in front of him bore little resemblance to the professional picture, and yet, the electricity he felt when he touched her hand caused his brain to short-circuit for a moment. Her natural beauty shown through even with no makeup and messy hair. Dark hair pulled back from her face. Warm but tired eyes. Dressed in simple capris, a pink T-shirt, and light blue sneakers.

She looked up at him with complete trust until her gaze moved to the helicopter, and then her wide-eyed, stunned expression turned to him with incredulity. Ignoring the strange reaction to meeting her, he hoped she was not going to fall into hysterics at their change in plans.

Looking up the steps, he saw a man coming toward

him, his pants bloodied and his leg bandaged. Recognizing the tour guide, he eyed him, watching with interest as Julie smiled widely at the older man.

"Oh, Hernando, our transportation is here, and you can go to your home now."

He eyed the tour guide and was not surprised when Julie turned and introduced him to Hernando. "Do you need some assistance?" he asked, staring at his injured leg.

Waving his hands in front of him, Hernando replied, "Oh, no, sir. I just need to get to my home but did not want to leave the girls alone." Grasping Julie's hand in his own, he said, "If you ever come back to our country, please look me up. I live in a small village outside of Tulum."

She leaned into his arms, hugging him, the affection pouring from her. "I can't thank you enough. For the amazing two weeks and all you've taught us. But, especially last night, keeping us safe."

Watching as Hernando patted her back, the older man held Walker's gaze over her shoulder. With a nod, he communicated that he would care for her now. She was his responsibility. Another unfamiliar emotion slid through him at that thought, but he pushed it down, giving his head a slight shake.

Hernando walked past the helicopter, stopping to shake hands with Drew on his way to the van, parked in the trees.

Swinging his head back around, he looked up the steps, not seeing anyone else, before dropping his gaze back to Julie.

She sucked in her lips, thoughts moving behind her intelligent eyes. Not wanting to give her a chance to ponder on the helicopter situation, he asked, "The girls? Are they ready?"

Blinking, she jolted slightly and said, "Yes. Um…let me get them." She turned to climb back up the temple steps, and he reached his hand out, placing it on her shoulder.

"I'll go with you," he said.

She hesitated, and he continued, "Ma'am, you've done an admirable job taking care of the girls in these extreme circumstances, but my partner and I are now in charge of them. I need to see how they're doing and what we need to be concerned with as we get them out of here."

Sucking in her lips, she held his gaze for a moment before nodding and leading him up the stairs and around the corner of one of the tall walls. The three girls jumped to their feet, Tiffany wavering slightly. They appeared to be in a similar state of fatigue as Ms. Baxter and their injured guide. As he quickly assessed them, it was obvious Tiffany was pale, a sheen of perspiration on her forehead. All three moved to stand next to Julie, and she kept her body slightly in front of them. *She's protecting them.* His admiration rose even more, but he focused on the girls as she made the introductions. He recognized them from the background dossier they had received from Senator Daniels, but she would not have known that.

"This is Tiffany Daniels, Andrea Tucker, and Jackie Dumont. Girls, this is Walker. Um…Mr…um…"

"Walker," he said. "Just Walker."

She fiddled with the strap of one of her bags, uncertainty flowing from her. Wanting to assure her that he had everything under control, he said, "Girls, here's what we're going to do. Our helicopter is not large enough to take all of you at one time, so we're going to make two trips—"

"Take them," Julie said quickly. "Take all three of them together."

"No!" Tiffany protested, the other girls following with their heads shaking.

Julie turned toward the girls, and she said, "Listen to me. It'll be safer for the three of you to go with…um… Walker, and I can wait."

"Actually," he said, wanting to make sure they understood who was in charge, "we've already got everything arranged—"

"I don't want the girls separated," she protested, her lips pressing together, her voice rising.

Throwing his palms up, he said, "Whoa, whoa, Ms. Baxter." Hearing a noise behind him, he spied Drew coming around the corner. Drew's gaze moved through the group, a smile on his face.

"This is Drew," Walker introduced. "I'm just explaining how this will work."

"There is no discussion," Julie said, a thread of steel in her voice. "I want the girls to stay together. Get them to safety first."

He shot Drew a tight-lipped look and then nodded. "It's already planned, Ms. Baxter. Drew can take all three girls back to Mérida but will have to leave them somewhere safe before he comes back for us."

"Oh," she said, a slight blush crossing her cheeks. "I see. Well, um…good."

"But, Ms. Baxter," Andrea began, her brow crinkling.

She turned to the girls and said, "We have no choice. The sooner you go, the sooner Mr. Drew can come back. And I'll be here waiting with Walker and will join you soon." Looking over her shoulder at him, she said, "And then we can go to the U.S.?"

"Yes, ma'am," he assured. Glancing back toward the helicopter, he said, "But we need to hurry."

Drew reached out and lifted the backpacks from the stone floor and smiled toward the girls. "Ladies? Follow me."

The group made their way down the stone steps and over the grassy knoll toward the helicopter. Throwing open the door, Drew placed the girls' backpacks under the seats as Walker grabbed his bag. Setting it on the ground, he walked over to Drew as Julie hugged the girls. He could tell she was whispering assurances to each of them and promises to join them in another hour. She stepped back as Drew and Walker assisted them into the helicopter and made sure they were buckled in safely.

Moving to the side so that he could speak to Drew privately, he said, "Keep an eye on Tiffany. She doesn't look well, and I don't know how she's going to do with the flight."

Nodding, Drew acknowledged, "I noticed she was

warm when I helped her in. I'll see if Joseph knows of a doctor who can take a look at her."

"Good idea."

Drew's gaze cut over to where Julie was standing, a forced smile on her face. "Are you going to be okay with little mama bear over there?"

Chuckling, he shook his head. "I think as long as she knows the girls are okay, I can handle her."

Before Drew had a chance to climb into the cockpit, Julie sidled up to them, leaning close to whisper, "I can tell Tiffany doesn't feel very good, and Andrea is my nervous one. Jackie likes to pretend that she's brave, but don't assume she's not scared as well."

Drew placed his hand on her shoulder, and said, "Now don't you worry none, Ms. Baxter. I'll get them safe and then come back for you. You'll be reunited in no time at all."

The sight of Drew's hand on Julie's shoulder sent another strange emotion slithering through Walker, but he refused to assess the reason. He watched as Drew fired off a two-finger wave and climbed into the cockpit. Just as Julie had predicted, Jackie was sitting in the copilot seat, a tentative smile on her face. Drew was already chatting, putting the girls at ease, and Walker jogged over to where Julie was standing. Moving her further back, they watched as the bird lifted, Julie's gaze staying on it until it moved out of sight over the trees.

She looked at him before her gaze dropped down. Wanting to put her at ease, he asked, "Have you had anything to eat today?"

"We had granola bars and water," she replied,

looking up at him, nervously fiddling with the strap of her bag while bravely maintaining eye contact.

He looked behind her at the Observatory Temple, and said, "It really is magnificent, isn't it?" Her face immediately relaxed as a beautiful smile curved her lips, and he knew he had chosen a topic to put her at ease.

"Oh, it is. We spent yesterday touring the entire area, and Hernando was such a fount of information. Have you ever been here?"

Shaking his head, he replied, "No. I don't often get a chance to take a trip just for a vacation, but I can certainly see the appeal here."

"How long do we have before Drew comes back for us?"

He rubbed his chin, calculating the time it would take for Drew to secure the girls, especially if Tiffany needed to see a doctor. "The flight time would only be about an hour, but he's going to need to make sure he leaves them in a safe place and checks on Tiffany."

A crinkle formed between her brows, and she nodded. "I'm so worried for them."

His hand lifted on its way to smooth the line from her forehead, but he quickly lowered it again, fighting the urge. He had never had a problem maintaining professionalism before and could not understand the desire to physically assure her that everything would be all right. Instead, he grunted, "They'll be fine. Drew will take care of them."

She blinked, rearing back slightly. "I'm sure. I didn't mean to imply that he wouldn't."

Before he had a chance to say anything else, she

turned and moved over to her backpack sitting on one of the steps. *Well, shit. That could have gone better.* He wanted to keep an eye on their situation, but as he and Drew flew in, they noticed little activity at the resort, and so far, no one had come to see what was going on. Looking up at the temple, he decided to climb the steps to give him a better view over the area.

By the time he had scrambled halfway up, he turned to see Julie coming behind him, her breathing labored. He stopped to wait for her, reaching his hand down to assist her up, taking her backpack from her. She hesitated for a few seconds before placing her hand in his. He watched her chest heave with the exertion of the climb before dragging his eyes away from her breasts. Hoping she had not noticed, he tried to think of something to say.

"I thought this would give me a chance to scope out the area while we wait," he mumbled.

"I may never be back here again in my life, so I wanted to take one last look," she said, looking around.

They continued to climb to the top together and then stood side-by-side, their gazes drifting over the area.

"This particular structure was built around A.D. 906. It's been suggested that it was an ancient Mayan Observatory and a way for them to observe changes in the sky. There are sight lines for at least twenty astronomical events that can be found within the structure."

Standing next to her, it was easy to see that she only came to the top of his shoulder, and he had to look down to see her face. She twisted her head and looked up at him, another smile gracing her face. Shrugging, she said, "I don't know a lot about the ancient history here, but I've tried to learn as much as I could."

"How did you become the girls' chaperone?" The question surprised him because he could not remember ever being so curious about a mission before. Normally, a mission was meticulously planned and carried out. Caring about why someone was in a position to need a mission was rarely an issue.

"I'm a counselor at their school," Julie said. "I was actually a last-minute substitution when their Ancient History teacher became ill. Senator Daniels asked if I would take over, assuring me that everything was already arranged, and I would just need to be the adult supervision."

Shaking his head, he said, "Three teenage girls. I can't imagine."

He looked down in surprise as she placed her hand on his arm, her eyes peering up intently into his.

"Oh, they're so mature. Drew won't have any problems with them if that's what you're worried about. It's been an absolutely amazing trip...well, with the exception of an earthquake...and then looters."

He chuckled and nodded. "Yeah, I can see how that would put a damper on your vacation." Looking around again, he asked, "What about some of the other structures here?"

"Much of the rest of Chichén Itzá is to our right. There are several more temples, a palace, and even their ball courts. It wasn't all built at the same time, but the city was added onto over several centuries. In the mid-to-late 1800s, vegetation from the rain forest had completely grown over almost all the buildings. In the early 1900s, some people from the Yucatán wanted to encourage tourism and so they began to build roads to some of these monuments, clear them off, and make them readily accessible."

Scanning the area, he could perceive no threat and allowed his gaze to move back to the woman standing next to him. The breeze was blowing the loose tendrils about her face. Her hands, which waved in excitement as she spoke, were now clasped in front of her as she calmly gazed out over the other ruins.

Turning toward him, she said, "This is going to sound like the strangest comment, but part of me is almost glad that I got to experience this without any other tourists around. Right now, only able to hear the sounds of the jungle, I can almost imagine myself stepping back into time."

Her comment caught him off guard, and he looked out over the area, trying to see it from her point of view. He appreciated the architecture. Admired the engineering. And understood a little bit of the history. But imagining being in a different time held no fascination for him. But seeing the smile on her face, it was easy to see that it meant something to her, and for some strange reason, he was glad she had that chance.

Noticing the dark circles under her eyes, he said, "I'm going to keep a lookout. Why don't you settle down in the shade and see if you can catch a little sleep?"

He wondered if she would argue, but she did not, a testament to how tired she really was. He watched over her as she found a spot at the top of the stone observatory temple, placed her bags against the wall, and lay down. He hoped she would be able to sleep until Drew came back for them, but as he continued to scan the area, he realized he missed the sound of her voice.

12

Drew glanced to the side toward Jackie who continually twisted around in her seat to look at the two girls in the back. "How's she doing?" he asked softly.

Jackie jerked her eyes up toward his and gave a jerky shake of her head.

Fuck! Forcing a smile on his face, he said, "We'll be there in a few minutes." The sound of retching met his ears, and he was glad Andrea had managed to find an empty plastic bag for Tiffany to throw up in. Continuing to radio to Joseph, no reply came in return. *Where the fuck is he? He knew we were coming right back!*

Circling the small landing strip, the hairs on the back of his neck stood up as he noticed no activity in the area at all. No cars or trucks on the roads nor parked near the hangar. Fear that his plane was no longer parked in the hangar gave the normally unflappable Drew a sense of dread.

"Girls, I need you to listen carefully. I've got to get

into the hangar to get the plane ready," he said, not giving voice to the possibility his plane may not be there. "I'm going to land as close to the hangar as I can so that we can be together. Jackie, I'm putting you in charge of the other two."

He looked over, seeing a flash of fear move across her face before being replaced with a quick nod. Smiling, he said, "Good girl."

"What do you need me to do?" Jackie asked, her voice shaky.

"I want you to get the other two out of the helicopter and see if you can get a little bit of water down Tiffany. She's getting dehydrated, and we need to at least get her to sip some water."

"I can do that," Jackie said. "What will you be doing?"

He hesitated for only a second before saying, "Just getting the plane ready. All I need you to do is just stay with Tiffany and Andrea." Calling Tate, he demanded, "Give me a status on the airstrip. It appears vacated, but I don't want to land in a hotspot."

"Satellite has shown little activity," Tate reported. "The two vehicles that were there earlier left not too long after you and Walker took off."

Breathing a sigh of relief that his plane would still be there, he added, "If no one's here, I can't leave the girls. I'm going in and will update you as soon as I know what I'm facing."

He set the bird down expertly and was pleased to see Jackie immediately unbuckle and twist around to assist the other two. "Get everyone out of the helicopter," he said to Jackie, "and bring them in. There will be a toilet inside, and I've got water bottles."

After assuring himself the girls were out of the helicopter, he got a better look at Tiffany and his concern ratcheted up. *Goddamnit, she looks bad.* He had to admit he had little to compare her to, considering the sickest girls he had been around were grown women who had drunk too much. AF Special Ops did not get sick, or if they did, they kept it to themselves. Blowing out a breath, he hurried into the open hangar, stalking straight to his plane. He knew he needed to give it a careful inspection before taking it back up into the air. *But take it where?*

Calling Tate again, he said, "Plane is here, but I need a new plan. Walker is not somewhere near a landing strip, and Tiffany is too fuckin' sick for me to leave her alone with the other two girls. You gotta give me directions because the best I can come up with is to get the girls to the resort in Cancún."

Mace came over the radio, saying, "That's the new plan, Drew. Get the girls to Cancún. Tate will get the flight papers for emergency landing to the airport. We've already been in contact with the resort, and they are expecting you. There'll also be a doctor on staff that will see Tiffany."

He almost asked about Walker but knew that Mace and the Keepers would be planning the next phase of the mission. "You got it, boss," he replied. Disconnecting, he turned around to check on the progress of the girls. It appeared each had been to the bathroom and were sitting to the side, their backs propped against the wall. Jackie and Andrea were nibbling crackers, and Jackie was assisting Tiffany, who was sipping water. Offering an encouraging nod, he continued inspecting his plane, readying it for takeoff.

Thirty minutes later, he loaded them into his plane, glad that it was much more comfortable than the old helicopter. Getting Tiffany and Andrea buckled in, he turned to Jackie. "Y'all are doing great. I got some extra plastic bags for Tiffany if she ends up throwing up on our flight. I'll get you to Cancún just as soon as I can. Should only be about half an hour."

The young girl turned her concerned gaze toward him, and asked, "What about Ms. Baxter?"

Shooting her his affable grin, he said, "Now don't you go worrying your head about her. My friend Walker will take good care of her and make sure she's safe until I can get back to them."

He watched as Jackie offered a small smile before climbing into the backseat of the plane as well. Hauling himself into the cockpit, he knew his words were true… Walker would take care of Ms. Baxter. He just hated missions that went awry and hoped that Ms. Baxter would cooperate with Walker as well as the three girls were with him.

Moving to the end of the runway, he twisted around to double check on the girls, receiving a thumbs up from Jackie and Andrea. With a short nod, he turned back around and took the plane into the air.

13

"Talk to me."

Walker listened to Tate's clipped voice on the other end of the phone say, "We've got to change plans."

Keeping his curses to himself, he glanced around, assuring that he was alone as he waited for Tate to continue.

"First of all, Tiffany Daniels is really sick. She's running a fever. On top of that, when Drew landed at Joseph's airstrip, it was abandoned. Drew cannot get hold of his contact, Joseph."

Dropping his chin, staring at his boots, Walker sighed. "What's the plan?"

"Mérida was closer to the epicenter of the earthquake and not a good place to try to go. He's flying the girls to Cancún. We've given him directions on where to land, and he'll take them to the resort they were going to stay at once they got there anyway. We've arranged for a doctor to take a look at Tiffany. He's going to need someone to stay with them before he can come back and get you and Ms. Baxter, so we're arranging that as well."

"Will he come back in a bird or do we need to get to a landing strip so he can fly in?"

"We're going to have you see if you can get somewhere he can get a plane in. We have your area under satellite surveillance. Whatever gangs and looters were nearby last night, they probably got hold of all the alcohol at the resort and passed out. But it looks like they're starting to move around again. Can you get transportation?"

Stifling his curse once more, he acknowledged Tate's question, saying, "No problem. I'll be in contact." Disconnecting, he scrubbed his hand over his face, feeling the stubble along his jaw, and sighed heavily.

"Is everything okay? Are the girls okay?"

The soft voice coming from behind him startled him, and he whirled around quickly. Pissed that he had let her slip up on him, something no SEAL should have let happen, he growled, "You need to stay where I tell you."

Her eyes opened wide before she blinked several times then snapped her mouth closed. He watched the telltale signs of her chin tremble before she straightened her spine and aimed a frosty gaze toward him.

"I will gladly go away from you, but I want to know about the girls first."

He kept his facial expression neutral, but inside was kicking himself for his rudeness as well as admiring the set of her jaw. "As you suspected, Tiffany is ill." The ice in her eyes melted instantly as worry took the place of her anger. Before she could speak, he added, "Drew is taking care of her, but unfortunately, our plans have changed. Mérida is somewhat unstable right now, and he doesn't have someone he can leave the girls with. We're in contact with our agency and have been instructed for him to take the girls to Cancún where they'll meet with someone who'll be able to care for them."

Her eyes darted to the side as she seemed to process the changing situation. Wanting to put her at ease, he said, "Before you ask, we can't stay here. Satellite intelligence is showing that groups of people at the resort nearby are still in the area. I'm concerned that they'll fill the roads around here and start scouring the area, looking for whoever they can find."

"Then we need to leave," she stated, her gaze glancing nervously toward the distance in the direction of the resort.

"Yes. We need to leave."

The words had barely left his mouth when she turned and began climbing back down the steps. Stunned, it took a few seconds for him to see that she was not going to give into hysterics. As he quickly followed her down, he realized this was the second time she had acted in a practical manner, defying his previous assumptions. And once again, his admiration for her increased.

Stay where he puts me? Who does he think I am? A dog? Julie seethed all the way down the steps of the temple, and when she reached the bottom, she plopped down on the hard stone. Practicality set in, and she had no idea where they would go or how they would get there. While the area surrounding the temples Chichén Itzá had been cleared of the jungle, it was still all around.

Suddenly very tired, she leaned forward, propping her elbows on her knees and her hands on her cheeks. She could not hear his footsteps but felt the electricity in the air as Walker came nearer.

He sat down next to her, his hard thigh pressing against hers. That slight gesture should have offended her, but instead, the warmth exuding from his body felt comforting. Sighing, she lifted her head and twisted to look at him. "So, what do we do?"

His lips curved slightly, and he shook his head.

"What?" she asked, her voice sharper than she intended. His grin widened, and his blue eyes held her captive. Swallowing audibly, she sucked in her lips, wondering what fatigue was doing to her.

"You just surprise me," he said. "That's all."

Her head tilted in question, but instead of explaining more, he continued, "So...next? I'm going to slip over to the resort and obtain transportation."

Blinking, her mouth dropped open. "We're going back to where the looters are? We're going to get transportation? How on earth are we going to do that?" Her voice rose with each word, and she shifted slightly away so that she could twist her body to face him, instantly missing the contact of their legs pressed together.

"I didn't say we."

"What?"

Speaking slowly, he repeated, "I didn't say *we*. I said *I* was going to go to the resort and obtain transportation."

"You? As in you by yourself?"

Chuckling, he replied, "That's generally what *I* means."

Narrowing her eyes, she asked, "Are you trying to piss me off?"

"No, ma'am. I'm telling you what my plan is. You'll stay here, out of sight, and I'll get to the resort, find something suitable, and bring it here for you. We'll then take back roads and get the fuck outta here."

Looking down at her clasped hands, she tried to still her racing thoughts. The idea of staying at the ruins by herself held no appeal, but uncertainty at how he did his job put her at a disadvantage.

"Hey," he said, giving her a slight shoulder bump. "You'll be fine here. Go back up to the top, stay hidden, and I'll be back before you know it."

Barely whispering, she asked, "What do I do if you don't come back?"

He placed his hand on her shoulder, giving it a little squeeze, and the tingle she had felt earlier returned. When Drew had placed his hand on her shoulder, she had felt nothing. Refusing to think on that, she looked up into his face again.

His icy blue eyes were now warm, and she sucked in a deep breath.

"I promise I'll be back, quicker than you'll realize.

But you've also got Drew's number if you need to reach him."

She let out a breath and stood. "Okay. I have no choice but to trust you."

"And do you?" he asked, his gaze roving over her face.

She remained quiet for a moment before lifting her chin. "Yes. I do." Shoulders hunched, she added, "I don't really have a choice."

"I can accept that, Julie," he said. "You don't know me. You don't know the kind of job I do. You don't know the kind of man I am. But you will."

He held her gaze, and his penetrating eyes stared deep inside of her, soothing the jagged edges of her fears. Somehow, she felt as though this man would do anything, go to any lengths to keep her safe. "Okay," she whispered, not able to come up with another response. If his smile was any indication, it was the only response he needed.

14

Walker could not remember the last time someone had questioned his abilities or doubted his word. Surprised that he did not feel insulted, it was hard to keep the grin off his face when he remembered the spirit coming at him this morning. Being honest with himself, he remembered thinking that she was going to be nervous, and possibly hysterical. Certainly not showing the backbone that she had already. *Maybe the next day won't be too bad.*

After watching Julie climb back up the temple steps and disappear out of sight, he slipped silently through the jungle forest by the side of the ruins. Approaching the resort, he moved with great stealth, making sure to stay hidden until he ascertained the situation.

A few people were milling around, tourists that still looked dazed as well as resort staff that appeared harried. He saw a few men with guns slung over their shoulders, uniforms giving them the appearance of being military or police, but it was hard to be sure considering many cartel members were part of the police. At least it did not appear that anyone was being abused.

Focusing on the task at hand, he scanned the parking lot, discovering the only vehicles left were older models. *Damn looters must have taken the nicer vehicles.* Unfazed, he found an old, green Jeep, with a high enough clearance in case they had to get off the road onto rough terrain and extra gasoline tanks. Bent low, he headed directly to it then changed his plan as he saw an employee nearby.

Walking up to him, he offered a slight smile and nod, adopting the battle-weary expression that most of the others wore.

"Sir, may I be of assistance?" the employee asked.

"I left my keys with the valet," Walker said smoothly. "Would it be possible for me to get them?"

"Oh, sir, I don't know how the roads are. We are encouraging our guests to stay until we can assure their safe transportation."

"I appreciate that, and I understand your position," he continued. "But I have government business in Cancún and must leave immediately. If you would be so good as to get the keys to this vehicle, I would certainly show my *gratitude*." Sticking his hand in his pocket, he pulled out a wad of cash as a symbol of being willing to pay for his gratitude.

The man's eyes dropped for a moment before lifting and meeting Walker's smile with one of his own. "Certainly, sir. I'll be right back."

Keeping an eye on the man, Walker observed as he went to a lockbox and pulled out a key. As the man placed the key to the Jeep in his palm, Walker handed him enough pesos to equal a month's salary.

Eyes wide, the man grinned and thanked him profusely before turning and hustling back to the hotel.

Having a key kept him from needing to pick the lock and hotwire the Jeep, which he could have done easily. But if anything happened to him, he wanted Julie to be able to get away, and the key would offer her that ability.

Keeping a sharp lookout, he saw no one as he pulled out of the parking lot, down the road toward the ruins, and then over the grass, coming to a stop near the observatory temple. Driving to the back so that he would be out of sight, he breathed a sigh of relief that the area still appeared deserted. He assumed that would not last for long. There would be some of the hotel residents who might decide to make a visit to the ruins, and there was always the possibility of new people coming by, even though the area had been affected by an earthquake. Not wanting to hang around and see who might make an appearance, he climbed out of the Jeep and looked up, hoping to catch Julie's attention.

Not seeing her, he was glad to find that she had listened and stayed well hidden. Using the back steps, he climbed to the top without breaking a sweat. "Julie?" Walking toward the dome of the observatory, he ducked his head, entering the building. "Julie?" Whirling around, he hustled back out, circling the perimeter of the dome. Not finding her nor seeing her as he scanned the area looking down, his heart began to pound, wondering where she could have gone. *Fuck! I should have taken her with me!*

Reaching the bottom, he ran toward the Jeep, skidding to a stop as he saw her walking toward him from the edge of the jungle nearby, carrying her backpack, large bag, and lugging his duffel along with her.

Irritation warred with relief, and he stalked toward her, his long legs making short work of the distance. He could tell the instant her eyes landed on him, a smile spreading across her face. He then watched it slide away as he grew closer. Now, her eyes were filled with concern. *Good. You should be concerned!*

She opened her mouth to speak, but he got there first. Hands on his hips, he leaned forward. "What do you not understand about staying where I put you?" he growled, not caring how rough his voice sounded.

She opened her fingers, dropping his duffle bag onto the ground with a thud. Straightening her spine, she pulled herself up to her full height, which he observed still put her eyes at his neck level, having to lean her head back to glare into his eyes. Her body shook with a slight quiver as she held his eyes. "Not to be indelicate, Mr. Walker, but I had to go to the bathroom. I couldn't wait. And I certainly wasn't going to desecrate this ruin, so I walked just to the edge of the woods where I could be hidden while still keeping a lookout for you." Leaning forward, mimicking his posture, their chests almost touching, she added, "And I lugged your duffle with me so that it would be protected!"

Lips now pinched tightly together, she sucked in a

deep breath through her nose and leaned back. Hefting her bag back up on her shoulder, she marched past him toward the Jeep.

His gaze followed her backside as she stomped away, incredulity mixed with admiration filling him. Trying to ignore the way her rumpled khaki pants cupped her ass as she headed away from him, he focused on the square set of her shoulders, her head held high, and her ponytail swinging as she walked. Bending, he grabbed his duffle and followed her to the Jeep.

Nothing was going as planned, and the sense of being out-of-control left her nervous. She wanted to throw her bags down and then follow by flinging her body onto the hard ground as well. A tantrum would not be unwarranted but would take too much energy. Crying might also make her feel better but might make her dehydrated.

Out of practical options, Julie reached the Jeep and leaned forward, resting her forehead on the passenger side window. Exhaustion threatened to take her legs out from under her, so she used the heavy steel to hold her up. *Why is he so grouchy? I'm just trying to do the right thing, and he's so...so...*

"Sorry," came his deep voice from right behind her.

She had not heard Walker approach but was not surprised. Keeping her eyes squeezed shut and her lips pressed together, she did not move. The electricity in the air shifted as he moved closer and she felt his heat directly behind her. Eyes still closed, her backpack was lifted from her shoulders, and she dropped her hands so that he could slide the burden from her. While her hands were still down at her sides, he lifted the strap of her bag, pulling it over her head. She sucked in a deep breath, letting it out easily, feeling the weight lift from her.

His warm presence was still close behind her, and she felt her ponytail move from the front of her shoulder to where it was hanging down her back again, the slight feel of his fingers in her hair causing her eyes to jerk open. Just as quickly as the sensation came it left, and he stepped back, leaving her uncertain if she had imagined his touch.

He stepped to the side and opened the back door, placing her bags inside. In a voice much softer than he had ever used with her, he asked, "Are you ready to go? We really need to leave."

Her body jerked slightly as his tone soothed over her. Straightening quickly, she nodded and reached for the door handle, finding his hand already there pulling it open. She looked to the side, forcing her gaze to lift to his, and offered her thanks before climbing inside.

"Buckle up," he ordered before closing the door, his voice no longer warm but at least not as gruff as it had been.

She obeyed but sighed as he rounded the front and climbed behind the wheel. Sparing a glance in his direction before focusing out the windshield, she wondered *Will I ever get used to his flash-changing moods?* Giving a slight shake of her head, she realized what a ridiculous thought that was. After all, by the end of the day, they would be in Cancún, she would be reunited with the girls, and she would never see him again.

As he pulled out from the edge of the jungle, she wondered why that last thought did not make her as happy as it should.

15

"What have you got for me?"

"We've got you on our radar," Tate replied. "You're going to need to avoid Highway 180D."

"What the fuck?" Walker groused, hearing that the major highway that could get them to Cancún in about two and a half hours was going to have to be avoided.

"There's been damage to a couple of overpasses that's got traffic snarled and maybe closed. Some of the back roads were dirt anyway, so that'll be your best bet for getting there."

"How about going north? Toward Espita? I know their tour was going to go to Ek Balam today anyway, and that would be on the way to Cancún."

"We want you to avoid that as well," Mace said, and Walker realized he probably had the entire Keeper crew in the compound working on this mission.

Continuing, Mace said, "I've got Clay here, and he's

been keeping an eye on the cartel movements over the past twenty-four hours."

He knew Clay was their best security specialist, and if anyone could dig out the detail on the drug cartel movement, it would be him. "Give it to me," he agreed. "I've stopped at the edge of the Chichén Itzá ruins, still hidden from the main road until you let me know where to go."

"Walker, we're going to send you south," Clay said. "You should be fine on the road toward Valladolid. Before you get there, go south again on a much smaller road to Chichimilá. You'll head straight south through the jungle to the small town of Chanchen I. From there you will go east to Cobá."

"How long is that going to take?" he asked, sparing a quick glance to the side, seeing Julie's wide eyes pinned on him, knowing she could not hear the instructions he was being given, only the irritation in his voice.

Attempting a slight smile, he felt sure it came out more as a grimace when her eyes widened even more.

"Without any problems that should take you about three hours," Clay answered. "There's a small town there where you should be able to get food and gas. It doesn't look like there's any major damage or cartel movement, probably because it's a poor area that doesn't get a lot of visitors."

"And from there to Cancún?"

"Best route to keep you from avoiding the major highway cutting through the Yucatán would be to have you drop down to the coast at Tulum and then follow the coastal highway all the way north to Cancún. And before you ask, that would take another couple of hours."

Tate had entered the information into Walker's GPS, and just as he disconnected the call, Julie hastened to ask, "What about the girls?"

His concentration focused on their surroundings as he pulled out onto the road, heading in the direction they needed to go. "I didn't ask about the girls." The road took them past one of the other smaller resorts near the ruins, and he was glad to see that there was some traffic out so that they would blend in. Hearing a huff in the seat next to him, he jerked his head around.

"I know you didn't ask about the girls," she said, her lips pinched. "I could hear you."

Unused to having to explain himself, he fought to keep his voice steady. "Where they are, they're safe, and Drew is taking care of them. Right now, they're not my concern. You are."

"Well, I'm concerned about them," she argued in return. "So if you're concerned about me, and I'm concerned about them, doesn't it stand to reason that you should be concerned about them as well?"

The inside of the Jeep remained quiet for a moment, the only sound heard by the occupants the engine running and their own breathing. Finally, tapping the button on his radio headset, he asked, "What's the status of the girls?"

Tate replied, "Drew has landed in Cancún. As soon as he gets to the resort, Tiffany will receive medical care. The other two girls are fine."

"Thanks, man," Walker said, before disconnecting

once again. Glancing to the side, he watched her eager expression. Not wanting to keep her in suspense, he said, "The girls are fine. They're safe, and Drew is getting the medical attention that Tiffany needs."

Julie's shoulders slumped as her body visibly relaxed, and a strange bolt of guilt slid through him.

"Oh, thank God," she cried. Once again, they fell into silence for a few minutes, before she said, "Thank you, Walker."

She had demonstrated her concern for her charges more than once, and as irritating as it was to have her question him, he once more respected her diligence. "No thanks needed, Julie. I should've asked the first time."

"I guess I've just gotten used to being around them for the past two weeks." Her shoulders hunched in a slight shrug as she added, "Actually, they were so easy to chaperone, it was more like being with friends. But I never forgot that I was the responsible one and don't see that duty ending until I hand them back over to their parents in Florida."

Relaxing his grip on the steering wheel as it appeared they were going to make good time on the road even if it was not a major highway, he said, "I'm sorry your trip came to such an abrupt halt." Casting his gaze in her direction again, he watched as her lips curved into a smile, her entire demeanor less rigid. Normally, making small talk with someone on a mission was not something he entertained or encouraged, but he found himself wanting to know more about her. *It'll just be a way to pass the time*, he reasoned.

"Tell me about what you enjoyed before everything fell apart."

He knew he had chosen the right subject when she twisted her body around, placed her knee in the seat and faced him, her eyes now bright.

"There was so much we learned, I almost don't know where to start," she said, reaching into a large bag at her feet and pulling out a colorful notebook. She flipped through a number of pages, then with her hands fluttering in excitement, she said, "Um, let's see. We actually started our tour flying into Villahermosa. That's where we met Hernando, and that evening, he gave us a wonderful beginning lecture on what all we would be seeing. Did you know that the entire Yucatán Peninsula is part of a large chunk of land that's partially submerged? It's flat, not very much above sea level. And," she said, waving her hand toward the front windshield, pointing at the thick vegetation on either side of the road, "it's dense with rain forests."

"Did you all do any exploring of the rain forest?"

Shaking her head, she wrinkled her nose and replied, "Only on the first day. That day we went to Kolem Jaa, where we had a short boat ride which I thought was beautiful. Then we did a zip line which was not supposed to be very scary, but I confess that I was terrified. Then there was a short rappel down through the water cascade, which I enjoyed mostly because it kept me cool. I'm embarrassed to tell you that that day concluded with Hernando taking us back to the hotel where we got a spa treatment. I'm not much of a daredevil." Sighing, she confessed, "The rest of the trip we were the type of tourists that went around in Hernando's nice, air-conditioned van, staying on major roads unless we were going straight to one of the Mayan ruins."

She looked back at him, scrunching her nose once more, and asked, "I guess that sounds pretty lame, doesn't it? Just being an ordinary tourist and not searching out the lesser-known areas to explore."

His brain short-circuited once more as he stared at her crinkled forehead, scrunched nose, and wide eyes staring straight at him. He could not figure out what it was about her other than she was the most unaffected woman he had been around in a long time. As he looked over at her again, he saw her head tilt and he remembered she had asked him a question.

"No, no. That doesn't sound lame at all. Not everybody's cut out for adventure, and that's fine. You came for a tour of the Mayan ruins and that's exactly what you did. On top of that, you came as a chaperone to three teenage girls, and believe me when I say that was very brave!"

Her face relaxed once more, and he nodded toward the large notebook and asked, "Did you keep all your notes in there?"

She blushed a delicate pink and nodded. "I like to have things planned. I found this planner and it was perfect. There was room for our itinerary, but also for me to make notes of what we saw each day. I feel better if I have a plan and can stick to my plan."

He wondered how the change in their plans had affected her, but wanting to keep the conversation pleasant, he asked, "So what are some of the ruins you saw?"

Grinning, her hands dancing in front of her again, she said, "We went to a couple of museums the next day and ended up at Palenque, which was straight out of a beautiful picture book. Old ruins with the jungle growing right up to them. The girls absolutely loved it, and so did I!"

With her eyes bright and her face glowing in a smile, she was beautiful in such a way that he had to force his gaze back to the road ahead while being tempted to continue to simply stare at her face. His fingers flexed, tightening on the steering wheel. *Let her talk, but I've gotta keep my eyes on the road. Distractions can be deadly, and I'll be damned if I let her distract me.*

She continued, seemingly oblivious to the fact that he did not look at her. "The ruins there were magical. Some of the stone steps of the temples closest to the jungle were covered in vines and trees that were growing straight up through the rock. You could climb up many of them and the views were breathtaking." She hesitated for a few seconds, but he kept his eyes on the road, merely giving her a nod of his head to indicate he was still listening.

"I think because the land is so flat that when you climbed to the top of the pyramids it felt as though you could see forever," she added.

He offered another nod, but this time she did not continue. The silence remained for a moment, and he finally gave in to his curiosity and glanced toward her. Her body had not changed as it was still twisted toward him, but her head was now facing the front. As he stared at her profile, he could see her lips pulled in, pressed tightly together, the animation gone from her expression.

He battled between appreciating the silence so that he could focus on the task at hand and wanting to see her smile again. "You can keep talking," he said, wondering what it was about this woman that made him want to hear her voice.

"I'm sure my babbling is a distraction that you don't need," she said, her voice soft, and he wondered if there was the barest hint of regret that he could hear.

"No, really," he insisted. "I'm sure the drive will go faster for both of us if you're talking, as long as you don't mind me not responding much."

"Oh, okay," she mumbled. She shifted slightly in her seat, the leg that had been propped up on the old bench seat now facing the front with both feet firmly on the floorboard. Her head turned away from him, and he had no idea what she was thinking. He started to ask her but halted, figuring if she wanted to talk, she would. But this time the silence in the old Jeep seemed out of place. Sighing, he kept his eyes on the road, determined to make the next couple of hours simply pass.

16

Julie stared out the window, the thick Yucatán jungle growing close to the road. So similar to some of the roads she had traveled with Hernando over the past two weeks, and yet, now, instead of seeing the beauty, it just made her feel more alone. Walker was obviously intent on his mission of getting her back to Cancún, for which she was grateful, but it made him poor company. Inwardly grimacing, she thought of how stupid that last thought was. *Jesus, Julie. He's not here to keep me company or to be entertained. And certainly not to entertain me.* Settling back in her seat, she considered the idea of taking a nap but hated to miss any part of Mexico.

"We should be to Tekom in just a little bit, and I'm gonna make sure the gas tanks are full. It looks like there'll be a place for us to get some food or snacks as well. We'll want to make sure we get some food to take with us."

She startled and looked to the side, seeing his blue

eyes staring at her. Uncertain if he expected her to have replied, she simply nodded.

"You still have to tell me about the rest of your trip. You were telling me about Palenque."

Gathering her thoughts, she said, "After that, we went to Chicanná. It was an ancient town but didn't have pyramids. Instead, it had the most striking buildings with detailed and ornate carvings. It was completely unlike anything we'd seen before."

Walker had fallen silent again, but as she glanced over, he offered an encouraging nod, so she continued. "Hernando told us that because of the ornate quality of the decorations it's suggested that it was a town for the region's most elite."

"A city for the rich," he stated matter-of-factly, eliciting a grin from her.

"Exactly. It's not unusual for our cities and towns to have neighborhoods for the rich and famous," she replied. "I guess that's not a modern idea at all. It's been suggested that it was tied into the city of Becán, which we went to next. It also has pyramids, the tops barely peeking above the jungle surrounding it. It's less structured to see than some of the others, so we were able to wander around the twenty or so ruins as Hernando lectured about the history."

"Sounds like you all packed a lot in a day."

Walker's hands on the steering wheel appeared more relaxed than when they first began their trip, and his voice was warmer as well. She felt some of the earlier tension slide out of her body as she leaned her head back against the seat. The old model Jeep did not have comfortable headrests, so she propped her elbow on the back of the seat and rested her head on her arm, still facing toward him.

Yawning, she continued, "That wasn't even the end of that day. We also went to Xpuhil. It was a small site but very old, probably being occupied about 600 BC. It had three tall towers that at one time would've been covered with ornate and intricate details, but looters over the centuries have stolen much of it. Hernando did tell us that there were secret stairways inside the towers that allowed the priests to sneak up to the top so that they could magically appear to the people."

"How are you able to remember so much?" he asked. "Your tour crammed so much into the days I would think it would all run together."

"Hernando was so much more than a tour guide. He was a really good teacher. And at the end of each day, the girls and I would gather either at the dinner table, or at the pool, or just in our rooms, and we would talk. We talked about what we saw and how it affected us. None of us had laptops with us, but they had small tablets and I had my planner. I was taking notes on a lot of what we saw and then in the evenings we would compare notes."

She looked over and saw him shaking his head, a slight smirk on his impassive face.

"What?" she asked.

"I'm still just amazed." He glanced toward her and then quickly added, "I'm not trying to profile all teenagers together, because God knows it's been a long time since I've been around teens. But when I was sixteen or seventeen, taking notes and studying while on a holiday is the last thing I would've been doing."

She laughed, "I'm not offended. It's been a long time since I was seventeen years old, and I doubt I would've been quite so into this either. But the girls seem to really soak up everything, and I just wanted to make sure the trip was something that they would remember. I certainly never got to take a trip like this when I was a teenager, and I'm glad they seem to appreciate that they were able to."

She yawned again and felt her eyelids grow heavy as the rough bouncing of the Jeep was no longer able to keep her awake.

Drifting to sleep, she imagined Walker whispering, "Rest easy."

Scanning the area as he drove into the tiny town of Tekom, Walker did not discern any unusual activity. The stone and concrete buildings did not appear to have been overly damaged by the earthquake, but then, it was hard to tell in their state of disrepair. He noted that not a lot of people were out, but neither were the streets empty.

His GPS showed that there were two small convenience stores in the town as well as a tiny restaurant and grocery. He had considered stopping at the restaurant to give Julie a chance to sit down to eat a meal and freshen up, so he stopped at the first convenience store to get gas and buy food for the road for later.

Glancing to the side, his hand halted on the way to her shoulder, hating to wake her. He sat for a moment and stared at her face, relaxed in sleep. Her lashes rested in crescents against her cheek. Her hair was still pulled back in a ponytail, although loose tendrils waved about her face. As her head rested on her arm, he looked at her wrapped wrist and chastised himself that he had not checked it recently. He could not remember the last time he had simply stared at a sleeping woman, preferring his encounters to be unencumbered with the entanglements of sleeping with someone. Life was simpler that way, with everything in its own box, including sex.

Blinking at the strange turn of his thoughts, his hand jerked roughly on her shoulder and he said, "Wake up, Julie."

Her eyes fluttered open, and she sat up quickly, looking around in confusion. As the fog in her eyes lifted, she rubbed the back of her neck and asked, "How long was I sleeping?"

"Only about fifteen minutes," he said as he climbed out of the Jeep. "Stay inside while I fill the tank with gas. I'll go inside to pay and grab some food for later on, checking things out as well. If all seems okay, we'll stop at a little restaurant down the block."

Grateful she did not argue, he filled the tank and the reserve tanks on the back. Several townspeople walked by, conversations and behaviors appearing normal, causing the tension in his shoulders to relax slightly. Stepping inside of the small building, he grabbed a bag and began filling it with water bottles and packaged food. At the cashier, the older woman grinned widely as she calculated his bill and gleefully took his money.

Tossing the bags in the back of the Jeep, he climbed behind the wheel and drove down the block to the small restaurant. There was no parking lot, a few other cars simply parking on the street in front of the restaurant. Foregoing that, he pulled around to the back of the building, parking in the shade. Once more glad that she was not peppering him with questions, they climbed from the vehicle and walked around the front that was lined by an ancient stone wall, green vines and trees all around.

The inside of the restaurant was simple, a few plastic tables and chairs crowded into the floor space, with others spilling outside the open door. Colorful plastic tablecloths covered the tables. Seated near the back, he ordered tacos with pork shavings and chicken enchiladas. Looking over at Julie, he asked, "Is that okay?"

She nodded enthusiastically, her smile genuine. "Hernando made sure that we ate authentic Mexican food while we were here, but he usually ordered, so thank you."

It did not take long for the food to come out, served by a smiling young man. They dug in, and he could not help but grin at Julie's exclamations of appreciation for the food.

"You like the food?" the server asked when he came back around to check on them.

Smiling, Julie nodded. "Your English is very good. I'm sorry that my Spanish is not nearly good enough to speak in your language."

Shrugging, the young man accepted her compliment and said, "We get English-speaking customers even if we're off the main road. I like to practice."

Walker watched as Julie and the server chatted for a moment, her smile infectious. The young man left so that they could continue their meal, and he was glad she dug in heartily.

"Oh, my God, this is so good," she groaned, touching her napkin to her lips. "I was getting sick of granola bars."

Her groan had shot straight to his cock, and his eyes were glued to her lips as she licked more of the sauce from them. Shifting in his seat, he dropped his gaze back to his plate, concentrating on his own food and trying unsuccessfully to ignore the sounds coming from her. *Jesus, what the fuck is wrong with me?* He knew the answer to that… *It's been too fuckin' long since I got laid. And that's not going to happen anytime soon.* Using all his discipline, he forced his cock to stop twitching every time she made a delightful moan, glad when she finished her food and pushed her plate back, a satisfied expression on her face. Losing his discipline battle, he thought of what he would like to do to give her an even more satisfied expression on her face. Wanting to get onto the road, he lifted his hand and waved toward the server.

The smile was gone from the young man's face, and as he took Walker's money, he bent low to whisper, "So, you parked in back? You go now. Quickly."

Instinctively understanding the warning, Walker

stood, his chair scraping back against the wooden floor. Grabbing Julie's hand, he barked, "Let's go."

He pushed her ahead of him toward the kitchen area and, twisting his head around to glance out the front, saw several vehicles with heavily armed men hanging on them coming to a stop at the convenience store they had been at earlier.

Once more grateful that Julie was taking direction quietly, he continued to push her along after the young man until they reached the back door. Grabbing her shoulders, he shucked her to the side, placing his hand in the middle of her chest to press her against the wall, ignoring her wide, frightened eyes. Peering out the back, he saw that all was quiet and leaned down to whisper his command. "Get into the backseat and lay down on the floorboard."

Giving her a slight shove, he forced her out the back door before he turned to the young man, pulling out some money from his pocket.

The server waved his hands in front of him, shaking his head. "No, no, sir. You and pretty lady be safe." Grinning, he jerked his head toward the front and said, "They will come in here next to get something to eat. I'll keep them busy. They eat long time."

With a nod of gratitude, Walker turned and darted out to the Jeep, pleased to see Julie not in sight. As he climbed in behind the wheel, he looked behind the front seat and saw her crouching in the floorboard behind him. "Stay quiet and we'll get outta here," he assured.

He started the Jeep and drove forward, continuing down the alley behind several buildings until he pulled back out onto the main road. Stone walls lined the asphalt road as long as there were still houses. Quickly though, as civilization was left behind, the jungle encroached on either side of the road.

"Can I come out now?" came the muffled voice from behind him.

Scanning the area, including behind him in the rearview mirror, all appeared clear. "Yeah. You can come on up." He was amazed at the speed with which she scrambled over the seat, her foot nearly hitting him in the head as she then plopped down.

Twisting to grab the seatbelt, she buckled and turned to him, asking, "What was going on?"

Wondering how much to tell her, he said, "Our server noticed some armed men coming into town and figured it was better for us to be leaving. While the townspeople seemed very nice, you never know who or what those men were."

He spared a look her way, seeing her lips open as though to speak before snapping closed again. She nibbled on her bottom lip, and he fought the desire to reach over and rub his thumb to soothe the sensitive skin.

"I don't even know where we are," she commented.

"We're heading south, but in about ten miles we'll get off this highway and head due east toward Cobá. I'm afraid that road won't be nearly as nice as the road we're on right now."

Her head jerked around toward him, and she said, "I hope you know by now that I'm not a fussy traveler. I know you're trying to get me to safety, and I'm not going to break. Honestly, you can just treat me like anyone else."

While he appreciated her words, he inwardly disagreed. The way his heart raced whenever he looked at her gave every indication that she was not like anyone else.

17

Drew was impressed. Expecting thatched umbrellas on the beach, bars overflowing with drunks, and crowded swimming pools in the resort that the girls were staying at, he was stunned at how wrong he had been.

The flight had been uneventful except for Tiffany's continued illness. Landing at the Cancún airport, Mace had arranged for transportation, and as soon Drew secured his plane, he carried Tiffany to the large, comfortable SUV. Placing her gently in the back seat, he offered a smile and said, "I promise we'll get to the resort in just a bit, and a doctor will be there to see you."

She smiled wanly, and he stood back to allow Andrea and Jackie to climb in on either side of Tiffany. Getting their bags into the back, he pulled out into traffic. The short drive took longer than he wanted, but pulling into the NIZUC resort and spa made it worth it. The modern flare of the resort, along with the low crowd in the lobby, made him want to personally thank Senator Daniels for his foresight.

Check-in was efficient, and he was assured that a doctor was awaiting their arrival. Following the bellboy to the luxury villa, he carried Tiffany through the door. A quick scan gave evidence to two large bedrooms, one with a king-sized bed and the other with two queens. Making his way straight to the king room, he laid Tiffany down.

Looking over his shoulder, he could not help but grin at Andrea and Jackie's tired-but-wide-eyed appreciation of their accommodations. "Girls, help Tiffany to the bathroom while I order some food. The doctor will be here soon. You two can get your things put into the other bedroom—"

"But we want to be close to her," Andrea protested, her eyes showing their concern.

Shaking her head, Jackie answered for him. "No, Andrea. Tiffany needs her rest. We'll be in the same suite, but we won't disturb her while watching TV or chatting."

Firing off an agreeing nod to her, Drew moved to the phone and ordered room service while the girls headed into the bedroom with Tiffany. He had no more finished ordering when a knock sounded on the door. Opening it, he was relieved to find the resort's doctor.

The older man, his short hair completely gray, smiled as he introduced himself. "Mr. Drew? I'm Dr. Lopez, at your service."

Drew looked at his identification before stepping back and allowing the man to enter. Curious, he asked,

"Were you not called to service in the remote areas that were hit with the earthquake?"

"I'm retired now," Dr. Lopez explained. "I'm on call for this resort only and to see an occasional private client."

Recognizing the word client as code for wealthy, he acknowledged "I'm glad you could see us then. Come this way."

As the doctor moved into the room where Tiffany lay on the bed, Drew was uncertain of the protocol. Looking over at Jackie and Andrea, he said, "I'm going to step out of the room, but I want you girls to stay in here." Lifting an eyebrow, he was glad to see Jackie give a short nod, indicating her understanding of his desire to have a female in the room with Tiffany.

Leaving the door open, he walked back into the main room of their suite, having a chance to appreciate the surroundings more. The tile floor, polished to a shine, was warmed with area rugs in neutral colors. The low modern couches and chairs, also in neutral colors of browns and tans, were sleek and inviting. Not one to notice décor, he could not help but note the cream-colored walls and wondered at the blandness of the color scheme. Walking over to the large window, he pulled back the blinds and recognized the reason for the neutral tones of the room. They did nothing to detract from the aqua blue waters, pure white sand, and green palms waving in the wind in the vista before him.

Hearing a noise behind him, he turned seeing Andrea stand in the doorway of the bedroom, her face pale. Stalking toward her, he asked, "Everything okay?"

She slumped into the nearest chair and nodded as she bent forward at the waist, resting her forehead on her knees. Jackie moved to the doorway, her eyes darting between Tiffany and the doctor in the bedroom and trying to keep an eye on Andrea in the chair.

"What the fuck is going on?" Drew asked, not able to read what was happening.

Jackie hurried to say, "The doctor is giving Tiffany an IV for fluids and an antibiotic shot. Needles make Andrea queasy, and she felt like she was going to pass out."

"Jesus," he said, heading into the kitchenette where he wet a towel with cold water before stalking back to Andrea, placing it on the back of her neck. Kneeling, he said softly, "Keep this on your neck and your head between your knees."

Hearing a sniffle, he bent lower to catch what she was saying.

"I... I'm s-s-sorry," she cried.

Taking an edge of the towel and wiping her face, he said, "Hey, none of that. You girls have done great. I couldn't have asked more from you."

"I don't mean to be such a wimp," she said, wiping her nose while breathing deeply.

"I think you're doing fine. You recognized that you thought you were going to pass out and you got out of the room and came in here and sat down. That kept you from passing out and cracking your head open on the floor. See? You did good."

That elicited a slight giggle from her, and he stood,

casting his gaze over to Jackie. "You stay with Andrea for a few minutes, and I'll go talk to the doctor."

Jackie nodded but stopped as she was passing him. Looking up with a slight grin on her face, she said, "Why did the doctor call you Mr. Drew? Isn't that your first name?"

Shaking his head, he replied, "Nah, my name is really Robert Drew, but no one calls me Robert …except my mom."

She laughed and said, "My real name is Jacqueline but only my mom calls me that, too." Cocking her head to the side, she said, "I guess this hasn't turned out to be quite the rescue mission you thought it was going to be, has it?"

Shaking his head, he admitted, "No. But my time in the military taught me that not everything goes as planned, so I think we're doing good."

Her smile widened as she hurried over to Andrea's side, rubbing her friend's back. Stepping into the bedroom, he thanked God the three girls were as mature as Ms. Baxter had assured. Assessing Tiffany as she lay in the bed, her eyes closed and resting, he then shifted his gaze toward the doctor.

Dr. Lopez looked up and smiled, "Mr. Drew, I can assure you that Miss Daniels will be fine. I have already received a call from Senator Daniels' personal physician and have filled him in on what I am doing. She's quite dehydrated, so I have given her an IV, and we will let the fluids get into her body while she is resting. I have also given her an anti-nausea medication. I have drawn blood which I will send off to a lab but am uncertain when I will get the results back due to the overloaded medical system in the area right now. Hopefully, I will know by the end of the day. But I suspect she may also have an ear infection and gave her an antibiotic injection so that it will act fast."

"When will she be able to travel?"

"I want her to stay here for a minimum of twenty-four hours," Dr. Lopez said, walking back over to his bag and collecting his medical supplies. As Tiffany's eyes blinked open for a moment, the doctor smiled at her before walking out of the room. As he passed by Drew, he added, "I'll be back this evening to check on her and again in the morning."

He walked the doctor to the door, securing it after he had left. Leaning his back against the closed door, he closed his eyes momentarily and sighed, slightly banging his head against the hard surface. While the girls' situation was much improved with Tiffany under medical care and Jackie and Andrea in a safe, comfortable location, he had only completed half his mission. He needed to get to Walker and Julie but needed them to be at a location where he could land his plane unless he could get his hands on another bird. Unable to leave the suite, not willing to take a chance on the girls' safety, he was going to have to handle everything from there.

A knock on the door sounded, and he jolted out of his musings. Throwing it open, he smiled at the sight before him…food. Letting the server in, Jackie and a revived Andrea bounded over, squealing in delight. Not knowing what they wanted to eat, he had ordered a smorgasbord. Tipping the server, they dove into the food. After the girls had eaten their fill, he finished his meal while keeping an eye on Tiffany, still sleeping peacefully.

Andrea and Jackie headed to the other bedroom where they decided to take a nap, and he moved to the table. Calling up LSI, he got hold of Tate and said, "Time for backup plans."

18

Julie kept her eyes on Walker, deciding she could no longer ignore his square jaw, blue eyes, and hair that she longed to reach over and touch. But while she was committing his profile to memory, she noticed he constantly peered into the rearview mirror. She would occasionally twist around, seeing nothing untoward. Not wanting to be kept in the dark, she finally asked, "Is there someone following us? Was it whoever you saw in the village?"

He hesitated, and she wondered if he was going to answer or ignore her when he eventually said, "I just want to make sure that I'm aware of our surroundings. So far, it doesn't appear as though anyone is following us, and I'd like to keep it that way."

"I don't understand, Walker. Who would be following us?"

"Under the best of circumstances," he explained, "Mexico can be a dangerous country for visitors who are not staying in one of the major tourist areas. Drug cartels, gangs, even the occasional overzealous soldier can demand money or more." He slid a guarded look her way and added, "It's particularly dangerous for a female. An attractive female, at that."

Attractive female? He thinks I'm attractive? As scary as his words before that had been, a thrill at the word *attractive* shot through her, a feeling she had not had in a long time. His gaze had shifted back to the road in front of them, and she fought to keep from reading too much into what he had said. Focusing back on their conversation, she prodded, "And these are not the best of circumstances."

Shaking his head, he replied, "No. With the earthquake in the middle of the Yucatán, it's pulled some the country's military and police resources to helping victims, leaving many of the areas around open for cartels and gangs to roam about freely. Just like they moved into the resort area to do looting, they'll be out on the roads looking for trouble as well. We were sitting ducks staying at Chichén Itzá and need to find a place where Drew can pick us up. And if he can't get a helicopter, then we're going to need to be near an airstrip."

"Is this why we're getting off the main road?" she asked as he made the turn onto the small dirt road that would take them to the Cobá ruins on their way to the coast.

"Yeah. I've got someone who can give us satellite information to let us know what's safe and what's not."

Thinking for a moment on what he said, she asked, "I don't know anything about you, other than you came to help us out. You must be very good at what you do for Senator Daniels to send for you."

Grinning, he glanced over and asked, "You fishing for information?"

"I guess I wasn't too subtle, was I?" she laughed. "But it hardly seems fair. You know so much about my trip, and I don't know anything about you at all."

"What do you want to know?"

"I suppose anything you want to share with me," she said. "It might sound overly dramatic, but I don't really know what you can share with me. I mean, do you work for some kind of secret, dark ops kind of agency?"

His head jerked around toward hers, and his eyes, filled with merriment for the first time since she had met him, stared at her. "Wow, you do have an imagination, don't you?"

The heat of blush hit her face, and she mumbled, "I guess I read too many novels."

His expression altered again as his eyebrows lifted. "What kind of novels do you read?"

Huffing, she crossed her arms in front of her in defense and said, "Hey, this was supposed to be about you. Now you're asking me questions again."

The smile stayed on his face, and she was not sure she had ever seen anyone so handsome. He could be dark and brooding, serious and demanding, warm and caring, and now smiling. She had only known him since early this morning, and yet, had witnessed a myriad of expressions. And every one of them she had memorized.

The road they were currently on was wide enough

for two vehicles to pass but surrounded by thick jungle and trees that sometimes overhung the street, creating a green tunnel for them to pass through. As beautiful as it was, she could not help but remember his warning of the types of people they might run into. Desperately wanting him to talk, both for the reason of wanting to know and for wanting to keep her mind off their situation, she asked, "Well if you don't work for a dark ops agency, tell me who you work for. I think I remember the word lighthouse from this morning, but I'm not sure."

"That's right," he nodded. "I work for a company named Lighthouse Security Investigations."

"Security…investigations…so, what kind of work do you do?" A nervous laugh slipped out as she added, "Besides rescue damsels in distress."

"We do a multitude of things, such as investigate crimes or suspected crimes, sometimes called in to assist the FBI. We work in high-profile security, again often contracting with the government. We have private clients as well, such as this case where Senator Daniels called us in."

She caught him looking at her, his gaze dropping to her lips, and she realized she was nibbling on her bottom lip again. It was a nervous habit of hers, and she quickly stopped, looking away. A realization struck her, and a small gasp slipped out as she exclaimed, "I don't even know your full name. Is that something I can't know?"

Grinning widely, he replied, "I might be on a mission

to rescue you, but it's not a state secret. My full name is James Walker."

"James Walker," she repeated. "Why do you go by just Walker?"

Shrugging, he replied, "Most of us go by our last names or a nickname. For me, that started back in my Navy days."

"Navy?"

"I was a Navy SEAL."

His pronouncement was just that. Short, clipped, with no fanfare. Her head whipped around to stare at his profile, and everything she had ever read about Navy SEALs came back to mind. At least, what she had read in the news or in novels. So many things about him fell into place. The way he spoke at times where it felt like he was giving an order that he expected to be obeyed. His constant vigilance of what was going on around them. His professional manner that took precedence over their conversations. His strong, muscular body and the way he carried himself with confidence.

Her voice softened, and she said, "I'd like to thank you for your service, but I don't know how you feel about that. I read where some former service members appreciate the sentiment and others don't care for it."

His lips curved softly, and he replied, "It's fine. And thank you."

"Was it hard?"

A tick appeared in his jaw, and his words were laced with incredulity as he questioned, "Hard being a SEAL?"

"Oh, no," she rushed, drawing his lowered-brow gaze over to her. She loved their conversation and the chance to get to know him more. Horrified that she had offended him with her question, she explained, "I know enough layman's information about SEALs to know you had to be the best of the best, but I assume you were doing it because you loved it. I was wondering if it was hard *not* being a SEAL anymore?"

Walker heard her simple question, asked hesitantly, and felt a strange pull in his chest. No one ever asked if it was hard not being a SEAL, only wanting to know about the glory days in uniform. Days that he remembered with pride and fondness as well as the desire to sometimes forget.

Flashes of memories moved through his mind like an antique Mutoscope, so fast he could barely discern each one as separate. Men he served with. Missions they were assigned. Cold water. Hot desert. Laughter mixed with blood. Camaraderie mixed with death.

A soft touch on his arm jolted his mind back to the present, and he swung his head around to see Julie's worried, lip-biting expression. Other than family, he had never had someone else look at him with such concern. A longing to stop the Jeep, pull her into his arms, and kiss the worry from her lips hit him with such force, the air left his lungs in a rush.

"I'm so sorry," she said in a hushed voice, her words barely above a whisper. "I should never have presumed to ask such a question—"

Hating that he was the cause of her contrition when

his thoughts had gone so astray in the middle of a mission, he jerked his head back and forth, saying, "No. You're fine. I was just…"

"Thinking," she filled in for him. "I could see your mind filled with thoughts."

Nodding slowly, he admitted, "Yeah." Clearing his voice, suddenly very self-conscious, he attempted a halfhearted chuckle, but before he was able to say anything else, his radio crackled.

"Ten-one-zero-one?"

Instantly alert at recognizing Tate's voice using police codes, he replied, "Walker, Ten-one-zero-six." He could feel the energy in the Jeep crackle as Julie's nerves vibrated but trusted her to stay calm as he found out what was needed.

"I've got your location on satellite as being about ten miles from Cobá."

"Road is shit, so it'll take another twenty minutes to get there," he estimated.

"Looks like there's movement close by. There's a small village south of Cobá that has cartel presence. Mexican federal police are concerned about the area from the coast over toward where the earthquake affected the smaller towns. That puts them moving right through where you're traveling."

"Does it look like we'll be intercepted?" he asked, praying the answer would be negative because it would be very difficult to ditch the Jeep and get Julie to safety in the dense jungle that was on either side of them.

"We've analyzed the situation in the area," Tate replied. "There are no tourists at the Cobá site today, probably due to the tour companies holding off a day or so until the Mexican government gives the all clear. We don't think it's safe for you to try to get all the way to the coast today, certainly not to Cancún, but probably not even to Playa del Carmen or even Tulum. Our intelligence concludes you should get Ms. Baxter to the ruins and stay there for the night."

"The *night?*" he asked, uncertain he was hearing correctly. The gasp coming from Julie served to indicate that she was equally concerned.

"Drew is getting help for the girls…and before you ask, they are fine. Drew reports Tiffany has been seen by a doctor, but they cannot fly back to the states until tomorrow. As for you and Ms. Baxter, we're working to get you to an airstrip so that he can pick you up. He's still checking, but there are no fuckin' birds that he can get hold of today."

Walker had kept his eyes on the road while talking to Tate, not wanting to spare a glance toward Julie, hating to see what he was sure was going to be panic in her eyes. Another touch on his arm drew his gaze sideways.

"It's okay," she said, her eyes searching his. "We'll do whatever we have to do. I trust you."

The tightness in his chest eased slightly, and he nodded his appreciation. "We're good, Tate. I'll let you know when we get to Cobá."

Disconnecting, he sighed before saying, "I know you wanted to see the girls tonight."

The road was rough, and he kept his eyes straight ahead. He felt, rather than saw, her nod.

"I did, but I feel better knowing that they're safe and Tiffany's getting medical help. Drew can't just snap his fingers and get a helicopter in to pick us up, and," she said with her arms waving around toward the jungle encroaching on either side of the road, "we're not anywhere where he can get us anyway."

His lips twitched in a grin, and he said, "You're making this almost too easy on me." Her head tilted and he continued, "You're not pitching a fit, complaining, moaning and groaning—"

"I beg your pardon," she said in an exaggerated offense, her hand splayed against her chest. "Not all damsels in distress are drama queens. Some of us are quite independent."

They both laughed, and he was glad for the ease of their conversation. He had been on a number of missions but could not remember the last time he enjoyed the company of someone other than his fellow Keepers or former Seal brothers. With another glance to the side, he found himself looking forward to spending more time with her. *As long as I can keep her safe, maybe a night together will be a good thing.* At the thought, his dick twitched, and he fought a growl. *Nope. Not going to go down that line of thinking. She's still a mission.* Now, to convince his cock.

19

Coming to the end of the dirt road at the intersection of the road leading to Cobá, Walker carefully watched for any movement. Turning to the right would take them to the small village that Tate had warned them of, but he saw no vehicles on the road. Pulling out toward the left, it only took a moment for them to see the small town of Cobá ahead.

"I'll bet you're glad to be back on pavement," he said, figuring the bone-jarring dirt road they had been on was not the most pleasant for Julie.

A sigh came from the passenger seat, and she replied, "I have to admit that the smoother ride does feel better."

Just then the tires of the Jeep hit a section of pavement that was potted with holes, and they both laughed. "I guess I spoke too soon," she quipped, her voice jiggling with the movement.

The town looked like the others they had passed

through, stone and concrete walls and buildings, some painted bright colors, others plain and bare. The biggest difference was that one side of the jungle fell away, leaving a large expanse of water visible. Lined with palm trees, it lent a calm, peaceful feel to the village.

The parking lot at the entrance of the walkway leading to the Cobá ruins was empty, giving credence to Tate's information. Spying the lowered-brow confusion on Julie's face, he said, "Almost everything is closed today, but I expect it to be back up and running tomorrow."

Nodding her understanding, she said, "But can we stay hidden when we're so conspicuous?"

He appreciated her understanding of the situation, but instead of replying, he drove straight past the small gate and onto the walking path leading to the ruins.

Gasping, she said, "I don't think you're supposed to drive on this!"

"I'm sure I'm not," he said dryly.

She remained quiet, and he drove along the dusty, packed dirt path, avoiding the occasional tall tree trunk growing in the middle of the path. It only took a few minutes until they came to the widened area near the ruins, the stone buildings and pyramids more easily seen. He continued around the back of some of the buildings near one of the lakes and parked, hidden in the jungle.

Neither spoke for a moment, then she finally shifted in her seat, looked at him, and asked, "It's only the middle of the afternoon. What are we supposed to do?"

A flash of what he would like to do moved through

his mind, but pushing it to the side once again, he smiled and said, "I suggest we explore the ruins." Her mouth dropped open in surprise, and he enticed, "Step outside your planner. This wasn't even on your itinerary, so use it to explore something new."

The surprise was replaced with a clap of glee, and she said, "You're right." Her hand moved to the door handle, then she hesitated. Shoulders slumped, she asked, "Will we be safe?"

He reached over and placed his hand on her shoulder, giving a gentle squeeze. "There's no one around today which makes us very safe here. Plus, the Keepers are keeping an eye on everything and will let us know if there's a change."

Her brow furrowed and she asked, "Keepers?"

Chuckling, he said, "That's what we call ourselves. Named after lighthouse keepers...rescuers of old."

Her smile curved her lips and his fingers stretched to the back of her neck, loving the feel of her soft skin underneath his fingertips. "I'll keep you safe, Julie. I promise."

Her smile returned, and his heart gave a little jolt. Dropping his hand, he winked and said, "Since I know nothing about Mayan civilization, you get to be my tour guide."

"I'm so glad I've got some bars on my phone," Julie said, peering down at her smartphone. The closest structure to where he parked was the ball court, which was much smaller than the one at Chichén Itzá but still a good size. "According to what Hernando told us there are hundreds of ball courts identified. The one thing they have in common is that they are a long narrow alley, flanked with two walls. He told us that the spectators would've stood on top and looked down."

Walker moved slowly along the walls before stopping and planting his hands on his hips, looking around. She caught up to him and said, "It seems they played some kind of a hip ball where they would bounce a rubber ball against the sides. He also told us that sometimes the games would be played with their captured enemies, and sometimes the losers would be decapitated."

She laughed at the expression on Walker's face when his eyes widened in disbelief. She threw her hands up in defense and said, "I know. I know. We said the same thing."

Shaking his head, he admitted, "I'm not really surprised. Even today, people can be pretty vicious."

Continuing to read, she said, "The layout of Cobá is different from the other ancient towns in that it is spread out over seventy km. Some of the buildings are almost a mile apart. It also has quite a few tall temples and was built near these lakes."

Veering off the main path onto one of the smaller ones, they pushed through the thick tangle of trees, coming out on the edge of a large, blue lake. "I'd love nothing more than to jump in and cool off, but I'm not sure we should." She looked up at him and shrugged, adding, "We were warned about parasites in the water before we came on the trip." Looking around, she said, "There are supposed to be some cenotes near here… underwater freshwater pools that are safe to swim in."

"Maybe we can look for those," he said, his eyes boring into hers with an emotion deep inside that she could not identify.

Worrying her bottom lip with her teeth, she sucked in a deep breath and offered a slight nod. "You want to do some more exploring?"

With a grand sweeping of his arm, he said, "Absolutely. Lead the way."

Walking back toward the pyramid, she felt the need to fill the silence. "These white roads we're walking on are quite unique. They're called sacbes and originate at the main pyramid and stretch out in all four directions."

Coming to the base of the main pyramid, they stopped and looked upward. With his hands planted on his hips, he said, "This is much taller than the one I saw this morning."

She agreed, and while she secretly hoped to see the view from the top, she had no idea if she would have the strength to make it that far. He turned toward her and stepped closer. Tilting her head back to keep her gaze on his, the air felt thinner the closer he came.

"Are you game?" he asked.

Not certain what he was referring to, her mouth opened slightly, but all she managed to utter was, "Uh…"

Grinning, he jerked his head toward the pyramid and said, "Let's see what it looks like from the top."

Her breath left her lungs in a rush as she nodded,

sure that her face was flaming hot with blush. *Maybe he'll just think I'm getting sunburned.*

They began climbing the pyramid, Walker turning and offering his hand on the uneven stones. Hesitating for only a few seconds, she placed her hand in his, now recognizing the electricity that seemed to pass between them every time they touched. He was staring intently at her, and she offered a slight smile in return before hiding behind her running commentary again.

"This is the tallest temple in the Northern Yucatán. They say there's an incredible view of the lakes and the surrounding jungle at the top."

"Then that's where we're heading," he said, giving her hand a slight squeeze. Looking down at her injured wrist, he asked, "Does it hurt?"

She shook her head, her eyes never leaving his. "No…I don't feel any pain."

Nodding, his breath left his lungs in a rush and they continued climbing.

The steps were not steep, but at one-hundred-thirty-eight feet in height, she began to wonder if they would ever get to the top. Halfway up she halted, her hand tugging slightly on his. Breathing heavily, she could barely smile when his eyes met hers. Seeming to understand she needed a break, he sat down, and she settled next to him.

He opened up a bottle of water and passed it to her, allowing her to drink first. After she took several long sips, she handed it back and watched as he tilted it up, swallowing deeply. The muscles in his throat worked as he swallowed, and she could not help but notice the heavy, dark stubble on his cheeks and neck. Fatigue pulled at her again, and she had to fight the desire to lean her head on his shoulder. Standing suddenly, she needed to put a little distance between them and said, "We can keep going now."

If he was surprised at her suddenness, he did not comment but neither did he let go of her hand. They continued to climb until they reached the top, and she was sure her legs would not go another step. Fighting the urge to plop down and rest, she stared out at the 360° vista, stunned at what lay before her eyes.

Above the line of the trees, it seemed as though they could see forever. The green forests and jungles of the Yucatán spread out as far as the eye could see. In the distance were the lakes, and the late afternoon sun glistened off the surface.

"Oh, my God," she breathed, turning to see Walker staring out over the horizon. "It's amazing, isn't it? More beautiful than I could ever have imagined."

He turned slowly, facing her, his fingers now linked with hers and said, "Yeah. More beautiful than I could have ever imagined." His blue eyes pierced hers, and she was no longer certain what they were talking about.

The barest hint of a breeze blew over the couple as they stood, her head leaned back as she held his gaze, and without her realizing he had even moved, suddenly they were standing chest to chest.

"I shouldn't do this," he said, his voice a growling whisper. "I shouldn't want this. Hell, I shouldn't even be thinking of this."

Staring up at him, her eyes traced the hard planes of

his face before moving to his lips. Focusing on the perfect symmetry of them, strong and soft, she did not even realize her tongue darted out to moisten her bottom lip.

His gaze fixated on her mouth, and his arms banded around her back as he ground out, "Oh, fuck it," just before he slammed his lips onto hers.

She gasped in pleasure as the strength she imagined would be in his body and lips was proven as she slipped her arms around his waist and held on tightly. He angled his head, maximizing their contact, his tongue tracing her lips before slipping inside, tangling with her tongue.

He tasted of beer, spices, and something uniquely him. Pure male. Pure Walker.

20

Tired of fighting the desire coursing through him, Walker plundered Julie's mouth as he tightened his arms and pulled her body impossibly close to his. He felt her hesitancy at first, and, determined to do the right thing, flexed his fingers just before letting her go to step back. But at the last second, her arms encircled his waist, digging into his thick muscles as she opened her mouth, allowing his tongue to sweep inside. She curled her tongue around his, and the simple, erotic movement shot a bolt of lightning straight to his cock.

For an instant, a flash of past women flew through his mind as he tried to find a comparison but came up short. Teenage fumblings. A few early girlfriends. Frog hogs in the bars near the SEAL bases. Recently, the occasional pickup for nothing more than a night of mutual pleasure. Kissing as a precursor to sex. Sex that was good for both partners, but never a longing for anything more.

But this…this woman in his arms had him rethinking everything he thought about kissing for the sake of kissing. He slid one hand to cup the back of her head, his fingers sliding through the silky strands of her hair, while his other hand slid down to her lower back, continuing to hold their bodies together.

His erection, straining against the zipper of his cargo pants, dug into the soft flesh of her stomach. Her lips were soft as petals, her breath minty sweet, and her eyes closed as they kissed with abandon, no longer able to say where he ended and she began.

An ache began to fill him, starting with his cock but moving to his chest. Pushing that emotion down, he refused to think that their connection was anything more than two consenting adults finding themselves in extraordinary circumstances. He felt her pull away slightly and peered down into her lust-filled eyes, her moist, kiss-swollen lips slightly open, and the realization that she was so much more slammed into him.

She drew in a ragged breath, her breasts pressing closer, and whispered, "Wow."

That simple word caused his male pride to swell, and he grinned. "I gotta tell you, I've been wanting to do that since I first met you."

Her smile widened, and she said, "That means this morning. I know it seems like we've known each other so much longer, but we really only met this morning."

He shook his head, and said, "Nope. I've known you since yesterday." Seeing her scrunched brow, he explained, "I saw your passport picture when we were planning this mission."

Her lips formed an 'o', and her eyes sparkled. "Well, that's different. Twenty-four hours is plenty of time to decide that you want to kiss somebody."

He tightened his arms, lifted an eyebrow, and quipped, "What about you? Haven't you had enough time?"

A giggle slipped out, and she said, "The moment I set eyes on you when you stepped out of the helicopter this morning, I thought, 'Now there's a man I want to kiss'."

Throwing his head back in laughter, he felt light. In the middle of the Mexican jungle, danger dogging their every move, rescue not imminent, and on top of a fuckin' ancient pyramid…happiness struck him right in the chest.

He dropped his chin so that he could stare at the woman in his arms. The top of her head came to his shoulders, her body fit and athletic while still having curves that could fill his hands and imagination. Determined to take care of her, he said, "Are you hungry? I've got food in the backpack."

Grinning up at him, she replied, "It's a tossup. Part of me would love to have a sandwich, and the other part just wants to keep you in my arms and stare at you a little longer."

"Love a woman who doesn't play any games," he said, giving her waist another squeeze. "Come on. Let me feed you."

He reluctantly let go and instantly felt cool where there had been the heat of her body. Moving over to a low wall at the top of the pyramid, they settled with their backs resting against the warm stone and the lowering sun casting a shadow across their bodies. It only took a moment for them to pull out the sandwiches, bags of chips, and water bottles that he had bought when they stopped for gas.

He watched as she ate eagerly, glad that she was not picking at her food. Finishing their simple meal, her eyes blinked slowly as though keeping them open was an impossible chore. Putting the refuse back into his backpack, he reclined using the pack as a pillow. Opening his arms, he silently invited her to join him, which she readily acquiesced.

Snuggling into his embrace, he wrapped his arms around her as she lay her head on his chest.

"I'll just rest a little bit," she mumbled, before falling silent.

He kissed the top of her head and wondered about the simple act of affection. He could not remember ever laying with a woman in his arms for simply rest, nor could he remember ever kissing their hair.

With those thoughts moving through his mind, he joined her in a siesta.

Julie woke with a start, trying to remember where she was. Her hip was stiff from the hard surface underneath, and she realized she had fallen asleep on the ancient stones of the Cobá pyramid, half-lying on Walker.

Her arm was thrown across his middle, her hand

resting on his rock-hard abs. She traced his face with her eyes, planes and angles, rough scruff and soft lips.

She inhaled deeply, unable to keep from sniffing him. She always hated walking past the boy's locker room at school, the odor nearly knocking her down. She equally hated going to the gym after work, the smell of heavily-sweating men overpowering. But Walker smelled completely different...warm musk, masculine, powerful.

He turned his head, catching her staring at him, and grinned. "Did you rest?" he asked, his voice like gravel.

She nodded, not embarrassed at having been caught gawking. Shifting her body so that she was higher on his, she kissed him. If he was surprised, he did not hesitate to slide his arms under her pits and pull her body on top of his, taking the kiss deeper.

Lifting her head, she asked the same question he had. "Did you get some rest?"

A slow grin curved his lips, and he replied, "Oh, yeah. I could go all night."

Unwilling to decipher the meaning of his words, she latched onto his lips again, tasting and tempting, a sensual burning flowing through her veins. A delicious ache began in her core, and she pressed her hips against his erection, feeling the full effect of his arousal.

His hands were heavy and warm against her back before sliding down to cup her ass, his fingers digging into the soft flesh. She sighed into his mouth, the kiss stealing her breath. He was as hard as she was soft. He surrounded her with his body, and she felt safe in his embrace.

She wanted to keep kissing this man she barely knew. She wanted to throw caution to the wind with him, not worrying if it fit into her carefully thought out plan.

She placed her hands on his shoulders and pushed up while spreading her legs and drawing her knees forward so that she ended up straddling his hips. The move shifted her core over his impressive cock, and she rocked gently, desperate for the feel of him against her sensitive flesh, hating the layers of clothes between them.

His hands, still on her ass, kneaded the flesh but did not move away. She kept her eyes locked on his, the blue piercing but full of questions. Julie had never played games with any man and had no intentions of starting now. Going with what she was feeling, she dragged her hands from his shoulders to the bottom of her shirt, watching his expression carefully. When he gave no indication that he wanted her to stop, she slowly lifted the T-shirt over her head, dropping it just to their side.

His blue eyes widened as they dropped from her gaze down her torso, and she felt the heady power of seduction. The setting sun cast a glow onto their bodies, and for an instant, she imagined she was a Mayan princess welcoming her warrior. As fanciful as that thought was, she could not help but grin as she unsnapped her bra, and with a shrug of her shoulders let it slide down to their bed of stone.

His hands moved slowly, gliding from her ass to her waist and upward until he cupped the full weight of her breasts, his thumbs circling her nipples. She gasped at the sensation and dropped her head back as she worshiped the sun beaming down on her body. Without realizing it, she had been shifting her hips, desperate for the friction her core so desired.

Her hands moved to her pants, quickly unzipping them. A swift movement from him caught her off guard as he rolled her to her back. The change in position allowed him to slide his hands into the waistband of her pants and pull them over her hips, snagging her panties as he went. His gaze focused on her abraded knees and shins, and he halted. "Shit, babe. I can't believe you were hurting and you didn't tell me."

She looked down and shrugged. "That didn't just happen. I got those when the earthquake struck, and I fell down some concrete steps. But they don't hurt," she rushed, not wanting him to stop. Lying on the warm stone, the slight breeze blew across her naked body, but she felt no shame. Her want was so great, and she could only hope he shared that desire.

With him now straddling her, he mimicked her motions by pulling off his T-shirt before standing over her, sliding his pants off as well. He grabbed a condom from his wallet and dropped it to the stone next to her.

She stared at the Adonis, his body bathed in the glow of the sunset, large and muscular. Her gaze dropped to his cock, jutting out from his body, a drop of pre-cum on the tip. She was so focused on staring at his body she almost missed his words.

Grinning, he repeated, "I want you to be sure."

Lifting her hands up toward him, she nodded. "I

want you. Of that, I'm very sure." Her gaze devoured him as he fisted his cock with one hand, kneeling down to place his face between her legs. As he began to lap her slit before sucking her clit into his mouth, it took no time for her to cry out her pleasure.

He kissed his way over her mound, circling her belly button, before moving to suckle each breast. Placing the tip of his cock at her entrance, he hesitated until she nodded and wrapped her arms around his back. Then, with one swift movement, he thrust, settling his cock deep inside her body.

21

If the ancient gods had placed a perfect woman on top of this pyramid for him, they could not have created anything more beautiful than the woman whose body was accepting his right now. Walker stared at Julie's face, illuminated by the sunset, and powered into her body. Her knees were bent, giving him easy access, but a slight grimace flew through her eyes, and he realized the hard stone underneath her back would never be comfortable.

Rolling them again, he brought her body on top of his. Taking his hands from her, he grabbed his pants and shoved them under one of her legs and her clothes under the other to give her padding for her knees.

She placed her hands on his shoulders and lifted slightly before settling back down on his cock. With his large hands spanning her hips, he controlled their movements and after a moment pistoned his hips up.

She gave herself over to the movement, sitting up

straight and lifting her head to the sky, her breasts bouncing with each thrust. He watched in awe as the sun cast her body in a bronze glow, sure that he was making love to a goddess.

As she dropped her chin and held his gaze, he grinned as she leaned forward, her breasts now hanging deliciously close to his mouth. He leaned forward, snagging a nipple and sucking it deeply. Moving between each breast, he heard her breath hitch in her lungs and knew she was close. Her inner muscles tightened around his cock, and she cried out her release, her fingers digging into the muscles of his shoulders.

Before her body had a chance to go lax, he felt his balls tighten and the burn in his lower back increase just before he powered his release into her. Thrusting until every drop was drained, he wrapped his arms around her as her full weight lay on top of him.

His breath was ragged as he fought to draw oxygen into his lungs. For several minutes his mind was blank, unable to pull together a coherent thought. Hating to lose her warmth, he shifted his hips so that his condom-wrapped cock could slide out, not wanting to lose their protection. With every breath, her breasts pressed deeper into his chest, and he felt his cock twitch again, knowing he would have no problem for a second round…or more.

As their sweating bodies cooled, doubt began to creep in. *Did I hurt her? Does she regret this? What the fuck was I thinking? Having sex with a mission?*

As though she knew the direction his thoughts had gone, she lifted her head, stared down at him, and smiled. Her eyes glowed with genuine pleasure mixed with a touch of insecurity.

"Wow," she whispered as a delicious blush filled her cheeks.

"You can say that again," he agreed, then wanting to remove all doubt, added, "That was the most incredible thing I've ever felt."

Her blush deepened as she worried her bottom lip. "So, um, having sex on top of a pyramid at sunset in the middle of the Mexican jungle isn't something you normally do?"

Cupping her face with his large hands, his thumb sweeping across her cheeks, he admitted, "I never mix business with pleasure. I've never been tempted before. But you? Beautiful. Smart. A cautious planner who just gave in to the perfect fantasy."

Her grin widened, and she said, "This whole trip is something I'll always remember, but what we just did made it truly unforgettable."

He was grateful she did not ask what he was feeling nor ask for promises beyond what they had at the moment. The way his heart squeezed at just the look in her eye, the sound of her voice, and the feel of her body lying on his, he wanted to keep exploring whatever was happening between them.

She shifted, rolling off of him, and said, "I feel really bad ending a very special moment, but I really need to…um…pee."

He chuckled as she scrambled to her feet and said, "I gotta take care of the condom." He pulled it off before tying it and bent to grab one of the napkins from their dinner. Wrapping up the condom, he looked over his shoulder as she stood with the sunset brilliant behind her. Stalking toward her, both still naked, he wrapped his arms around her, pressing her face against his chest. He felt his heart squeeze as her hands encircled his waist, and he pressed another kiss against the top of her head.

Forcing his arms to let go, they found her clothes, sliding them on.

He bent and ran his fingers lightly over the roughened skin and said, "That could not have been comfortable with your knees taking most of your weight."

She stepped closer, wearing nothing more than her bra and panties, and wrapped her arms around his neck, pulling him down. With his lips a whisper away from hers, she said, "I love that you're being so sweet and that you worry about me, but I'm fine. Every second of everything that we did was perfect." Lifting on her toes, she touched her lips to his, her tongue darting out to barely lick his lips before she settled back on her heels.

She stepped away and turned to slide on her pants and T-shirt, but he was sure with the blush crossing her cheeks that her boldness was out of character. Shaking his head, unable to keep the grin from widening, he chuckled once again.

A heavy rope was attached down the middle of the steps, and because of the darkening shadows, he had her turn and face the pyramid, hold on to the rope with her hands, and back down step-by-step. Planting his body just in front of hers, he was assured that she would not slip and fall. Finally arriving at the bottom, she stood and turned, her eyes wide with need, and said, "I've got to go! Don't peek!"

She ran around the corner of the pyramid and disappeared behind some trees. It had been on the tip of his tongue to say that considering his mouth had been on her and his cock had been in her, seeing her pee should not be embarrassing. Waiting until she came out, an air of contentment on her face, he kissed her forehead and jogged behind the same tree, not wanting to mortify her by pissing in her presence.

Returning to her, he found her nervously looking from side to side. Before he had a chance to ask her what was wrong, she said, "It didn't seem so dark up on top of the pyramid, but down here it is."

Her gaze held the specter of fear, and he wanted to erase all traces of it. Stepping closer, he linked fingers with her again and said, "Don't worry. I've got you."

Julie tried to still the tennis balls bouncing around in her stomach as Walker linked fingers with her and declared for her not to worry because he had her. The desire to read so much into those words was overwhelming, but she knew that was ridiculous. Never one to feel that sex had to be everything, she also didn't want it to be nothing. *But men so often don't feel the same way.*

Determined to not make things awkward between them, she allowed him to lead them through the dark shadows of the trees, glad that the bit of moonlight striking the white pathways helped guide them back to the Jeep. The jungle that had seemed so beautiful earlier now felt claustrophobic.

"Where are we going to sleep tonight?" she asked.

Shooting a smile her way, he said, "When we get back to the Jeep, I'm going to check in with my group. I'll get an update on what's going on in our area and find out how the girls are doing."

Appreciating his concern for not only her but the girls as well, she nodded. They soon reached the Jeep, still hidden from sight with the thick tangle of trees all around.

"I'm glad I'm with you," she said as they climbed inside. "I don't think I would've ever found it by myself!"

Walker leaned over the bench seat and flipped the back seat down flat. "I'm gonna find out what the latest news is. See if there's any way we can make some kind of a bed out of the back of this."

She looked at the space, her nose scrunching as she considered what she could use for bedding. "I can try, but I can't guarantee how comfortable it will be."

Laughing, he replied, "As a SEAL, I learned how to sleep on a bed of anything. In fact, we just took a nap on stones. Don't worry about me, just make it as comfortable for you as you can."

With her nose still scrunched, she nodded and scrambled over the seat, causing him to duck so that her foot did not hit him in the head. As she moved around the back, he placed his call.

"Tate? I'm clear," Walker said. "If you've got a lock on our location, then you know we're still lying low at the Cobá ruins."

"That's good," Tate replied. "There was earlier movement on the roads around you, but I see no problem with you staying there tonight. Have you got accommodations?"

Glancing toward the back of the Jeep where Julie was grunting as she tried to unfold an old blanket she found, he grinned. "We've got food, and water, and we'll sleep in the Jeep tonight."

"I'm sorry Ms. Baxter's having to rough it," Mace cut in to say.

"Don't worry about it," he said, capturing her gaze as she blew out a breath, puffing her hair out of her face. "She's a trooper."

"Glad to hear it. Drew says Tiffany is responding to the medication, but the doctor has concerns about her infection. He came back this afternoon to check on her and is giving her permission to fly out tomorrow, but Drew's working on a plan to get to you two. He's got a lock on a bird."

Walker grunted as Julie poked him in the shoulder with her sharp finger. "How's Tiffany? Ask him. Ask him now."

"Mace, give me just a minute," he said before turning to Julie, saying, "She's okay, responding to medication but he's concerned about infection. The doctor is going to let her fly tomorrow once Drew can get to us."

Jerking her head back and forth, she said, "No. They need to get Tiffany back to the States and get her to a hospital. We can't take a chance on Drew picking us up first. He can take the girls and then come back for us."

The idea of spending another day with Julie battled with the desire to make sure she was safely back in the States as well.

"We could hear that," Mace said. "She's speaking from emotion, but I need to know your assessment of the situation, Walker."

"If the roads are safe tomorrow, we can get over to the coastline at Tulum. That was where her tour guide was from, and if he's amenable, we can stay with him for a little bit. It's a quick trip up the coast from there, to a place where Drew can come back and pick us up with his plane either tomorrow evening or the next day." As the words left his mouth, he watched as Julie's head nodded up and down emphatically.

"You look safe tonight, but we're gonna monitor the situation during the night and talk to Drew. Will let you know first thing in the morning what the new plan is," Mace said.

Disconnecting, he looked at Julie's face, so easy to read her emotions, but asked anyway, "You okay with this?"

She scooted close to him, with the back of the seat between them, and wrapped her arms around his neck. "Walker, I've got no problem spending tomorrow with you since the people you work with indicate there are no scary people around us right now."

Unable to keep the grin off his face as she said the

words 'scary people', he remained quiet as she continued to speak.

"What's most important is getting Tiffany the medical help she needs and all of the girls back to the States. I'm sure their parents are frantic, and I'd never forgive myself if she became even sicker here."

He leaned forward and kissed her, determined to keep it light. Glancing over her shoulder, he asked, "So how's the bed coming?"

With a sly smile sliding across her lips, she asked, "Why don't you come back here and try it out yourself?"

With a quick scramble over the back of the seat, he pulled her down beside him, wrapped his arms around her, and with his mouth held just a whisper away, said, "I think we're gonna like it just fine."

22

Staring at the empty dinner plates, Drew walked to the two open bedroom doors, taking a glance at Tiffany sleeping peacefully. Throwing his hand up in a wave toward Andrea and Jackie as they sat in the other bedroom playing games on their phones, he turned and moved back to the living area of their suite. Plopping down on the sofa, he scrubbed his hand over his face in frustration. *I need to be picking up Walker and Ms. Baxter, not being alone with three teenage girls!* He took his responsibilities seriously but could not help but feel awkward at the situation.

A knock on the door jolted him from his musings, and he stood. Throwing open the door, he turned and said, "You can go ahead and take the trays down now, and we've marked our breakfast choices for in the morning."

"Well, hell, Flyboy. If that isn't just the kind of greeting a girl wants to get!"

His head flew around so quickly he almost lost his balance. Staring in open-mouthed shock at the slender, dark-haired woman standing in the doorway, for once he was almost speechless, only able to mutter, "Babs?"

Cocking her head to the side, Babs planted her hands on her hips and quipped, "Have you been drinking?"

Snapping his mouth shut, he groused, "Of course I haven't been drinking!"

He heard a noise behind him and heard, "Mr. Drew? Is everything okay?"

He stared at Babs as she lifted an eyebrow and asked, "Are you going to ask me in?"

Blinking, he stepped back, saying softly so that only she would hear, "Abso-fucking-lutely."

He watched as she stepped into the room, her dark pants molded to her legs and ass, and still could not believe she was standing there. She marched over to Jackie, with her hand stretched out and a wide smile on her face.

"Hi. I'm Barbara but known as Babs to all my friends. I work with Drew, and our boss thought that since you were separated from your chaperone, you could use another female around here."

He watched as Jackie and Andrea came forward, shook Babs' hand, and glanced up toward him. Wanting to put them at ease, he reiterated, "Since we're stuck here for the night, it's best if there's another female chaperone."

The girls appeared to understand and led Babs into

Tiffany's room to check on her. Now that Babs was here to act as a stand-in chaperone, relief flooded him. Dropping his chin to his chest, he stared at his boots for a moment, feeling as though he could finally suck in a deep breath and not choke on it. He had no idea how long he stood there until a pair of black, heeled boots were standing right in front of his feet.

Lifting his head slowly, he allowed himself the pleasure of close observation of Babs' legs and hips, narrow waist, and firm, pert breasts encased in a dark green T-shirt.

"You ever going to get your eyes up on my face?" she asked.

He glanced over her shoulder, glad that the girls were still in Tiffany's room, and grinned as he met her gaze. "You wouldn't begrudge a man a long drink of water if he's been in the desert, now would you?"

"You drama queen," Babs laughed. "You just saw me yesterday!"

"Well, it feels like a lot longer."

She shook her head at him as though he was an errant child and then glanced back toward Tiffany's room. "Have you checked in?"

"I was going to do that but was waiting until the girls went to sleep first. With you here now, I'll step outside and give 'em a call.

Nodding, she said, "Go do what you gotta do, Flyboy. I'll watch after the girls."

He moved to the door as she walked toward the bedrooms. He called over his shoulder, "Hey, Babs?"

When she stopped and looked back at him, he grinned. "I'm glad you're here."

With a wink, she headed into Tiffany's room. With his heart much lighter, he stepped outside, pulling up his phone.

Ten minutes later, he stepped back into the suite, his gaze immediately going to Andrea and Jackie's door, hearing Babs' laughter as she said goodnight to the girls. His breath trapped in his lungs as a strange sensation passed through him. Something different. Undefinable. And yet, so right.

He watched her sometimes when she was joking with the others and hoped no one noticed. Occasionally, he caught her looking at him but had no idea if there was something there or if she was treating him differently. Blinking, he broke the spell of his musings as he heard her approach.

As she walked back into the living area, she lifted her gaze to his and time stood still. No quips. No jokes. Just that unidentifiable emotion that seemed to be binding them together across the distance of the room.

Neither spoke for a moment, until both swallowed nervously, breaking the spell.

"Tiffany's fine, resting peacefully. Andrea and Jackie are going to bed. I think they're exhausted, so hopefully, they'll sleep well."

"Good, good," he muttered, foolishly trying to remember what he was going to say.

"Did you talk to Mace?"

Nodding, he forced his mind back to the task and

said, "Yeah. Complete change of plans." Nodding his head toward the sofa, he indicated for her to sit. Following, he sat in one of the chairs facing her on the sofa. "Walker and Ms. Baxter are safe, and with the news that Tiffany needs continued medical care, they both suggested that I get the girls back to the States first thing in the morning. With you along, that means as soon as I get the four of you to Florida, you can take charge of the girls until they're reunited with their parents, and I can focus on getting back here. That'll also give Walker a chance to get to an airfield."

Babs' face gentled in a smile, and she said, "No problem. I'll take care of the girls and you can come back and finish the mission."

He glanced down at the sofa she was sitting on and said, "You can sleep there, and I'll—"

"Don't worry about it, Flyboy. Tiffany takes up very little of a king-sized bed, and I can lay on one side. That way I'll be close in case she needs anything during the night." Nodding down at the sofa, she said, "So you get the sofa." Grinning, she stood and walked toward Tiffany's bedroom, stopping when he called out.

"Babs." As she stared back at him, he hesitated, suddenly unsure of what he wanted to say. "Uh…thanks for coming. It means a lot that you volunteered to do this."

A soft smile barely curved her lips, and she whispered, "Don't you know? I do anything for…" she swallowed audibly before finishing, "the Keepers."

As she left the room, he flopped back in his seat, his

breath rushing from his lungs in an audible whoosh. He stared after her for a moment, rubbing his chest. He wondered what she meant, and the more he thought about it wished what she had actually said was that she would do anything for him.

23

Walker had slept fitfully in the back of the Jeep. He knew that one of the Keepers would have been on duty all night long, monitoring the movements on the roads around, and his Spidey senses never set off an alarm that made him feel like they were in danger. While the old Jeep bed was certainly not comfortable, as a SEAL he had slept on much worse.

Feeling Julie shift slightly, he looked down as she lay sleeping in his arms. This was what kept him awake. Her warm body. Her delicate scent. The soft puff of her breath on his arm. One leg laying across his, her knee hitched perilously close to his cock.

The jungle surrounding the Jeep kept them in the dark, but he was now able to see the barest hint of dawn peeking through the leaves.

Turning his attention back to Julie, it was hard not to focus on the soul-altering orgasm she had given him the evening before on top of the pyramid. It was as though the ancient gods had come together and sent him the perfect woman. *And there's no fuckin' way this'll be anything more than just passing sex between two people caught in extreme circumstances.* She had a life to get back to in Florida, and he had his life in Maine.

He had never been opposed to casual sex when on a vacation, but there was nothing about what he felt for Julie that seemed casual. Blowing out his breath, he could imagine Drew asking if he gave up his man card with all the agonizing thoughts flying through his mind.

She stirred again, this time her eyes fluttering open before they focused on his face. Her lips curved into a smile, and his heart squeezed at the sight, wishing he could see that every morning.

"G' morning," he greeted, kissing her lightly.

Her eyes widened, and she slapped her hand over her mouth. "I've got morning breath," she complained.

"Not with that mint gum you were chewing last night," he said, laughing. "Anyway, I've been laying here wanting to kiss you good morning for at least an hour, and nothing's gonna put a damper on that."

This time he took the kiss deeper, sweeping his tongue into her mouth, still tasting a bit of the mint. The urge to lie on top of her pressing his aching cock against her soft stomach was overwhelming, but he did not want her back against the hard surface.

Lifting his head with reluctance, he stared down at her kiss-swollen lips, seeing her pout, and she looped her hands around his neck and tried to pull his lips back to hers. Shaking his head, he explained, "I can't explain what's going on here between us, but you deserve someone to make love to you on a soft bed."

She nibbled on her bottom lip, her brows lowering slightly. "Oh…sure…um…yeah…"

His fingers curled around her neck, his thumb sweeping across the soft apple of her cheek while his fingers tangled in her silky tresses. "That doesn't sound good, Julie. That sounds like you just thought I gave you a brushoff, and babe, that's the last thing in the world I gave you." Her forehead creased deeper, and he said, "What I mean is that I want to make love to you. I'd do it right now, right here, if I thought that was the best thing. But what I want to do with you and for you is make it good and make it right. And for that, I want you comfortable."

Her smile widened as his words sank in, and he gave her a squeeze before sitting up. "I'm going to step outside and check things out. As soon as I can tell that things are okay, I'll let you know so that you can go to the bathroom. We'll have some breakfast and then as soon as I'm sure it's clear, we'll get back out on the road and get to Tulum. If Hernando can give us a break in our trip, we'll spend a few hours with him, giving Drew a chance to get the girls to the States and then back to us."

"Aye aye, Captain," she quipped, pretending to salute.

"Smartass," he laughed, popping her on her ass as she rolled over to grab her bag. Climbing outside, he pushed his way through some of the jungle, finding a place to relieve himself. Returning to the Jeep, he found her sitting in the front seat, nibbling on a granola bar, running a brush through her hair. "Don't go too far," he instructed. "I promise not to peek."

Rolling her eyes, she put her hand in his as he assisted her down from the seat. Not wanting to make her self-conscious, he nonetheless wanted to keep her close by. Satisfied that she just went behind a tree, he was still relieved when she popped back up, ready to go.

"Nice to see that it doesn't take you long to get ready in the mornings," he said.

Cocking her hip, she said, "Now who's being a smartass?"

She climbed into the passenger seat and pulled out a granola bar, handing it to him. Munching on it as he started the Jeep, they pulled out of their hiding place, his heart warm once more at the ease he felt around her. *God this is dangerous...I could get so used to this.*

"The road seems better today," Julie commented, looking at traffic passing them by. "Yesterday it seemed so deserted."

Nodding, Walker agreed. "According to my coworkers who are monitoring the situation, the worst-hit areas are near Mérida, and that's where so much of the police, military, and government assistance went to. Of course, that's left this side of the Yucatán with less police, so we still need to be vigilant."

"I texted Hernando, and he said that he lives north of the town of Tulum, not too far from the archaeological ruins there." She glanced sideways and worried her lip.

"I don't know if we'll have time, but if we get a chance, I'd love for us to visit the Tulum ruins."

He smiled and said, "Drew won't be able to get us right away, so Ms. Baxter, it looks like you get to play tour guide with me again today."

He wiggled his eyebrows, and she burst out laughing. "I played tour guide yesterday, and you know how that ended up once we got to the top of the pyramid."

"I love it when you play tour guide," he joked, eliciting another giggle from her.

They had passed a little shop that served Starbucks coffee just north of Cobá, and she had clapped and waved her hands in excitement as he ran in to get some. Now, sipping her coffee, she watched as the miles passed by. The paved road was only two lanes but much wider than the roads they had been on yesterday. The jungle still grew right to the edge giving no shoulder, but what little traffic was out flowed steadily. The small towns were slightly more modern than the small villages on the back roads.

Taking another sip, she asked, "How old are you?"

Brows lowered, his head gave a quick shake in surprise, and he replied, "How old am I? Where did that come from?"

"I thought it would be nice to get to know each other more. Well, a little bit better than just carnal knowledge."

He had just taken a sip and choked at her words. Sputtering on hot coffee for a moment, he repeated, "Carnal knowledge? I'm not sure I've heard it put that way before."

Shrugging, she said, "Well, I *am* a lady."

He grinned, catching her eye, and nodded. "That, Ms. Baxter, you are."

"So, your age?"

"I'm thirty-one. My dad is retired from the Navy, and my mom is a second-grade teacher, getting close to retirement."

"Are you an only child?"

"Nope. Got a sister named Sarah. She's married and has a couple of kids."

She continued, "Have you ever been married?"

"Not me. You?"

She sighed, drawing his attention over to her. Nodding, she said, "Yes. A long time ago."

His surprise sounded in his voice as he asked, "What happened?"

"I think it was probably a very typical story," she confessed. "We met in college, got married just as we graduated before we had really gone out into the world and tried life. There really wasn't any big problem other than we just shouldn't have gotten married. He was a musician, and while his band never made it big, he wanted to travel, be a gypsy, live a nomadic life, and go from bar to bar, venue to venue. I, on the other hand, was teaching and then got my master's degree in counseling and got a job at the prep school in Florida." Shaking her head, she added, "You know how they say opposites attract?" Gaining his nod, she continued, "I don't always think that's a good thing. Todd was a free spirit, and I was a planner. Todd wanted to go with the flow, and I liked knowing what was going to happen.

Todd didn't mind traveling and waking up in a different place every day, and I had a job where I knew exactly what I was going to be doing the next day."

"How long were you married?" he asked.

"It's embarrassing to say, but we were only married for two years. I knew we had grown apart, but divorce never entered my mind. One weekend he came home, gave me a kiss, and declared that he was going to file for divorce." Twisting her body so that she was facing Walker, she said, "You know what's crazy? I wasn't expecting it, but I didn't fall apart. I was sad because we'd been friends, and I knew we were never going to stay very close after the divorce. But I wasn't devastated. We actually divorced amicably. So, by the time I was twenty-five, I had been married and divorced. I'll be thirty on my next birthday and have discovered that I'd rather be on my own than be with the wrong person."

He reached across the bench seat and placed his hand on her leg, giving a little squeeze. "I'm impressed, Julie," he admitted. "I'm impressed that the two of you decided to not stay in a marriage that wasn't working."

"When I'm counseling teenagers who are devastated with a breakup, I always tell them that we can learn something from every relationship that we're in. I truly believe that," she said, placing her hand on his, linking their fingers together.

He glanced away from the road again, holding her gaze for a few seconds, and asked, "And what are you learning from us?"

Laughing, she said, "I'm learning that not everything

has to be perfectly planned. Some things are just better surprises."

"Surprises, huh?" With a grin, he jerked on the steering wheel, pulling them off the main road into what looked like an empty parking lot. No one was around, and just like with Cobá, he drove past the gate that would normally have kept vehicles out. Parking just behind a tall wall, he looked over and winked. "Come on. Let's go find another surprise."

24

Julie had been right, Walker thought. This whole trip had been one big surprise. From thinking it was a simple in and out rescue, to having to improvise every step of the way. And the biggest surprise of all was discovering how much he liked being with her.

Grabbing her hand, he pulled her from the Jeep, and they followed the wooden board walkway into the jungle. Glad that she was not protesting, she continued to pepper him with questions.

"What is this place? It's not open. Should we be here?"

The drive from Cobá to Tulum was less than forty miles, and since they had left so early in the morning, they were almost to Tulum before anything was open. They would soon be at Hernando's house, and he wanted more time with her alone. And the opportunity to see a cenote was too great to pass up.

Tall trees and thick, lush ferns dominated the area

with the wooden pathway cutting in between. Suddenly the space opened up, and the morning sunlight beamed down on a pool of water bordered by the jungle and a limestone wall.

Clapping her hands in excitement, Julie cried out, "A cenote!"

Staring down at her obvious delight, Walker felt that same squeeze in his chest and lifted his hand to gently rub over his heart. He could not remember the last time he had been around a woman who took such delight in simple pleasures and beautiful sights. It had been over a month since his last date, set up by a mutual friend. He had taken her to an expensive restaurant, and the woman was dissatisfied with everything from the food, to the service, to the way the bartender mixed her drink.

A grab on his arm jerked his attention back to the beauty in front of him, and he grinned.

"Oh, my God, Walker. It's like a little secret paradise. Isn't this the most beautiful thing you've ever seen?"

She had asked the same thing last night at the pyramid, and he gave her the same answer, referring to her each time. "Yeah, it is."

Moving to the end of the walkway, she sat down, dipping her toes into the water. She leaned back with her hands propping her up and tilted her head to the sun. "These are made when there's a collapse of the limestone and it exposes groundwater underneath," she explained. "There are so many of them in the Yucatán, some like this one that have been built up around it so that visitors can easily find them. There are also others that are just small swimming holes that haven't been commercialized."

While she had been talking, he had reached back, grabbed hold of his T-shirt, and jerked it over his head. Shucking his boots and cargo pants, he took a running leap off the edge and cannon-balled into the water. Rising to the surface, he slung his head around, sending water droplets in all directions. Immediately refreshed, he opened his eyes and swam toward the wooden platform, Julie's delighted laughter ringing out.

Lifting an eyebrow, he teased, "You comin' in or am I coming to get you?"

She moved her head back and forth, throwing her hands up to the side. "I don't have a bathing suit with me!"

"You can always go skinny-dipping. That won't bother me at all."

"Walker! I can't go skinny-dipping in case somebody comes around."

"Seriously, babe? Your bra and panties cover more than what most women wear to the beach."

He was only going to give her a moment before he pulled her in, but he watched as she nibbled on her bottom lip before finally standing, still looking around. As she must have determined that they were quite alone, she slid her pants and shirt off, walking to the edge in her underwear.

"Is it cold?"

Shaking his head, he said, "Come on, babe. It's so refreshing, it'll be worth it to feel like you're washing off all the dust from the trip."

Those words must have done the trick, because she grinned, gave a small running hop, and jumped in.

As she rose to the surface he was right there, his arms encircling her. Her hair was slicked back away from her face, and her eyes sparkled with excitement. Her sun-kissed face glowed with health, and a smattering of pale freckles dotted her cheeks. As he stared at her delighted smile, he knew he had told her the truth. She was the most beautiful thing he had ever seen.

He reluctantly let his arms loosen so that she could swim about freely. They circled each other, splashed and played, teased and tempted in their little, private corner of paradise.

Swimming closer, she wrapped her legs around his waist, her arms around his neck, and they floated toward the bedrock cave wall. Lush, green jungle ferns were hanging down over the edge, creating a curtain around them.

"Can you keep us afloat?" she asked.

Chuckling, the sound rumbling from deep in his chest, he replied, "Babe, I was a SEAL. I could do this all day in full uniform with a fuckin' heavy pack. Believe me, I got you."

Her eyes were wide, and her mouth formed an 'o' just before she leaned in and kissed the underside of his jaw. Allowing her to take the lead, she left no doubt as to where she wanted them to go as she rubbed her panty-clad core against his already-eager cock. With her arms about his neck, his hands were free to roam. Sliding one underneath the waistband of her panties, he cupped her ass, pressing her even tighter against his hips. The other hand moved to the front, pulling her bra cups down to expose her rosy-tipped breasts.

Shifting her upward, he kissed his way from her jaw to her neck and downward over her full mounds. Latching onto a wet nipple, he suckled and teased, drawing her deeply into his mouth, eliciting moans from deep within her. He was barely aware of her fingernails digging into his back as he moved one from one breast to the other.

His hand cupping her ass slid lower, his forefinger moving through her slit, delving inside, eliciting another gasp from her lips. His cock swelled even more. Sliding another finger inside, he scissored them, crooking his forefinger until he found the spot that had her screaming his name.

Slick and tight, her inner muscles clenched against his fingers, and his body shuddered with want. As she came down from her orgasmic rush, her head flopped forward onto his shoulder, her face tucked into his neck, where she began to pepper his skin with soft kisses.

Knowing he did not have a ready condom, he groaned in frustration but told himself it was enough that she had come. His cock had a different idea, though, as it pressed against her stomach.

With her arm still encircling his neck, she leaned back and peered deeply into his eyes. Nibbling on her bottom lip, she whispered, "It's okay, you know. I mean, if we do it without a condom."

His eyes jerked wide at the thought, but he shook his

head. "No, no. I don't want you to do anything that would make you uncomfortable."

Her face softened into a sweet smile. "I'm on the pill, and I'm clean. I haven't been with anybody in…" she blushed, admitting, "a really long time."

"It's been a while for me, too," he confessed. "I'm clean and get tested all the time for my job."

Tilting her head slightly to the side, she said, "Then I guess we trust each other, right?"

They had only known each other for twenty-four hours, but in that time with all they had been through, he knew trust was something they absolutely had. And something he would not break with her. "Oh, yeah."

Cupping the back of her head, he pulled her in for a kiss, their mouths meeting in a wild tangle of lips, tongues, and teeth. This was no gentle good morning kiss, but one of heat and passion, want and need. Her soft breasts rubbed against the hard planes of his chest.

With one hand, he jerked his boxers down and tossed them to the wooden deck where they landed with a splat next to his clothes. Her panties quickly followed. Wanting her ready, he slid his fingers deep inside of her core, eliciting more moans. Sliding his fingers back out, he held open her sex and placed his cock at her entrance.

Seeing a slight grimace cross her face as she bit her lip, he halted, terrified of hurting her. "Are you okay?"

Her eyes snapped open, and she nodded in jerks as her fingers dug into his shoulders once more. "I just need you. Now."

He grinned, and with a shift in their bodies, plunged

his cock deep inside. *Jesus, she's amazing!* Having never gone ungloved before, the feeling of bareback sex had his thoughts go haywire as electricity zapped between them.

She threw her head back, her eyes closed, and her lips curved in a smile so sexy he almost came right then just from looking at her. The sun was now streaming through the jungle leaves, turning the water around them a brighter aqua. Not one for fanciful thoughts, he nonetheless realized that just like last night on the pyramid, they made love in a timeless place that would have certainly been used by ancient lovers.

She shifted on his hips slightly, and all thoughts flew from his mind other than the connection of their bodies. With his large hand spanning her narrow waist, he shifted her up and down on his shaft, hoping she would come again soon, knowing he was not going to last.

As the friction increased, he felt her walls tighten once again, and she cried out her release, her voice captured by the jungle. As she fell languidly forward, he continued to easily move her until with gritted teeth, his body strained, his orgasm pulsed deep inside of her.

They clung to each other, circling slowly in the buoyancy of the water, deep in the shadows of the cenote edge where the lush jungle green dipped over the water. As rational thought returned, he knew they needed to be on their way before other visitors would come for a swim.

With a kick of his strong legs, he brought them back to the dock. Pulling her bra cups back over her breasts, he reached one hand out and snagged her panties. Hefting her ass up onto the dock, he slid her panties back over her feet and upper legs as far as he could. Ascertaining they were still in private, he nodded, and she stood, quickly jerking them up onto her hips.

With his palms pressed against the wooden dock, he hefted his body up out of the water and grabbed his cargo pants, pulling them on commando. Her blatant staring gave evidence to her appreciation of his body. Julie's quiet, unabashed desire did more for his ego than the Frog Hogs of his SEAL days when they would hang in the bars, run their fingers over his muscles and talk about how big he was.

As her head popped through the T-shirt she pulled on, he grabbed her waist and bent to place a kiss on her lips. "Thank you," he said softly.

Cocking her head to the side, she asked, "For what?"

He had no idea how to put into words everything he was feeling. The way she looked at him. The way she trusted him. The way she gave herself to him. So he answered the only way he knew how. Kissing her lightly again, he said, "For everything."

25

"Are you peeking?"

Julie was in the back of the Jeep, peeling off her pants and dropping her wet panties into the floorboard. Grabbing a clean, dry pair from her bag, she shimmied them up her legs and then caught Walker's gaze, hot on her through the rearview mirror.

His deep chuckle reverberated through the vehicle, and his white-toothed smile widened. "Of course, I'm peeking. But considering I've seen you naked and my cock has been buried deep inside of you, I'm not sure why that should surprise you."

Rolling her eyes, she fastened her pants and slipped her sneakers onto her feet. Climbing back into the front seat, almost hitting him in the head again, she replied with a pretend haughtiness, "It's one thing if I choose to display myself for you. It's quite another for you to take liberties in peeking."

"Ooooh, display yourself," he repeated. "I like that,

babe. You can display yourself for me anytime you want, and you can be damn sure I'll love taking liberties."

Laughing, she watched as their driving trip across the Yucatán peninsula of Mexico was almost over. After passing through several tiny villages, the coastal town of Tulum was much more modern. A four-lane highway ran through the city with a palm tree median in the middle. Two, three, and four-story buildings were not uncommon to see. Modern stores and restaurants lined the street, and looking down side roads at intersections, she could see subdivisions of modern homes and apartment buildings.

"Wow, it's like we stepped back into modern times," she said, looking around.

"Looking at the map, Tulum is right on the coast with beautiful beaches. There's a coastal highway that runs along the Pacific all the way up to Cancún, so this area becomes much more populated."

She knew he had spoken to his coworkers just before they arrived at Tulum, and with his calm demeanor assumed that there was no trouble lurking. As they continued down the main road, she turned to him and said, "It's weird. I should be glad that we are safe, in a more populated area, and Drew will soon be able to pick us up to take us back to the States. And yet, seeing all this modernization, I miss the jungle and the ruins."

Nodding, he sighed. "I know what you mean."

She hoped he would elaborate more, but he remained quiet, and she did not want to ask about his thoughts further. Staring at his profile that she had now committed to memory, she thought back on the past day with him. She lived by her planner, taking pride and pleasure in lining up each day. But it was as though the earthquake had ripped that from her. Having to change plans quickly. Having to make snap decisions. Going off with a man she did not know and trusting him explicitly. Worrying her bottom lip with her teeth, she added another item to the list. Falling for that man and knowing it had nothing to do with their extreme circumstances, but simply who he was as a man.

She blinked as he slowed down and turned to the right, and she saw the sign for the Tulum ruins. Determined to enjoy the last ruins she would see on this trip, she climbed from the Jeep after he parked in the large lot. As he walked around the front, linking fingers with her, she looked up and quipped, "This is the first time you parked in the parking lot instead of just driving through all the barriers."

He wrapped his arm around her shoulders and pulled her in close, giving her ass a swat, once more mumbling, "Smartass."

They walked down the long pathway toward the ruins, their arms around each other. The sky was blue with only a few white, fluffy clouds passing by. The jungle grew next to the pathway, but the vegetation seemed much more arid than it had been deeper in the center of the Yucatán. It was still early morning, but there were visitors already moving about. Closer to the ruins, her breath halted in her lungs as she spied the castle sitting on top of tall cliffs overlooking the

Caribbean Sea. Pulling out her phone, she snapped several pictures before looking up some of the information.

"Because of the coastal and land routes meeting here, it was probably a huge city of trade at one time. It actually had a wall around it to protect it on all sides, with the cliffs protecting it next to the sea. Of all the buildings, the three major ones that everyone sees are the castle pyramid and two temples."

They made their way over to the seaside, where they had a private, white sand beach surrounded by palm trees, and a view of the ancient ruins rising from the rock cliffs nearby. They stood, not speaking, Walker behind her with his arms wrapped around her front, tucking her in tightly. The breeze from the ocean blew gently over them, rustling the palm leaves above. The aqua water lapped with gentle waves upon the sand.

Suddenly overcome with emotion, her breath hitched, and a tear slid down her cheek. Hoping Walker had not noticed, she winced when he turned her in his arms, placed his hands on her cheeks and tilted her head back so that he could see the trail of tears.

Grateful he did not question her and simply bent and kissed the tears away, she leaned forward, pressing her cheek against his strong chest, the feel of his heartbeat comforting. "I know you must think I'm so silly—"

His deep voice rumbled against her cheek as he interrupted, "Nothing silly about any emotion you're having."

Her hands flexed around his waist, her fingertips digging into his back muscles. Deciding to throw caution to the wind, she leaned back and peered up into his face, his eyes full of concern holding her gaze. "I know I'm just a mission…a rescue. But I have to tell you that the past day with you has meant more to me than you can realize. I…I just want to thank you for that."

The rough pad of his thumb swept over her cheek again, and he shook his head. "I don't know what we are, and I can't even pretend to put a label on it now. But I know what you aren't. You aren't just a mission. You aren't just a rescue. You aren't just a woman I happened to cross paths with. Whatever you are, whatever we are…it's a fuck of a lot more than that."

His words washed over her as gentle as the breeze, soothing their way through her body. She loved his honesty. She loved that he would not pretend to just give her words. But, more than anything, she loved that his feelings were as wrapped up in her as hers were in him.

Sucking in a deep breath through her nose, she let it out slowly and twisted slightly in his embrace so that they were both facing out toward the sands, surf, and ruins. "I know we need to go, but I just want to soak this moment in, one last time."

He pulled his phone from his pocket and turned them so that their back was to the view. With his arm held out, they smiled for the camera as he took a selfie of them. With a few taps of his finger, he sent the picture to her.

Without sullying the moment with words, they slowly began the trek back to the Jeep.

"Hernando!" Julie cried out.

It had only taken them ten minutes to drive north to Chemuyil, the small town where Hernando lived. Following his directions, Walker had easily made it to the bright yellow, two-story concrete house.

Scrambling from the Jeep, she rushed to the open arms of the older man, his effusive greetings cut off by her exuberant hug. Feeling a hand on her shoulder, she twisted around and spied a grin on Walker's face.

"Give the man a chance to breathe," he laughed.

Stepping back, she blushed, and said, "It's so nice to see you again."

"Oh, my dear Miss Baxter, you have no idea how pleased I was when you called to say you would be nearby. Please let me introduce my wife, Rosalita."

Standing slightly behind Hernando was a short, slightly plump woman, her dark hair streaked with bits of silver. She reached out and grabbed Julie's hands, clasping them tightly, saying, "You are most welcome to our home, Ms. Baxter. My Hernando has told me so much about you and the wonderful girls he had on the tour. We are so sorry that your visit to our country has been marred with such difficulties."

"Oh, please call me Julie. And this is Walker."

She stepped to the side so that Walker and Hernando could greet each other before he shook hands with Rosalita. Uncertain how to act in front of the older couple, she tensed slightly as Walker placed his hand on her shoulder. Deciding she was fine with the slight display of affection, she relaxed and shot him a grin.

If Hernando and Rosalita thought the action was untoward, both were too polite to say anything as they ushered them into their home. They were immediately met with delicious smells coming from the kitchen, and several more people that they were introduced to as members of Hernando's family.

Rosalita moved closer to Julie, and said, "If you would like to freshen up, it will be an hour before we eat."

"I would love to, if it's not too much trouble."

Waving her hands dramatically in front of her, Rosalita said, "My house is your house, Miss Julie. Please, make yourself at home." Rosalita led the way upstairs, through the master bedroom into a nicely appointed bathroom. As her hostess went back downstairs, Walker walked into the bedroom, carrying her bags.

"Figured you'd want these."

Laughing, she said, "I promise to save some hot water for you."

He stepped closer, and said, "It would save water we took a shower together."

"I will not scandalize our hosts!"

His chuckle rumbled forth. "No worries. I'll just have to make do with my imagination."

Still grinning, she disappeared into the bathroom, delighting in the floral scented soap Rosalita had provided. As she ran the soapy washcloth over her body, she could not help but remember the feel of Walker's hands on her breasts and between her legs. Stifling a groan, she hurried through her shower, hoping the blush would be gone by the time she made her way back downstairs.

As she rounded the bottom of the stairs to head into the kitchen, Walker placed his hand on her stomach, bent, and stole a quick kiss.

Whispering, "I'll think of your naked body sharing that space while I'm taking my shower."

Now that he had managed to put the blush back on her cheeks, she watched his muscular ass as he headed up the stairs. Moving into the busy kitchen, she found Rosalita and asked if she could help. Twenty minutes later, they all sat around, the delicious aromas now emanating from the platters filling the table. The food was so much better than what she had had in the restaurants at the resorts, the flavors exploding on her tongue.

She noticed Hernando and Walker had their heads bent at the other end of the table as they talked quietly.

Rosalita touched her hand and whispered, "I would normally fuss that my husband is not being a good host, but I know he has concerns from some things he has seen in the area in the last day. I know he wants to make sure Mr. Walker can keep you safe."

With a few of Hernando and Rosalita's grandchildren at the table, Julie did not want to ask for any further explanation, but her eyes continued to dart over to the seriousness on Hernando's face.

26

Walker said his goodbyes to Hernando's family and stepped back to allow Julie to be enveloped into their hugs. He had stepped outside after lunch to find out the latest on Drew's plans, a sense of urgency after having Hernando's warnings during their meal.

He had hoped that Rosalita's conversation would have kept Julie's attention away from the other end of the table, but he should have known that with her sense of perception, she would have been aware of the undercurrents. As soon as the meal was over, she insisted on helping Rosalita with the dishes, and bending near him to take his plate, she had whispered, "What's going on?"

Unable to let her know anything at that time, he managed to put her off but could feel nervousness rolling off of her in waves.

Drew had shocked him when he said that Babs had shown up in Cancún the evening before to act as chaperone for the girls. Drew was completely trustworthy, and from what Julie had said, the girls were trustworthy as well, but with Babs' presence, it safeguarded everyone. Drew had flown Babs and the girls back to Florida, officially turning their care over to Senator Daniels. Babs had planned on staying in Florida, but Andrea and Jackie's parents came with Tiffany's to pick up their daughters. He was relieved to find out that Tiffany was better and the other two girls were fine, knowing that Julie would be concerned.

Now Drew was flying back to Mexico and should land in Cancún within a couple of hours. Because they had stayed a little longer with Hernando's family, it would take them almost two hours to get to Cancún, but hopefully, with no problems, they would be able to meet with Drew easily, giving him a chance to check his plane and refuel.

Now, he just needed to get Julie in the car so that they could get on the road, hopefully staying ahead of any problems. With her last goodbye said, she trotted over to him, and he assisted her into the Jeep. She held his eyes for just a few seconds, but with a quick shake of his head, he silently indicated that he would talk to her when they were on the road.

Five minutes later, as they pulled onto the main road heading north toward Cancún, she turned to him and said, "Okay, I know something's happening. Is it the girls? What was Hernando telling you? Are we facing problems?"

"Good God, babe. You're firing off questions quicker than I can answer. First of all, I talked to Drew, and he's gotten the girls back to Florida—"

"Oh, thank God! How's Tiffany?"

Softening his voice, knowing she was worried, he replied, "She's going to be fine. Senator Daniels and his wife, along with Andrea's and Jackie's parents met them at the airport, so he and Babs were able to relinquish their care of the girls."

"Babs? Who's Babs?"

Lifting one hand from the steering wheel, he scrubbed it over his face before reaching over and placing it on her shoulder. Sliding it toward her neck, his thumb rubbed her tense muscles, and he said, "She's part of our crew. I'm not sure why she came, because she never goes into the field. Ever since our boss hired her, she keeps us all straight but works in the office. I'm assuming she volunteered to come down, knowing that it would be best if the girls had a trusted female chaperone overnight and for the flight back."

Nodding, Julie agreed. "Well, for whatever reason she came, I'm glad she did. That was really nice of your boss to think of that." She leaned into his hand, and he continued to massage her neck, eliciting a slight moan from her which shot straight to his cock.

Forcing his thoughts to something less pleasant, he said, "And now for what Hernando was telling me." He felt the tension immediately returned to her neck and longed for a time when they could be together and just enjoy each other's company without any trouble hanging over their heads. Not knowing if that time would ever happen, he sighed heavily before saying, "Hernando says that much of the police and military have definitely left the coastal area and headed to the mid and northwestern part of the Yucatán to help with earthquake victims. He said that during the day he is not seeing much of a change, but everyone is hiding out in their homes at night. Cartel members have been roaming the streets at night, and everyone is afraid. His advice to us was to get to Cancún as soon as possible and get out of here."

She relaxed slightly, and asked, "We can be in Cancún in two hours?"

"Yeah, probably less. It's only about 60 miles, but I'll need to stop and get gas. Other than that, it's a straight shot. The whole way will be in daylight, so we should be fine."

"And then we fly out of Mexico?"

With that question, he heard a different tone in her voice…almost wistful, but he was unable to truly define it or even explain it, and definitely too scared to ask. Perhaps it was his own dread at saying goodbye to her that he was projecting into her voice. "Ye…" Clearing his throat, he repeated, "Yes. Then we can leave Mexico."

An hour and a half later, Julie shifted her eyes over to Walker and wiggled slightly in her seat. Hating to ask, her motions must have let him know what was happening because he chuckled.

"I'm assuming from your tightly crossed legs you need to find a bathroom," he asked.

Huffing, she said, "Yes, I'm sorry."

"No worries, babe. We're almost there. We're not going to the main airport in Cancún since Drew...uh... didn't exactly have the correct flight plans. He's just landed at a small airstrip this side of Cancún, and we should be there in just a few minutes."

"I'm fine. I can wait. I probably should have had you stop in Playa del Carmen since it was the largest town we've traveled through. In fact, it's the largest town I've been in since Mérida."

Nodding, he agreed. "There are loads of beaches and resorts there making it a destination stop for lots of tourists. I think even some cruise ships let off near here."

"I saw a sign for a ferry that takes people over to Cozumel. I guess that's another reason why it was so big."

"Planning your next trip to Mexico?" he asked.

Sighing, she shook her head and replied, "Right now, I'm not sure when I'll ever plan another vacation."

Shifting again, she breathed a sigh of relief as he flipped on the blinker and pulled down a narrow road leading to a small airstrip with only a few hangers nearby, the jungle encroaching the back of the buildings.

"How did Drew find this little dinky airstrip?" she asked, looking around.

"It was found on our satellite search of the area."

She noticed his sharp gaze darting all around. "Do you think there's a problem around here?"

He looked over at her and smiled as he shrugged. "Occupational hazard, I guess. Plus, to be honest, it seems like drug cartels have a heavy presence around all the airstrips." Turning his gaze back forward, an audible sigh of relief left his lips and she followed his line of vision, seeing an airplane parked just outside the hanger.

"Thank fuck," he said, relief filling his voice. "There's our ride home."

As soon as he put the Jeep in park, she threw open her door and hopped down to the pavement, glad to see Drew, but halted as soon as she heard Walker call out with enthusiasm, "Babs!"

Her desire to go to the bathroom fled as she watched the dark-haired, athletic beauty walk with a confident swagger straight into Walker's arms.

"Well aren't you a sight for sore eyes," Babs called out, giving Walker a hug.

"God Almighty, Babs. What on earth has got you down here with this reprobate?" Walker asked, jerking his head toward Drew.

"Trying to keep his ass out of trouble," Babs said. "Leave it to him to find a sketchy airfield to land in."

Julie watched as Drew walked over and clapped Walker on the shoulder, saying, "Aww, you know this girl couldn't stay away from me. She had to tag along to make sure I didn't get tangled up with some Mexican beauty."

Feeling like the odd one out now that Walker was amongst friends, Julie looked toward the hangar, wondering if she would find a bathroom there.

Before she had a chance to ask, Babs walked over, a wide smile on her face. Sticking out her hand, Babs said,

"You must be Julie. I'm Babs." Jerking her head toward the men, she added, "I work with these knuckleheads. Usually, I work in the office, but our boss thought they might need a babysitter. It's so nice to meet you."

Unable to keep from responding to Babs' friendly reception, she smiled in return, shaking her hand. "It's nice to meet you, too. Thank you for coming to get me."

Drew and Walker had walked over and must have heard her last statement, because Drew replied, "Don't thank us. Walker's been filling us in on everything the past couple of days, and I have to say that he's done nothing but sing your praises for how well you've handled everything. It's nice to finally meet the woman who has impressed Mr. Unimpressable."

"Jesus, shut the fuck up," Walker grumbled.

Babs threw her head back and laughed, saying, "I think Drew's got you on that one, Walker. If the shoe fits…"

The sound of vehicles in the distance cut through their conversation. Drew's face took on an immediate seriousness and he said, "We need to get in the air. We got here just in time to meet you, but I've already refueled."

"I'm sorry," Julie rushed, "but is there any chance I can run to the bathroom before we get in the plane?"

Nodding, Babs said, "Yeah, follow me."

Babs took off toward the hangar, walking at a fast clip with Julie rushing to keep up with her. Slipping through an outer door, Babs nodded toward another door toward the back. "There's a toilet in there."

Thanking her, she hurried inside, seeing a tiny room

with a toilet and sink, but much to her disdain, there was also a window. Having no other choice, she quickly took care of her business and washed her hands. As she turned off the water, she heard raised voices from just outside the window.

She peeked out in curiosity just as a man cried, "No! No!" Her eyes widened and a gasp flew from her lips as she stared at a man with a gun in his hand, holding it against the head of another man on his knees. Before she could react, he fired.

Jumping, her back slammed against the door, the doorknob painfully digging into her spine. The man turned and looked toward her as she whirled, threw open the door with a bang, and ran out.

Babs looked up in surprise as Julie snatched her hand and jerked her toward the outer door, still running to the front of the hangar. Seeing Drew already in the cockpit and Walker standing next to the plane, she cried out, "Go! Go! We've got to get out of here! I just saw a man get shot!"

27

Used to reacting under extreme circumstances, Walker wasted no time in grabbing Julie's hand and racing to the plane. Picking her up by the waist, he tossed her in, careful to not hurt her.

The engine came to life as Babs followed Julie inside and Walker hopped in afterward, slamming the door and securing it.

"Buckle up," Walker ordered to the women in the back as he buckled himself into the copilot seat. While Drew taxied to the end of the small runway, Walker explained, "Julie saw someone get shot behind the hangar."

Saying nothing, Drew maneuvered the plane around once he reached the end of the runway. "Goddamnit!" he shouted.

Walker jerked his head around following Drew's line of vision and saw two military-type, open-top Jeeps careening around the back of the hangar, men hanging on with automatic rifles in their hands. "Heads down," Walker ordered. "Head to your knees." He spared a glance behind him, seeing Julie's wide-eyed fear etched on her face, but following Babs' example, she bent over, clutching her knees.

The sound of rapid gunfire coming their way elicited another round of cursing from Drew. From the back seat, Babs said, "You want to get us out of here, Flyboy?"

"Not helping," Drew growled, sending the plane hurtling down the runway amidst the gunfire. Another round of cursing met more gunfire, and while Walker trusted Drew's abilities completely, as he saw the gunmen's Jeep park at the end of the runway, weapons facing them, he hoped like hell they could get airborne.

Just when it looked as though they were not gonna make it, Drew went wheels up, and the plane flew over the gunmen and disappeared over the tree line, keeping them out of range. Drew cackled out, "Fuck that, you Fuckers!"

Walker leaned back in his seat, gaining control over his erratic heartbeat, not understanding why the adrenaline was coursing through his body after all the missions he had been on as a SEAL and with Lighthouse.

Hearing Julie's small voice in the back seat asked, "Are we okay?", he knew he had the answer. He had never cared for one of his missions before. *Jesus, how can I care so much for her after only a couple of days?* He had no answer to that question but scrubbed his hand over his face before he turned to Drew.

"We get hit?"

"I'm sure we did," Drew reported, "but from what I can tell, nothing major was hit. We'll be over Key West in less than an hour, so if we have to set down there, we can. If not, we can make it all the way to Lake City."

Turning in his seat, he watched as Julie and Babs sat up straight in their seats, their hands clasped together. Babs' lips were tight, but she gave him a curt nod indicating she was fine. Looking toward Julie, he saw that she was anything but fine.

"Babs? Change seats with me."

Without complaint, Babs unbuckled, and she gave Julie a hug before scooting past Walker. As she buckled into the copilot seat, she shot Drew a grin, saying, "You got me as copilot again. Aren't you lucky?"

"Hell, Babs," Drew drawled. "Anytime I can get you near me, I feel lucky."

Walker ignored the banter from the front seat and reached over to put his arm around Julie's shaking body. "Baby. Baby, look at me."

Her chest heaved as the air left her lungs in a rush. Twisting her head, she met his gaze. Blinking, she said nothing but clung to his arm.

"Baby, we're fine. It's okay, we're fine," he soothed. Lifting his hand, he pushed her hair back away from her face and cupped her cheek, pulling her close. Placing a light kiss on the corner of her mouth, he felt her cold lips quivering. Reaching behind the seat, he grabbed a blanket and spread it over her, recognizing the effects of shock.

He wanted to ask her what she saw but was uncertain how much he should pressure her. Tucking the blanket around her, he enveloped her in his embrace as best he could, hoping his body would provide some comfort.

After a moment, her shaking slowed, and she whispered, "Walker?"

"Right here, babe."

"I don't understand what I saw," she said, her voice barely audible. Her eyes searched his, and she continued, "I mean, I know what I saw. But I don't…it didn't…"

Giving her a squeeze, he said, "Julie, babe, it's okay. You don't have to talk about it now."

Shaking her head, she said, "No. I need to."

He knew that Babs and Drew were quietly listening from the front, and he said, "Okay, babe. You just tell us whatever you want to."

"There was a window in the bathroom. I thought it was dumb, but since there didn't seem to be anyone around, I used the toilet and then was washing my hands when I heard voices outside. Men's voices. But I knew it wasn't you and Drew. So, I looked." Her shaking began again, and a tear fell from her wide eyes as she said, "Oh, God, Walker. I looked."

"Fuckin' hell," Drew cursed softly from the front.

Walker ignored Drew, continuing to soothe, "Shhh, baby, it's okay." But now that Julie was talking, it was as though she had to get it all out.

"There was a man…on his knees…with his hands behind his back…another man held a gun to his head…and fired…"

Her body bucked with a sob, and he unbuckled her, pulling her over into his lap, blanket and all. Continuing to comfort her until she stopped shaking once more, he let her rest with her head tucked underneath his chin.

Neither he, Drew, or Babs spoke about the incident, all in silent agreement to fill in Mace when Julie was no longer in earshot. Closing his eyes, Walker leaned his head back, settling her deeper into his embrace, and sighed heavily.

With the key in her hand, Julie opened the front door to her apartment. Stepping over the threshold, she felt as though everything should be normal when, in actuality, nothing was. The living room looked the same, the blue loveseat facing the flatscreen TV with the yellow, comfy chair angled in the corner. The matching end tables with matching lamps stood at either end of the loveseat. The sliding glass door that led to her small, enclosed patio. To the right, her U-shaped kitchen that opened to a breakfast nook with her glass top table. And just down the hall was the large bedroom and bathroom that made up her space.

If she closed her eyes, she could almost imagine that she had just walked in from work and was ready to decide what she wanted to fix for dinner. But the heat at her back let her know that Walker was standing just behind her, and nothing was the same as before.

Drew had determined that his plane was fine and they were not losing fuel, so they made it all the way to the small airport near Lake City, Florida, where she lived. She assumed she would be saying goodbye to them all there, but Walker had insisted on taking her home.

Drew wanted to inspect his plane before flying it back to Maine and had said that he and Babs would be spending the night near the airport. Babs had rolled her eyes and quipped that they would be spending the night near the airport *in separate rooms*.

Julie knew they were trying to lighten the mood, but all she could do was force a smile onto her face as she hugged them goodbye and thanked them for all they had done for her and the girls. Walker had insisted on driving her to her apartment and spending the night to make sure she was all right.

And now, here she was. Turning, she stared as Walker walked into her living room, his large body dwarfing the space.

"You've got a nice place here, Julie," he said, a soft smile on his face.

Shrugging, she said, "It's small, but it works for now. I honestly haven't decided if I'm going to stay in Florida, but then I also haven't been looking for another school, so I guess I'll be here at least one more year."

Cocking his head to the side, he said, "I never asked you where you are from. I just assumed you were from Florida."

Shaking her head, she replied, "I grew up in Pennsylvania, but it's so hard to get a teaching job there. After my divorce, I wanted to get away, and the job at the school here was available. I've been here for four years and really need to decide if I'm going to stay. If so, I'd like to get a bigger place…maybe even a house."

They stood for a moment, and then she said, "This is weird."

Confusion crossed his face, and he asked, "Weird?"

She swallowed deeply, then said, "I've spent the past couple of days racing across Mexico, and a few hours ago I watched a man get killed. Now I'm standing in my living room having what seems like a normal conversation with you. How bizarre is that?"

He stepped forward, wrapping his arms around her again, and she encircled his waist with hers. "I know it's bizarre, sweetheart. I know everything the last several days has been completely bizarre, but you're home. You're safe. The girls are safe. I'm not downplaying what you saw at all, because it was horrible, and since you're a counselor, I'm going to assume I don't have to beg you to get some crisis counseling. But you can go to sleep tonight knowing that you and the girls are safe."

She leaned back and stared up into his face. His words made sense, and she nodded. "You want something to eat?"

Grinning, he said, "Absolutely, but I'm not about to make you cook."

She pushed away from him and walked into her kitchen, opening the freezer door. Calling over her shoulder, she said, "I'll have to go to the grocery store soon, but I do have some homemade lasagna that I put in the freezer, knowing that when I got back, I would want something home-cooked. I've even got some frozen garlic bread."

Groaning in appreciation, he said, "As long as you only have to nuke it, babe, that sounds great."

She grabbed the food from the freezer, unwrapped it and placed it in the microwave. Setting the timer, she watched as he slowly made his way around her living room, looking at the various pictures she had displayed. He looked so strange amongst her things, and yet, so right at the same time. Giving herself a mental shake, she thought *This isn't real. He'll leave tomorrow and go back to his life in Maine, and I'll be here in Florida. What we had will fade to nothing more than a memory.* She knew she was lying to herself as soon as that thought crossed her mind. *Maybe a memory for him, but for me? This is as real as it gets.*

Pushing that thought aside, she grabbed some plates and set the table. Determined that if this was going to be their last night together, she wanted it to be memorable.

28

Slow and easy, Walker rocked into Julie's warm body, his strokes long and slow as he dragged his cock along her channel, allowing the friction to build. He wanted every second to last. Every second to count. He had seen it in her eyes from the moment they stepped into her apartment...the doubt, the worry, the questions.

He did not want her to doubt what they felt for each other. He did not want her to worry about what they had experienced. And he sure as fuck had no answers to the questions that swirled between them. He had no idea how to make a long-distance relationship work or if she would even want to.

After dinner, he led her into her well-appointed bathroom, where they filled her garden tub, and he climbed in, settling her between his legs with her back resting against his front. As the warm water soothed their tired bodies, he took great pleasure in washing every inch of her, following the sponge with his lips. Finally, as the water cooled, he climbed out and wrapped her in a thick towel, taking equal pleasure in drying her off.

In a surprise move, she dropped to her knees on the plush bathroom mat and took his swollen cock in her mouth. She worked the length of him, licking and sucking as her fingers dug into his ass until he thought he knew he would explode in her mouth. He tried to warn her and pull out, but she clung tighter, sucking as he came with a roar as she swallowed every drop.

Barely able to move after her ministrations, he grasped her under her arms and lifted her up, seeing her lust-filled eyes as she licked her lips.

Determined to give back everything she had just given, he scooped her up into his arms and carried her into her bedroom, glad to see she had a queen-size bed. Bending, he jerked the comforter down before laying her gently onto the sheets.

Disappearing between her legs, he licked and sucked her sex, pulling her clit into his mouth until she cried out her own release.

Now, with his cock buried balls-deep inside her sweet body, he propped his weight up off her chest with his forearms planted on either side of her face. She lifted her knees and met him stroke for stroke, her hands running up and down his back. Their eyes never closed, staying focused on each other. The crescendo built, and he heard the gasps slipping through her lips and knew she was close. Angling his hips so that his pelvis hit her clit as he thrust harder and faster, her fingers dug into his shoulders as she cried out his name, and he swore he had never heard anything so sweet in his life. The last few thrusts as her channel clenched onto his sensitive cock, he came again, continuing to plunge deep inside her until every drop was wrung out of his body.

Shifting slightly to the side before he dropped down, his arms shaking with exertion, he rolled, pulling her with him. After a moment, when he could finally catch his breath, he continued rolling to his back, draping her body over his. One hand cupped the back of her head that was laying on his chest, and the other hand moved slowly up and down her spine, over her ass, and back again.

The emotions swirling in the room were so thick they were almost tangible. He wanted to promise her... *What? We'll call and text and see each other once a month on a weekend?* His mind raced with a million ways of how to tell her goodbye the next day without it being a true goodbye.

She shifted over him, leaning up and peering down. "At the risk of scaring you off, can I ask what this is between us?"

He chuckled, and her body jiggled as it rested on him. "Jesus, Julie, you've just asked the question that I've been trying to figure out the answer to."

Her head nodded up and down slowly, a sigh leaving her lips. "We've known each other for such a short time, and every moment of that was in an extreme circumstance. It would be so easy to dismiss what I feel as just exhaustion, or dramatic emotion, or even imagination.

But that's not me, Walker. I'm not some infatuated teenager. I know what I feel for you, and I know it's real. I don't have a label for it now, but I don't need one. You're in my heart, that I know. What I don't know is how I'm going to be able to say goodbye to you tomorrow morning knowing that our time together will be over."

Walker stared into the eyes that he had grown to know so well, seeing nothing but honesty looking back at him. Lifting his hands, he thread his fingers into the hair at the side of her head, pulling it away from her face so that he could see her clearly. "Babe, you've just managed to put into words everything I was thinking. What I feel for you is real also. What we've experienced together may have been extreme, but that doesn't mean that what's in my heart is any less real than a couple who's known each other for a long time. I can't tell you what's going to happen after we say goodbye tomorrow, but I'm not willing to let you just walk out of my life."

Her voice, barely above a whisper, asked, "What are you saying?"

"I don't know," he admitted, his gravel voice rough with emotion. "I just know that I want you in my life. Somehow, someway."

Her lips curved into a slow smile, and of all the times he had ever thought she was beautiful, right now, with hope shining in her eyes, she was the most beautiful he had ever seen. Settling her gently by his side, he leaned down and grabbed the sheets and comforter, tucking them up around her. He knew they had a long way to go, finding their way together, working to become a couple. He needed to return back to Lighthouse and she needed to deal with what she had seen in Mexico. As they fell asleep, he vowed to make his way back to Florida just as soon as he could arrange some days off.

As sleep claimed her body and he found himself easing into rest, he pushed all thoughts away from his mind. Nothing else mattered at the moment except for the woman in his arms.

Julie stepped into her apartment the next afternoon and leaned her back against the front door. Swallowing deeply, she closed her eyes, willing her mind to empty. But it was to no avail. The day had been too busy. Too emotional. Too painful.

Images of the day filtered in behind her tightly-squeezed eyes. Waking in her bed with Walker's large body wrapped around hers had been the most perfect way to start her morning. But knowing it was only one morning had caused her heart to ache. She had looked forward to a time when she could make love with him on a comfortable bed, but the reality was that whether they were on top of a stone pyramid, in the back of a cramped Jeep, or in the water with the jungle all around, it did not matter. Making love with Walker was exquisite no matter where they were.

They had climbed out of bed with the slow movements of two people who knew their time was limited. A long shower together. Breakfast of oatmeal and coffee. And then finally standing at her door as they said goodbye.

She had wanted to memorize the sight of him in her apartment so that when he was gone, she would be able to feel his presence still there. But as they stood at the door, clutched in an embrace, she knew that when he left, her apartment would never feel the same.

With his large hands planted on either side of her face, his rough thumbs moving over her cheeks, he had peered deeply into her eyes before lowering his lips to hers. They had shared kisses of abandon and kisses of deliberation. They had shared the light touching of lips and breath-stealing, nose-bumping, tongues-tangling kisses. But nothing had prepared her for a goodbye kiss.

It was filled with a mixture of hope and sadness. Filled with what they wished could be mixed with what the reality was.

And when he finally lifted his head, touched his forehead to hers and said goodbye, her tears flowed freely. With promises left unsaid, she watched as he walked out the door, not knowing if or when she would ever see him again.

Determined not to fall apart, she left soon after he did and drove to the Daniels' house. Tiffany's mother had left a message that they were going to be all together that morning and would love to see her. As she walked into the large, stately home, she was overwhelmed with emotion as her gaze landed on Tiffany, Andrea, and Jackie. Tears and hugs ensued, first by the girls, and then by their parents.

Senator and Mrs. Daniels ushered the gathering into

their large, comfortable family room, and as she sat down on the sofa she was immediately surrounded by the girls. Everyone clambered for details of her Mexican escapades, and she gave them an abbreviated version.

Andrea and Jackie's parents all clucked over her tales while Tiffany's parents declared they wanted to send a bonus to Hernando for going above and beyond the call of duty when the earthquake hit. She assured them that Hernando and his family were fine, but she would get them his contact information if they would like to provide him with the gift.

"The only thing we missed on our tour was seeing Tulum," Jackie said. "Did you get any pictures?"

Nodding, she pulled out her phone and quickly found the pictures of the ruins by the ocean. Handing her phone over so that the girls could scroll, she said, "It really was beautiful, and I'm so sorry we didn't get to see it together. I would've loved to have heard Hernando's lectures about it."

The girls had been exclaiming in delight as they looked at the pictures then suddenly grew quiet. The parents were all conversing together, and Julie glanced over in question at Jackie who was still holding her phone. Reaching for it, she saw what had given them pause. It was the selfie that Walker had taken of the two of them alone in their own tropical paradise with the palm trees around, the white sand in the background, and the ruins in the distance.

Glad that the adults' attention was not on her, she reached for her phone, but could not think of anything to say. All three girls looked at her with a mixture of pleasure and sadness on their faces...the very same emotions that she felt when she was reminded of her time with Walker.

"Now that we're back home, it almost seems like it didn't really happen," Tiffany said softly.

Jackie nodded emphatically, saying, "Yeah. I woke up this morning and wondered if I had dreamed the whole trip."

Andrea rolled her eyes and held out her slightly sunburned arms. "The only thing I have to do when I think it's a dream is look at my arms."

Everyone laughed, but Julie knew what the girls meant. The only problem with her dream was that it was not only mixed with the feelings she had developed for Walker but the sight of a man dying in front of her. Giving herself a quick shake, she plastered a smile on her face.

Standing, she thanked Senator and Mrs. Daniels for offering the chaperone position to her and accepted all the parents' heartfelt thanks. Hugging the three girls goodbye, she made them promise to write down the memories of their adventures so they could share them with their classmates in the fall.

On the way home, determined to take care of her normal business, she stopped at the post office, pharmacy, and grocery store. As she walked up and down the food aisles pushing her cart, she grabbed items and tossed them in the cart, occasionally wondering if it was something that Walker would like to eat. Standing at the checkout line, she wondered how long it would be before he would no longer invade her every thought. Sighing heavily, she wished that day would never come.

And now, back in her apartment, she sighed once again, feeling lost. Glancing to the side, she saw her bags that Walker had dropped near the door when they came in the day before. Opening the one that contained some clothes, she pulled them all out and tossed them into her dirty clothes hamper. Her personal items went back into the bathroom, and a few of the salvaged pamphlets that she had gathered over the trip landed on her coffee table. Her passport went into the locked file cabinet she kept in her closet, and her wallet was laid by her purse so that she could make the switchover from pesos to dollars.

The last item in her bag was her beautiful planner. Pulling it out, she flipped it open and looked at the plans she had made leading up to the trip, each item carefully marked off when accomplished. She looked at the copious notes she had taken each day, having planned on matching them with the photographs she had taken.

The last several days in her planner were glaringly blank, and yet, had been filled with more than she could have ever written down. The places she and Walker had gone. The things she and Walker had done. The feelings she and Walker had shared.

She dropped the planner on the kitchen counter next to her wallet, no longer wanting to stare at the blank future pages. Not able to continue writing down what she and Walker would be doing together, they lost their appeal.

She put away her groceries, poured a glass of wine, and walked to her sofa. Plopping down with her feet on the coffee table, she sat and sipped her wine. And reminisced. By the time she finished the glass, her cheeks were wet with tears.

29

Walker woke with a jerk, his internal alarm clock having not gone off. Drew and Babs had dropped him off at his apartment once they landed in Maine, having orders from Mace for him to take the rest of the day off. He had been informed that the Keepers would meet first thing the next morning.

At first eschewing the idea of crashing in the early afternoon, he quickly gave up protesting when it appeared Mace would not relinquish. Neither Drew nor Babs said anything to him about Julie on the way home, but he knew they were not stupid. He knew it was obvious that there was something between the two of them that went way beyond the mission and his desire to make sure she was safe.

Sitting up in bed, his forearms resting on his bent knees, he heaved a sigh. He had slept for hours but, with a heavy heart, he did not feel rested.

It was still dark outside, and with a glance at his

clock, he knew that dawn was still several hours away. He wondered what Julie was doing. Was she was resting? *Hell, is she thinking of me?*

Climbing from his bed, he walked through his apartment, once comfortable but now seeming lonely. She had never been in the space, and yet, it felt like it was missing something. Now that he had been in her apartment, he wondered if she still felt him there.

Starting a pot of coffee, he leaned his hip against the counter and scrubbed his hand over his face in disbelief at the trail of his thoughts. Grabbing a cup of the hot, black brew, he walked over to the sofa and sat down, propping his bare feet up on the coffee table.

Snagging his phone from the end table, he scrolled through messages, pondering if he should send one to her. Seeing that he had sent one to her the previous day, he tapped his finger on it to remind himself what it was.

Fuckin' hell. He stared at the picture of the two of them on the beach at Tulum, having forgotten that after he took the selfie of them, he sent it to her phone. Her hair was pulled back in a ponytail, but loose tendrils were blowing in the breeze from the ocean. If he looked closely, he could see the smattering of freckles across her sun-kissed cheeks. Her eyes, bright and clear, sparkled as she stared toward the camera. And her smile —*her fuckin' gorgeous smile*—lit up the screen and filled his vision.

Dropping his phone to the sofa cushion next to him, he closed his eyes and leaned his head back, visions of Julie and memories of their time together slamming into his mind. Finally, when he could take no more, he stood, downed his mug of coffee in a few gulps, and headed to the shower. Needing something to do, he decided to get his day started by going to the Lighthouse early.

An hour later, he walked into the house, not surprised to see Marge at the stove fixing breakfast and Horace having a cup of coffee at the kitchen table. He also was not surprised when Marge turned, and as soon as her eyes landed on him, marched directly into his space and gave him a hug.

With a hearty slap on the back, she said, "Good to have you home, Walker." As she pulled away from him, she looked him in the eye and asked, "You okay?"

She was too perceptive for him to bullshit, so he simply asked, "Drew and Babs been talking?"

Lifting her chin slightly, giving the effect that she was peering down at him even though she was staring up, she said, "I don't listen to gossip. I'd rather hear it straight from you."

Horace chuckled, and Walter slid his glance sideways, seeing the older man's bright eyes pinned on him.

Shaking his head, he said, "It was an interesting mission, but everyone got home safe, so that's all that matters."

Marge tapped his chest right over his heart and asked, "And this? Is this safe?"

"I'm not sure," he said honestly while sighing. "I'll have to get back to you on that one."

Marge opened her mouth to speak, but Horace got there first, saying, "Best get to your breakfast, Marge. I think something's about to burn." She snapped her mouth shut and hustled over to the stove, leaving Walker to shoot a grateful look toward Horace. With a nod, he headed down the hall toward the elevator. Time to get back to work.

Sitting at the large table in the compound, Walker looked around at his fellow Keepers. He had spent the previous two hours writing up his report on the mission, part of that time spent sitting with Sylvie as they went over the expenses. Drew had already turned in his report, still assessing the repairs on his plane.

Tate and Josh were at one of the computer stations. Clay and Blake were out of the building on their own missions. Bray and Cobb were sitting at the other end of the table, files spread out in front of them. Drew had just gotten off the phone with one of his airplane mechanic contacts, grumbling about the expense as he walked over and sat down next to Walker. Mason and Rank sat on the other side of him.

Leaning back heavily in his chair, he shook his head. "I've written up everything Julie said. Drew and Babs were there, and none of our descriptions give us anything to go on. The best I can come up with is that she witnessed a cartel execution. That's certainly what it looked like with those who came after us."

Drew nodded emphatically, agreeing. "I feel like fuckin' shit, choosing that airstrip, but I didn't have the right papers to land at the Cancún airport. I tried getting hold of Joseph, my ex-military contact down there, but haven't heard from him since he first got us that bird in Mérida. I figure Mexico was calling up everybody to try to help with the earthquake victims."

Walker shook his head, looking over at Drew. "Don't take that on, man. Like always, we go with the best intel that we have at the moment, and then we fuckin' make it work."

Drew grimaced, continuing, "That lack of intel could've gotten Julie ki—"

"I'm fuckin' serious, man," Walker interrupted, leaning toward Drew. "You and Babs got there before us, and nothing bad had happened. It was just fuckin' bad luck that Julie went toward the back of the building."

"He's right," Mace pronounced. "Bottom line, you got all four women out safely."

Nodding, Drew stood from the table and clapped Walker on the shoulder. "You're right, thanks. I'm going to keep seeing if I can get hold of Joseph, just to make sure he's all right and hope he got the bird that I left in Mérida. I'd really hate like hell if it was stolen away from him."

Mace finished reading over Walker's report before closing the file folder. "I'll have Babs get this into the computer, along with her and Drew's reports. I know the way it ended left a bad taste in your mouth, but the mission was successful. All four women were brought home safely in the midst of a lot of fast decisions you two had to make. Good job."

Drew ambled back over to one of the computer stations, and Walker caught a shared look between

Mace and Rank. Throwing his hands up, he said, "Before you ask, I'm fine—"

"Let's take a walk," Mace said.

Walker understood that it was actually an order, so he stood and followed, noting Rank came along as well. Assuming they were going to the top of the lighthouse, he was surprised when Mace detoured and they walked along the grassy knoll behind the lighthouse, overlooking the rocks leading to the shore. Adirondack chairs, worn and weather-beaten, were placed near the edge, and Mace offered the silent invitation to sit with a jerk of his head.

The three men settled comfortably, no words spoken for several minutes as the sun shone down on them, only occasionally broken by the clouds. Allowing himself the luxury of closing his eyes, he felt the breeze from the ocean on his face and for a moment could almost imagine that he was back at Tulum with Julie. But then the differences crept in. The sound of the water crashing on the rocks was not the same as it was washing up on the white sand. The breeze was pleasant but did not have the tropical heat that had blown across them. Even the sound of the sea birds was not the same.

Heaving a sigh, he opened his eyes, feeling the other two men staring at him. Knowing Mace would speak when he was ready, Walker kept quiet.

"Your mission was completed, and your ability to think fast on your feet and make the necessary changes is what got everyone home safe," Mace began. "But you don't look like the same man who left out of here, so I need to ask if you're okay."

Tightlipped, he replied, "I'm fine, boss. And even if I wasn't, it's my situation to figure out."

"With all due respect, Walker, something happened down in Mexico that's got one of my best men walking around with a struggle on his face. I'm not going insult you by pretending that Drew didn't talk when he got in, so what I need to know is what are you going to do about Ms. Baxter?"

Staring out over the water, he tried to still the ache that had settled around his heart. "I live and work in Maine. She lives and works in Florida. In a fantasy world, we could make that kind of long-distance relationship work, but I don't live in fantasy. What we had was extreme and fast. I have no idea if we could've made something last out of that, but with that distance between us I can't figure out a way to even see if that could happen."

"So you've given up," Rank said.

Swinging his head around to stare at his best friend, he growled, "Easy for you to say. Helena was only two hours away when you two first hooked up." Swinging his head back to Mace, he added, "Hell, Sylvie was just an hour away."

Nodding, Mace said, "You're right, it's not the same. And before I met Sylvie, I would've never given two thoughts to trying to make something work. Only you can decide if she's worth it. Worth the time, energy, effort, and trouble to see if there's something there. And if there is, only you can decide to go for it. I'm just letting you know, as your friend and your boss, I'll support you in whatever decision you make."

Mace pushed up from the chair, and with a chin lift walked back into the lighthouse, leaving Walker and Rank still looking out over the ocean. Neither spoke as the waves crashing sounded in the distance.

Finally, looking over at Rank, he said, "She's worth it."

A wide grin spread across Rank's face, matched only by the one on his own face.

30

"Have you given any more thought to what I suggested yesterday?" Walker asked.

Julie, perched on her sofa, leaned forward to stare at her planner, open on the coffee table. "Of course, I have. That's all I've been thinking about!"

Ten days had passed since Walker had walked out of her apartment, and for the last nine days, they had talked on the phone every day. She had been shocked when he first called, uncertain if she would ever hear from him again. But in typical, honest Walker fashion, he had told her that he did not care about the distance, he wanted to keep getting to know her better. Considering that was exactly how she felt as well, she could barely keep from twirling around the room every time he called.

So far, he had not been sent on another mission that took him away from being able to call her every night, and for the last three days, they had spoken each morning as well. The first day their conversation was stilted and somewhat forced until they quickly got back into the swing of learning about each other and enjoying conversation, just like in Mexico.

Staring at her planner, she could not help but grin when she saw the tiny little heart stickers placed on each calendar day for the last nine days. Yesterday's heart had an exclamation written next to it because he had asked if she would be able to fly to Maine to spend some time with him.

Giving her head a quick shake to focus back on what he was saying, she continued, "I've got three more weeks off before I'm supposed to go back to work, and you said that you have some vacation days that your boss is going to let you take. So, I've looked up flights, and I should be able to get to Maine next weekend."

She could hear the enthusiasm in his voice when he whooped over the phone. Laughing, she said, "So I take it that meets with your approval?"

"Abso-fuckin'-lutely," he said. "Just let me know which airport you'll fly into and when, and I'll be right there."

She grew quiet and he asked, "Are you still there?"

Sucking in a deep breath, she said, "We're really doing this, aren't we?"

She knew he understood exactly what she meant when his voice softened, and he agreed, "Yeah, babe. We're really doing this."

"I was surprised…when you first called me nine days ago."

"I should've called you ten days ago," he said, eliciting a giggle from her. "I left you in Florida and felt like I left part of myself there. I've never done that before. So, I took a day, moped around, and finally, my boss and a good friend talked to me."

"What did they say?" she wondered aloud.

"My boss told me that he'd support whatever decision I made, but he said only I can decide if you were worth whatever it was going to take to see if this would work out between us."

She sucked in a quick breath, but before she had a chance to respond, he continued. "It didn't take long for me to figure it out," he said. "I know you are absolutely worth it."

Her head felt light as the import of his words washed over her. "I think you're worth it, too," she said softly.

"I gotta confess, babe, that I keep thinking about us being together again. But when your sweet voice hits me in the gut like it just did, I want to make love to you right now."

She groaned, flopping back on her sofa, and said, "I haven't made my airline arrangements yet, but now I want to push them up and leave tomorrow!"

He laughed and said, "You'll get no argument from me."

"Instead of flying on Friday, how about if I fly up on Thursday? I know you'll have to work on Friday, but that will give me a day to putz around your apartment, snoop through your closets, and discover all your secrets."

"And what will you do when you discover the skeletons in my closet?" he quipped.

"I don't know," she continued playing along. "I guess it depends on how big the skeletons are."

"Babe, you can come anytime you want. In fact, you can snoop through my whole apartment. I've got absolutely nothing to hide, and just knowing that you'll be here waiting for me as soon as I get off work will have my friends wondering why I'll have a big-as-fuck smile on my face."

She laughed but was already grabbing her laptop to check out new flight arrangements. "Well, if I do come up early, I can stop over in Boston."

"Boston? What's in Boston?"

"The Museum of Fine Arts has an exhibit of Mayan artifacts." She waited to hear what he would say, but the phone line was quiet for a moment. Finally, she could hear him chuckling on the other end.

"Mayan artifacts? You don't think you got enough of that in Mexico? Hell, babe, come whenever you want. You don't need an excuse."

They chatted for a few more minutes before she said, "I hate to let you go, but I'm going to have to. I promised my upstairs neighbor that I would pop by this evening."

"Hmmm, do I need to be jealous?"

"Let's put it this way…Randolph would be more interested in you than in me."

Chuckling, he said, "Okay, babe. I'll let you go, but make sure to let me know your flight arrangements. Can't wait to see you."

Disconnecting, she placed her phone on the coffee table next to her planner. She had already put a sticker in the area for the next weekend when she would be in Maine. Now that she was going to leave a day earlier, she decided another heart sticker was in order. Glancing at the clock, she determined she had just enough time to find a new flight before she had to get ready to visit her neighbor.

Walker headed through the main compound room passing Babs' desk. He glanced at her, grinning at the way her dark hair was piled on top of her head, purple tips springing out like Medusa.

She lifted her eyebrows and said, "Well hell, boys. Looks like everybody's got a grin on their face today. Makes me wonder who might be getting some."

Stopping, he said, "I know why I'm grinning. Don't know about anybody else."

She held his gaze, then smiled in return, her voice softening. "I take it things are going well with Julie?" He nodded, his smile wider, and she continued, "I knew the minute I saw you two together you had something special. I'm really glad for you."

He walked over to the conference table as Drew came from the back hall, whistling. "You must be getting your plane fixed for you to be that happy," he surmised.

"Nothing major was hit, so I just have to get the fuckin' holes repaired. I've got a buddy who'll take care of it so it won't cost Lighthouse too much." Drew started to turn away, then whirled back around. "I almost forgot to tell you. Joseph finally got hold of me."

"Did he get his bird back?"

Nodding, Drew grinned. "He said everybody had been called up to help out the areas that had been hit the worst by the earthquake. Police, rescue, military, former military. He said it took him about three days to get back there, but the bird was in the hangar where I left it."

"Too bad he was out of commission when you were trying to find a good place to pick us up," he said.

Nodding, Drew ran his hand through his hair, pushing the front up, and agreed. "I told him what happened, and he wanted to know why the fuck I flew into that airstrip. I told him it was the only one I could find where I could land and not have to worry about having the right papers. He said it was known in the area for being used by drug runners."

"What'd you say to him?"

"I told him that next time I need him to keep his fuckin' phone charged!" Drew laughed, settling down at the table.

Sliding into the seat next to him, Walker scanned his tablet for the upcoming missions for the week. Nothing major. Nothing taking him out of town. Unable to keep his grin from spreading, all he could think about was the weekend and Julie flying to Maine.

"What I want to know is if Mr. Tall, Dark, and Handsome is in Maine, what are you doing down here in Florida?"

Julie looked over at Randolph with affection as he poured another glass of wine for them both. She was sitting in a comfortable chair in his living room while he reclined on the sofa. His apartment was identical to hers, and yet, could not be more different in style.

Randolph decorated in an eclectic mixture of sleek furniture that could be described by some as masculine, punctuated by colorful throw pillows and shelves filled with odds and ends. The first time he had invited her up, it took almost an hour for her to make her way around the living room, looking at the collectible figurines, antique silver picture frames, cut glass bowls, and brass candlesticks. Nothing matched, and yet, everything seemed to fit.

He had explained that he was the only son of his parents and the only nephew of three maiden aunts. Years of family bric-a-brac had been passed down to him. Laughing, he said he knew it was the hope of his aunts and mom that all their collectibles would eventually be handed off to his wife and child until they finally had to accept that he was never going to marry and procreate. That last word had been said with great flourish and air quotes, causing her to laugh out loud.

She stared affectionately at the older man who had befriended her on the day she moved into the apartment several years ago. So easy to talk to, she found herself telling him all about the divorce and how she was ready to start anew. Now, she had just told all her tales of her time in Mexico and the man who came to rescue her.

"I told you I'm going to visit him in a few days," she replied, taking another sip of wine.

"Visit shimizit," Randolph retorted, pinching his lips as he made a face of disgust, waving his hand to the side before pointing a finger directly at her. "Take it from a man who tried to live his life fitting into someone else's mold before I finally said 'screw it' and started living the way I wanted, you do not want to pass up a good thing."

"Sounds like there's a story in there," she deflected, tucking her legs up under her as the wine relaxed her body.

"Oh, child, you know I always have a good story. And yes, I let more than one good man get away because I was too busy trying to live the life my mama wanted for me. But tonight is about you, not me. You've told me about Mexico. You've told me about Walker." He took another sip of wine, then waggled his eyebrows, saying, "And don't think I don't know that you left out the juicy parts."

She had just taken another sip of wine when her laughter exploded, and she nearly choked. Coughing and sputtering, she set the wine glass down as Randolph jumped up, ran over, and began slapping her on the back.

Crying, "I knew it. I knew it. I knew there was good stuff you left out of your story," Randolph grinned while continuing to pound her back.

Finally, gaining control of herself, she shook her head

as he made his way back to the sofa and settled in again. "There are some things I'm just not going to tell you," she announced, pushing her half-empty wine glass to the side. Shrugging, she added, "But just because two people have a connection in the middle of an intense situation, how do you know there's anything to really build upon?"

"You don't."

She blinked, staring at Randolph as he stared back at her, his expression stern. "If you're looking for the ability to look into the future and see exactly who's right to be paired with whom, you're going to be one very unhappy woman. Who's to say the man that you meet in the fresh food aisle of the grocery store and strike up a conversation with about the size of cucumbers is going to end up being your forever love?"

She fought to keep the grin from her face but remained silent, knowing that once Randolph was on a tangent, there was no stopping him.

"Who's to say that the boy you grew up with and played with on the school playground is going to be your forever love? And what about the man that you meet in your office and have lunch with for three years, getting to know each other slowly? Does that guarantee love?"

Leaning back in his seat, he picked up his glass of wine, crossed his legs with elegance, and took another sip. "Is the gist of what I'm saying finally sinking in?" he asked with a lifted brow and a slight smile.

Nodding, she laughed. "You're trying to tell me that just because Walker and I met in an unusual way doesn't mean that we don't have just as good a chance at having a real connection as someone else."

Throwing his hand into the air, he shouted, "Hallelujah! Give that girl a gold star and a one-way ticket to Maine!"

Standing, she picked up her glass and walked toward his kitchen. "My ticket is definitely not one-way. You forget I have a job here in Florida." After rinsing her glass and putting it in his dishwasher, she walked toward the front door where he was waiting for her.

Enveloping her in an affectionate hug, he whispered, "We have one life to live, my dear. Keep your options open and allow the possibilities to take hold."

31

Bolting awake, Walker sat up in bed, his attention sharp as he searched for the reason why he awoke. It was just like the night he woke before getting the mission to go down to Mexico. Once again, there were no sounds to be heard, and while his Spidey senses could detect no immediate threat, something did not feel right. Knowing sleep would not come right away, he silently slipped from his bed, pulling his weapon from the drawer of the nightstand. Stealthily moving through his apartment, he checked each room, looked out the windows, and scanned the area. Nothing. Giving his head a little shake, he moved into the kitchen and drank a glass of water, trying to still his heartbeat.

Securing his weapon, he crawled under the covers and punched his pillow, willing sleep to come again. With thoughts of Julie filling his mind, he counted down the hours until he would see her again and finally fell into a fitful sleep.

Julie's eyes jerked open, uncertain what had woken her. She sat up quickly, cocking her head to the side as she listened. She had not wakened so quickly in the middle the night since before the earthquake in Mexico. Just like then, she was uncertain if she had heard a noise. At that time, it had sounded more like a rumble deep in the earth. Now, it sounded like a metal chair leg had been scooted across the concrete patio.

The patio was reached through the sliding glass doors leading from her living room, but her bedroom also had a window that overlooked the area. She sat in bed, trying to listen over the sound of her pounding heart, but was unable to detect any other sounds coming from outside. Knowing sleep would not come if she did not check, she slipped out of bed.

Not wanting to be seen if there was an intruder on her patio, she moved to the side of her window, and without touching the curtain was able to peek onto the patio from the barest slit of space between the wall and the curtain.

Randolph had often told her that she should leave her patio light on at night to illuminate the area, discouraging anyone who might be looking for an easy apartment to break into. It was a habit she had gotten into, but now that she peeked out, she realized the light was no longer on. *What a dumb time for it to burn out.* Still not seeing or hearing anything, she decided that drinking wine at night caused strange dreams, and she relaxed.

Stepping away, she jolted as another sound came from the patio. Pressing her shaking fingers against her lips to quiet her breathing for fear that any noise might give her away, she leaned forward again to peek through the curtain slit.

Even with the security light not on, she could barely see a man standing on her patio, right at the sliding glass door. The moonlight gave just enough illumination for her to spy dark pants, dark shirt, and a dark cap. He lifted his glove-covered hand to the door, and unable to stay quiet, she cried, "No!"

He jerked around, saying, "Mierda," before turning away. She bolted toward her nightstand, grabbed her phone, and dialed 9-1-1.

An hour later, sitting on her living room sofa, Randolph at her side with his arm around her, she had described what she heard and saw to a policeman. There had been no break-in, no fingerprints on her door, and she knew from the way the police were speaking to her that they either did not believe her or had no evidence to pursue an investigation.

"You don't have a bulb in the light fixture outside," one of the policemen said as he entered her living room through the sliding glass door.

"I do, but it must have burned out," she protested.

Shaking his head, he repeated, "No, ma'am. There's no bulb there at all."

Frustrated, she knew the light had been working before. Giving up on that argument, she said, "Well, maybe he took it or something because it was there."

"Ma'am, had you been drinking last night?"

"Just a few glasses of wine, but I hardly see what that has to do with anything!"

As the police left her apartment with a promise to increase their patrol of the neighborhood, Randolph walked down the hall toward her bedroom. Assuming he was double checking her room even though the police had just been there, she walked into the kitchen and filled a glass with water. Drinking thirstily, she set the empty glass into the sink and gripped the counter.

As Randolph walked back into the room, she looked up and said, "I know what I saw. I know what I heard. It sounds crazy, but he mentioned a place I had just been to… Mérida"

He lifted his hand, holding her phone, and said, "Darling, I believe you. Now you need to tell him."

She stared at her phone for a couple of seconds, not understanding what Randolph was telling her. Reaching for her phone, she barely had it to her ear when she heard, "Why the fuck did you not call me after you called the police?"

Her eyes popped open wide as she stared in incredulity. "Walker?" Shooting her gaze back over to Randolph, she watched as he shrugged, feigning indifference to her glare before he moved to her sofa and settled in.

Putting the phone back to her ear, she said, "The police just left. I haven't had a chance to do anything, much less even think to call you." Glancing at the clock on her stove, she added, "It's almost three o'clock in the morning, Walker."

"Babe, the time of day or night is irrelevant. Some

fucker tries to break into your apartment, I should be the second call you make after police."

Shoulders slumping, she did not reply, not having any idea what to say. The events of the past hour continued to play through her mind, and as the adrenaline begin to wear off, she felt very tired.

"Julie? Babe? Please tell me what happened. Your neighbor only gave me the basic information, that someone was on the patio and you called the police."

She looked over, and Randolph was motioning with his hand for her to come to him. Walking over, she plopped heavily onto the sofa and leaned her shoulder against his.

"I woke up, thinking I heard a noise on the patio. I couldn't imagine that someone was there considering that I keep my patio light on. I also didn't want to move the curtain to peek out and possibly be seen—"

"Good thinking!"

Continuing, she said, "At first I didn't see anything, and realized my patio light was off. Then I heard another noise. A man, all dressed in black, moved to the sliding glass door that leads into the living room. I was so scared, I shouted 'no' when I ran to get my phone to call the police because he ran away. The weird thing was that he mentioned the place we had been in Mexico." She gasped, "Oh, God, Walker, what does that mean?"

The phone line was silent for just a few seconds before Walker asked, his voice carefully measured, "Mexico? What the fuck? Did you tell the police that?"

"Of course, I did, Walker," she snapped, wondering

why he sounded so cold. "It seemed to just give them one more reason to think that I had dreamed up the entire incident. There was no evidence of somebody on my back porch by the time they got here, so I'm not sure they even believed me."

"What place did he mention?"

"He said 'Mérida,'" she replied.

The phone line was silent again for just a few seconds, only this time when Walker spoke, his voice was soft but firm. "Are you still with Randolph?"

"Yes, he's sitting right here."

"Okay, babe. Here's what I want you to do. Get your shit packed together. Clothes, shoes, toiletries, whatever you need. I'm calling Drew and we're coming to get you."

"Do you think that's necessary, Walker? I'm already planning on flying to see you at the end of the week."

"Babe, I'm holding onto my shit here because I want to get you safe, and right now, am wishing I could jump through the phone line."

She smiled slightly, realizing his steady voice was him trying to stay calm when he was really worried for her.

He continued, "So, yes, I think it's necessary, and that was before someone tried to break into your apartment. Just think of it as we're moving your vacation up a few days."

She closed her eyes and tried to think of a reason why she should not go ahead and let him come get her but came up blank. The reality was she really wanted to see him. Wanted to feel his arms around her. Wanted to have him kiss the top of her head. Sighing, she said, "Okay."

"I want Randolph to stay there while you're packing everything up, and then I want you to go to his place until I get there."

A protest was on the tip of her tongue, but she remained silent. She did not really want to be alone and figured that Randolph would not let her stay in her apartment by herself anyway.

"Okay," she repeated. Then adding for good measure, she said, "You know you're not always going to get your way, don't you?"

"Only when I think you might be in danger," he responded, his warm words soothing over her cold body. "Text me when you get settled into Randolph's apartment, and I'll let you know when to expect me to get there. If you have any other frights, call the police again and then call me immediately."

Giving her promise, she disconnected before tossing the phone to the coffee table. Randolph shifted slightly, his arm curling around her shoulders, giving her a hug.

"Before you start fretting, let me just say that the way that man acted when I told him what had happened has solidified in my mind that he's a good man for you."

She twisted her head and looked at him, and said, "I know he's a good man."

He shook his head and said, "You're not hearing what I'm saying, Julie. He's a good man, but he's also a good man for *you*." Giving her shoulder another squeeze, he stood and held out his hand to assist her from the sofa. "Now, let's get some packing done."

Five hours later, Walker walked through Randolph's front door, immediately scooping Julie into his arms. With his powerful embrace wrapped around her, she felt safe for the first time since she first looked out of her window. Closing her eyes, she pressed her cheek against his chest, his steady heartbeat filling her with comfort. When he pressed his lips to the top of her head and kissed her, she felt complete. They stood like that for a moment until she was aware of murmurings in the room.

Leaning her head back she smiled up at Walker and whispered, "Hey."

"Hey, back," he grinned, this time leaning down to capture her lips in a soft kiss.

She stepped back, seeing Drew chatting with Randolph, and immediately greeted him as well.

"Is this all your stuff?" Drew asked, bending to grab her two suitcases. When she nodded, he hefted them and with a chin lift toward Randolph headed out the door.

She introduced Walker and Randolph, listening as Walker thanked him for being such a good friend and Randolph waving away his thanks, insisting that he was thrilled to have her heading to Maine a few days earlier.

She moved into his arms, hugging him goodbye. He kissed her temple and then leaned in to whisper, "I've now seen him with you, I can amend my former statement. He's not only a good man *for you*, he's the *right man for you*." She blinked away the tears that threatened to fall, and as she moved back into Walker's arms, Randolph called out, "And Drew? Now that man could be the right man *for me!*"

Laughing, she waved goodbye as Walker led her down to the rental SUV. Within the hour, they were in the air, flying to Maine. And she wondered once again if her life was ever going to fit back into her planner.

32

Several hours later, Drew guided the plane to an easy landing at the airport near Brunswick which was not too far from where Walker lived.

Walker looked at the seat next to him and stared at Julie in the early morning light. She had fallen asleep about an hour out of Florida and had not woken up, even during landing. Drew taxied to the private hanger that LSI rented, and Walker debated on trying to wake her up or carry her to his SUV.

"I didn't want to say anything unless she was sleeping, man," Drew said as he unbuckled himself from the pilot's seat, twisting around to look at Walker, "but who the fuck do you think was at her house?"

Walker shook his head slowly and said, "I've got no fuckin' idea. If it wasn't for the man calling out the town in Mexico, I would've easily thought it was just a random burglary. Maybe someone who thought she was still gone, although she's been home for almost two weeks." Scrubbing his hand over his face, he felt his rough stubble, and worry pulled at him.

"You going to take her back to your place, or do you want her to go to the safe house?" Drew asked.

"I'm going to take her back to my house and let her sleep for a couple more hours," Walker said. "Tell Mace that I'll be in this afternoon and bringing her with me. Until we know what's going on, I don't want to leave her alone."

Drew climbed down and opened the door to the cabin. Trying not to jiggle her, Walker unbuckled her from her seat and bent to pick her up. Julie's eyes fluttered open, and she looked around in sleepy-eyed surprise, obviously trying to figure out where she was. When her gaze landed on his, she said, "Oh, are we here? I must have fallen asleep."

Scooping her up into his arms, he chuckled. "Babe, you're so exhausted you've been crashed for over two hours."

She tried to protest, saying, "I can walk, you know."

Hugging her tightly, he replied, "I know. I just like having you here." Drew followed behind with her bags before giving them a wave goodbye.

"It'll only take us about twenty minutes to get to my apartment," he said. Shooting a glance toward her, he added, "I thought we could get a couple more hours of sleep, and then I need to go into my work."

She turned and looked at him, her voice soft, and said, "That's okay, Walker. I know you need to work. I'll be just fine at your place—"

"Oh, hell no, babe. I don't want you out of my sight unless you're with someone I trust."

She stared at him, her brow crinkled in worry. "Really? Do you really think I'm in danger? I mean maybe it was just…I don't know…random?"

"Sweetheart, I don't know what to think. But I think we're taking a big chance if we just assume that it was a random break-in attempt. But don't worry. The people I work with will already be looking at things by the time we get there. Hopefully, we'll have an answer soon."

Reaching over, he engulfed her cold hand in his much larger, warmer one. Hoping to take the frown from her face, he added, "Just think of it this way. We can start our vacation together sooner."

That earned him a grin which he accepted readily. He drove through an older section of town, parking outside a block of brick apartments. After assisting her out of his SUV, he reached into the back and grabbed her bags. They were not heavy, but it also looked as though she had not packed light. Inwardly grinning at the thought that she might be staying for a while, he ushered her into the front door after entering the security code. Immediately to their right was the elevator, and with a short ride up to the third floor, he led her to his apartment.

Entering, he set her bags down but suddenly found himself unsure what she would think of his space. The wooden floors were clean but slightly worn. The outer walls of the rooms were exposed brick, and the inner walls were painted a basic white.

She walked around slowly, her gaze taking in everything. She moved past his kitchen, through his living room with its comfortable but clearly masculine furniture, and over to the large picture window that overlooked a small park behind the apartment buildings. Wishing she would say something, he stood rooted to the spot, his palms beginning to sweat.

Suddenly, she whirled around, and with a wide smile announced, "I love your place."

Blowing out a breath he had not realized he was holding, he met her smile with one of his own as he stalked forward. Wrapping his arms around her, he kissed the top of her head and said, "I know you're exhausted, but do you want to eat something before we try to take a nap?"

She shook her head, and said, "No, but I could definitely use the bathroom."

While she was in the bathroom, he brought her bags into the bedroom. His apartment had one large master bedroom and one smaller one that was set up with the daybed as a sofa, a desk in one corner, and a few weights in the middle of the floor for when he felt like a workout without going to the gym. He definitely wanted to share the bed with her but also did not want to make any assumptions.

As she came out of the bathroom, he rushed, "I want you to have this bed, and if you'd rather sleep by yourself, I can take the daybed in the other room or the sofa."

With a sweet smile curving her lips, Julie walked over and encircled his waist with her arms, once again placing her cheek on his chest. "I've been waiting to share a bed with you since you were at my place."

Leaning her head back, her grin widened, and she added, "But as tired as I am and as much as I want to be with you, I'd even take the back of the Jeep."

Throwing his head back, he laughed. "No worries, my bed is much more comfortable than the Jeep." A few minutes later, his words proved true as they fell asleep, curled up in each other's arms in his large, king-sized bed.

Julie had no idea what to expect from Walker's workplace, but leaving town and driving out into the country was not what she expected. After he turned down a long drive that meandered through thick woods and popped out at the edge of a lush, green meadow, the ocean in the background, a tall, white lighthouse next to a large, white, red-roofed house was a total surprise.

For a moment, she stared in stunned silence as he parked his SUV next to the house alongside other SUVs, trucks, and a few motorcycles. Finally coming out of her stupor, she swung her head around, finding Walker looking at her, a questioning gaze on his face.

"This is amazing, Walker!" she enthused. "I had no idea that the Lighthouse Security was actually going to be at a lighthouse." Swinging her head back around so that she could view the ocean down below what appeared to be a cliff behind the house, she repeated, "Amazing. Absolutely gorgeous."

He reached over and took her hand, then said, "Before we go inside, let me explain how this will work.

We'll be meeting with some of my other coworkers here in the house. If I know the woman who runs the place, she'll probably have food ready for all of us. They'll want you to be comfortable. I want you to be comfortable. The only thing that's important is your safety."

She smiled softly, his concern touching. "Don't worry about me, Walker. I'm good."

He leaned over, kissing her lips gently. A sigh slipped from his lips, his warm breath washing over her face. "Waking up with you and knowing we needed to get here, not having time to make love to you the way I really wanted, was hard. Now, kissing you may have been a mistake because all I want to do is take you back to my bed."

Her gaze dropped to his lap, noticing the bulge at his crotch. Unable to hold back a grin, she laughed as he shot her a warning gaze. He adjusted himself before climbing down from the SUV and assisting her down as well. With fingers linked, he walked her into the house.

Entering, she should not have been surprised at the number of people inside considering how many vehicles were parked nearby. But seeing the hustle and bustle of large men and a few women moving between the kitchen and a door leading to outside tables, she found herself pressing closer against Walker's side.

Recognizing a familiar face, she smiled at Babs who elbowed her way through the mass of men, pulling her in for a hug.

"Good to see you again, Julie," Babs said. Turning toward the crowd, Babs stuck her fingers in her mouth and whistled loudly, effectively bringing quiet to the group.

Shaking his head, Walker laughed. "Everyone, I'd like you to meet Julie Baxter."

An older, stocky woman with short gray hair, warm eyes, and a bright smile came from behind the counter. Shaking Julie's hand, she said, "I'm Marge Tiddle, housekeeper here. Over there," she nodded toward a man with a twinkle in his eye and his gray hair cut military short, "is my husband, Horace. Welcome to the lighthouse." Looking at Walker, she said, "Take her on outside. Might as well introduce her to everyone before we sit down to eat."

As Walker led her out of the kitchen, two very pretty women came from the hall, both with welcoming smiles. Sylvie, she learned, was married to Walker's boss, Mace. And Helena was with his best friend, Rank.

As they made their way outside, she saw several large tables pushed together with chairs all around. A lot of food was already placed out on the tables, and several men were manning grills. Seeing another familiar face, she smiled as Drew came over and offered a hug.

Walker introduced her to the other men that were there, telling her that it was not the entire group since some of them were out on missions. She tried to use her trick of repeating each name after she met the person to help her remember, but they all began to run together. Besides Drew, the two she did remember were Rank, since he and Helena were sitting on one side of them, and Mace. The owner of Lighthouse

Security was not a man to easily forget. Like the other men, he was large, but with his dark hair, dark eyes, and penetrating gaze, he appeared to be a man very much in charge. He would have been someone that would have made her nervous except for seeing the smile on his face whenever he looked at his wife, Sylvie, or their son, David.

The conversation stayed light until after they had eaten, when Sylvie took David back to their home nearby, and Helena, Marge, and Horace went back inside the house.

Feeling all eyes on her, she squeezed Walker's hand under the table. When asked about the man who tried to break in, she repeated everything that she had told the police.

"And you're sure you didn't recognize him?" Tate asked. She had remembered his name since Walker had introduced him as the one who had been on the computer looking for any surrounding security cameras or traffic cameras near where she lived.

She said, "No. I had my security light on which surprised me that he even tried to get in." Shaking her head, she grimaced, and amended, "I mean, I thought I had my security light on. But when I looked out there was no light. The cops told me the bulb was missing."

She observed several shared looks between the men but was uncertain how to interpret them, so she remained quiet.

Mace looked at her, his rough voice softening as he asked, "And he mentioned one of the cities you had visited in Mexico?"

Nodding, she said, "Yes. That's why I knew he must've been after me. He said 'Mierda'."

Babs jerked her head around and asked, "Mierda or Mérida?"

Blinking, Julie stared in dumbfounded silence, not understanding what Babs was asking. "I'm sorry, but I didn't hear a difference in those two words." She glanced sideways at Walker, but he appeared equally confused.

Everyone's attention focused on Babs now, and she explained, "Mérida is a city in Mexico, the one that Walker and Drew first flew into, and I believe was on your itinerary. Mierda means…well, it literally means *shit*. Both in the actual word for feces and as a curse word, just like we use it. If it was the second one, then he wasn't specifically mentioning a city in Mexico, he was just cursing."

Julie slumped back, the various scenarios moving through her mind as she realized she could not identify exactly which word the man had said. As realization slowly dawned, her stomach dropped and she clapped her hands over her face, moaning, "Oh, my God. He may have just been a random man trying my door then cursing, and I made a big deal about it like he was someone from Mexico after me!"

"Whoa, whoa, there," Walker said shaking his head. "It doesn't matter which he was or what he said. He was still a man trying to get into your apartment in the middle of the fuckin' night."

The other men protested as well, but Mace's voice cut through the others. "Julie."

The authoritative tone underlined with kindness had her dropping her hands and lifting her head to look at him across the table.

"Walker is exactly right. We have no idea who the man was, but Tate is working on the security cameras in the area, and hopefully will be able to get a picture, vehicle description, or license plate number quickly."

With a chin lift, Tate stood from the table and said, "I started a search this morning. I'll get back to it right now."

Several of the others stood offering nods of their own and headed back into the house behind Tate. It ran through her mind that she wondered where the offices of LSI were, but as Walker pulled her closer into his side, she pushed that thought aside.

Looking at first at Walker and then at her, Mace said, "Julie, perhaps you'd like to spend a little time with Sylvie. I'm sure she'd would enjoy showing you the lighthouse."

She nodded her understanding that Mace was politely trying to distract her so that his men could talk and discuss the situation without her around. Instead of being insulted, relief flooded her. Smiling softly, she agreed, "That would be lovely. I know you have work to do, and I'd love a chance to see the beautiful lighthouse."

"Shit, my phone's got a low charge," Drew interrupted. "Hey, Babs, where are the extra chargers?"

Rolling her eyes, Babs thrust out her hand, palm up, and said, "Just give it to me, Flyboy. I'll get it charged and get it back to you."

Drew slapped the phone in Babs' hand and grinned.

"I knew there was a reason I loved having you around," he quipped before turning and heading toward the house.

Julie watched as a specter of something undefinable but almost sad flashed through Babs' eyes. The look was gone so quickly she was not sure she had actually seen it.

Walker stood, assisting her to her feet, turning her body so that she face-planted into his chest once again. Feeling his lips on the top of her head, she smiled as her arms encircled him.

"Baby, I'm going to be with Mace and the Keepers for a little while, but I don't want you to feel abandoned. The others can keep you company, and if you get tired, there are guest bedrooms you can rest in."

Leaning her head back, she looked up, seeing the worry in his eyes. Standing on her tiptoes, she kissed the underside of his jaw and said, "Really, Walker, I'm fine. You go do whatever it is you …uh…do."

He chuckled, and she felt the rumble deep in his chest and gave him another squeeze before stepping back. Babs walked over and linked arms with Julie, and said, "Hope you're not afraid of heights, 'cause the view from the top of the lighthouse is amazing."

Catching the wink Walker sent her way, she smiled and walked arm in arm with Babs into the house, still wondering where all the men were going to work.

33

As soon as Babs led Julie away, Mace and Walker joined the others in the underground compound. Once seated, Tate immediately flashed several pictures on the screen.

"She lives in a neighborhood off of a main highway, so going through the street cameras has been slow work. Her apartment building does not have security cameras, but there is an intersection camera right at the beginning of her complex. When I cross-reference the people driving on the complex after nine PM, I've been able to determine that they either live there or can see who their vehicle is registered to. I'm not saying it isn't one of those, but I'm not convinced I've come across them yet."

Bray looked over and asked, "So someone could have come in earlier and just waited, or they could have come in by foot?"

Walker nodded, and said, "Her apartment complex is near a busy shopping center with a highway that goes by, and it's not a gated community. Someone definitely could have walked over or walked by." Looking around at the others, he said, "I know. I know. It's a security nightmare."

"Do you think this had anything to do with what she saw in Mexico?" Rank asked.

Dragging his hand through his hair, Walker grimaced. "It's too much of a fuckin' coincidence, and I've never believed in coincidences. Whether the man said 'Mérida' or cursed 'mierda' to me is inconsequential."

"She did witness an execution," Drew said, his face serious. "I know the cartel has a long reach, but someone would have to have figured out who she was, where she lives, and managed to get into this country. If that's what happened, we're not dealing with just any lowlife drug runner."

"She said the man was wearing a uniform," Walker said, shaking his head slightly, a headache beginning to bloom behind his eyes. "I didn't think that much about it at the time other than I wanted to get her to safety." Shrugging, he added, "Plus, as we saw, a lot of people have military or police-type uniforms. Hell, some of the military and police are working for the cartels, so who the fuck knows who they were associated with."

"I thought about showing her some of the various uniforms that the military and police wear in Mexico, but if they're so easily bought and worn by others, I don't guess that makes any sense," Tate said.

Mace had been quiet during the exchange, but as the

Keepers looked toward him, he said, "I agree with Walker in that the coincidence is too great that she witnessed an execution in Mexico and within two weeks someone is trying to break into her house in the middle the night. I also agree that even if the two incidences are not related, we'd still be worried about her security." Looking over at Walker, he asked, "LSI can easily take on her security if you want us to get her set up."

Walker hesitated, then said, "I'd like to say yes, boss, but then…well, I guess I'm hoping to convince her to stay. I know that sounds premature, but—"

"Nothing premature about fallin' in love and wanting that person with you," Rank said, his smile both wide and sincere.

The others around the table chuckled and grinned as well, but Rank's comment caught Walker off guard. *Love?* He and Julie had not begun to define their relationship, and he certainly had not given his feelings a label. *Can you love someone after only knowing them a few weeks?* Uncertain how to respond, he just said, "I want her to have the best security, Mace. Let's hold off on getting it into her apartment in Florida right now. She was planning on spending a week here in Maine anyway, so that'll give us a chance to see what we can find out."

As everyone continued work, he moved to a seat next to Tate so that they could look through the camera feeds together. Feeling a clap on his shoulder, he twisted his head around, seeing Rank settling in the chair next to them, a sheepish expression on his face.

"Sorry, man. Didn't mean to put you on the spot like that," Rank said.

He stroked his chin, shaking his head. "Don't worry about it. We just haven't defined what we have yet."

Rank's lips quirked upward as though he was stifling a grin. "I get you. I didn't know how to define what Helena and I had for a while either. But it finally hit me...I thought about her all the time. I wanted to be with her all the time, I didn't want to have to travel back and forth on the road between her house and mine but was willing to do it. We hadn't known each other all that long, but if that's not love, I don't know what is."

Rank stood and moved away to one of the other workstations. Turning back toward the computer screen, Walker felt scrutinized and looked to see Tate staring at him. "What? Now *you* got an opinion about my love life?"

Shaking his head, Tate laughed. "It's not me that just said the words *love life* instead of relationship. Sounds to me like you already know what you've got."

Jaw-dropping open, he mumbled, "Just stick to looking at the street cameras." With Tate's laughter ringing in his ears, the two men turned their attention back to the computer screens and scanning the feeds.

The stairs continued upward in the spiral leading to the top of the lighthouse. Helena and Babs were behind Julie, and Sylvie and David were in front, the exuberant little boy commenting nonstop on the lighthouse.

"There are sixty-five historical lighthouses in Maine, and my teacher says that we are often referred to as The Lighthouse State. They've been around for hundreds of years and get lots of visitors. This one doesn't, of course, because my dad owns it, and it's no longer a working lighthouse."

David stopped suddenly, and his mom almost ran into them. He turned around, looked at Julie, and asked, "Did you know that a lot of them are on islands and the only way to get to them is by boat?"

She laughed and asked, "Would you like to live in one of those?"

His eyes widened, and he nodded with enthusiasm. "Yeah! And if the weather was bad, then I wouldn't have to go to school!" Sylvie rolled her eyes as David turned around, bounding up the last of the steps.

Reaching the top, they walked along the outer edges of the lighthouse lens, and she admitted, "This is the first time I've been up in a lighthouse. These lights are so much bigger than I could've imagined."

At the door leading to the outside observatory deck David stopped, obediently waiting until his mother could take his hand. Stepping through the door herself, Julie could understand why Sylvie was nervous. "Oh, my, we are up high."

"It's eighty feet tall," David announced proudly.

"I'd be out of breath if I hadn't just been climbing all those pyramid steps in Mexico," she laughed.

Moving out of the way so Helena and Babs could step out on the deck as well, Julie looked out over the blue ocean, the waves crashing against the rocks below.

It looked so different from the ocean view in Florida, and yet, it was hard to put into words why. The gulls appeared larger. The force of the waves appeared stronger. And as she listened, she realized it was the crashing sound of the water against rocks that was so different from the waves upon the sand in Florida. Strangely mesmerized, she stared out over the beauty of the coastline. To each side was the lush, grassy lawn ending in thick, evergreen forests all around.

From down below, she heard Horace call up, "David? You goin' into town with me?"

Sylvie smiled with benevolence at her son's renewed excitement and called down to let Horace know he was on his way. Watching, she cautioned him to take the stairs slowly as he bounded down toward his next adventure.

The cool breeze tossed Julie's hair about, and she said, "I've never been to Maine, but it's just as beautiful as the pictures I've seen. After living in hot Florida for several years and having just come back from the summer heat in Mexico, this is absolute heaven." At the mention of Mexico, she noticed that the three other women shifted their gazes to her.

Helena held her gaze before smiling widely. "Since Walker and Rank are such good friends, I'm hoping we can spend some time together while you're here."

"Not too much time," Babs quipped. "After all, I'd say they got some reacquainting between the sheets to do."

Laughing, Sylvie shook her head. "Babs...the things you say."

"Hello, ladies. I'm only saying what you're thinking."

Huffing, Babs continued, "At least the three of you are getting some regular. I'm the one who has to go out and look for it. Do you have any idea how hard it is to find a guy who's got looks, talent, cares about his mind as much as his body, and even has a clue how to give me a good O?"

Julie let go, her laughter causing tears to leak down her cheeks. "Oh, God, I needed that."

Babs grinned and said, "Anyway, I think it's great you're with Walker. I think all the Keepers are good men and deserve to find someone special."

She licked her bottom lip before she nibbled on it. "I know I'm with Walker for now. I mean, we're not seeing anyone else. I just don't have an idea what the future holds. I don't even know what you'd actually call us. We've never talked about labels or exactly what our relationship is."

Sylvie leaned back against the glass windows of the lighthouse, crossing her arms in front of her, nodding. "It's hard at our age, isn't it? When you're young it's so easy to say that someone is your boyfriend. When you get older, that almost sounds silly, and yet, I think we naturally want to be able to define what we mean to each other."

Throwing her hands to the side, Julie agreed, saying, "Yes! I work with teenagers, and the word boyfriend and girlfriend are thrown around all the time. That's the common word for defining two people who want to be together and are dating exclusively. But when you hit your adult years, boyfriend and girlfriend almost sound too juvenile."

Helena joined then, adding, "*Lovers* doesn't sound right either, even if that's what you are. You'd never introduce him as, 'Hey, meet my lover.'"

With a lifted eyebrow, Babs shook her head. "Lover. Boy toy. Fuck buddy. One-night stand. I've got all kinds of words I can use."

Laughter erupted from the group again, then Julie noticed a faraway look in Babs' eyes as Babs added, "Not really the words I want to use, but…well, someday…maybe." Babs gave a quick shake of her head, her wistful expression morphing into delight once again as she clapped her hands together and rubbed them briskly. "Who cares how you define your relationship with Walker? The bottom line is y'all are together!"

A ring tone sounded out, and Babs jumped. "Shit! I was supposed to charge Drew's phone, but I guess it must have a little bit of a charge left." She pulled his phone from her pocket, glancing at the screen as she let the call go to voicemail. "I swear he's such a juvenile, always taking pictures of people so he can see who's calling, saying he's bad remembering names."

Julie glanced down at the screen as it lay in Babs' palm, blinking to clear her vision as she stared at the picture that appeared. Her heart stuttered for several beats before pounding out of her chest. Her fingers flew to her lips as she stared in horror. "Oh, my God! It's him!"

34

By the time the four women were racing down the concrete steps of the lighthouse, Sylvie had already called for Mace to meet them. Blocking out everything but the sight of the man's picture on the phone, Julie barely heard Sylvie use the words *immediate* and *emergency*.

She stumbled, glad that Helena was in front of her and Babs was holding on to her arm, helping to steady her. At the bottom of the steps, the three women hustled her into a large, open room, furnished as a den but large enough to hold a lot of people. She heard noises coming from behind her, but they barely registered as the room began to fill with the Keepers, led by Walker, who stalked toward her, pulling her into his arms.

She stared, wide-eyed, into his face, repeating, "It's him. I'll never forget that face. It's him." He opened his mouth, but Babs stepped forward.

"Drew," Babs said, stepping up, gaining everyone's attention, "your phone rang, and a picture ID came up from the caller. Julie saw it and freaked."

Drew's gaze jerked between Babs and Julie, shaking his head, and asked, "What the fuck? Who was it?"

Julie swallowed deeply, forcing her heartbeat to slow and her voice to steady. Her gaze shot around to the other Keepers standing in the room, faces concerned. Mace had a hard expression she imagined could freeze boiling water, but his eyes were kind as they stayed on her.

She looked at Walker, and his penetrating gaze held her attention. "Julie? Babe?"

"It was the man from the airport in Mexico. The one in the uniform. The one with the gun." Swallowing again, she finished, "The one who shot the other man."

The room was deadly silent for a moment just before it erupted into a cacophony of cursing, filling the air with, *fuckin' hells*, *what the fucks*, and a few *holy shits*!

"Quiet!" Mace demanded, his voice not loud but carrying an air of authority that caused the occupants of the room to instantly obey.

Drew, unable to stand still, stalked over to Babs with his hand out, growling, "Let me see." Babs handed the phone to Drew, and with a few taps of his fingers he brought up the last call. Staring at it, he staggered back a step, eyes wide and mouth gaping open. With a clenched jaw, he looked at Julie and asked, "Joseph? It was Joseph?"

Her head nodded in jerks, not trusting her voice in

the face of Drew's obvious anger, unsure who the emotion was directed toward.

"You're telling me this piece of shit that I trusted was the one who put a gun to a man's head, blowing it off right in front of you?"

She began to shake. Walker growled. Babs grabbed Drew's arm, giving it a jerk as she hissed his name.

The hard lines of Drew's face fell as he sucked in a ragged breath, cursing, "Jesus, Christ. Oh, God, Julie, I'm so sorry."

Not knowing the whole story behind Drew and the man…Joseph, she remained quiet but was glad that Babs continued tugging on Drew's arm, saying, "It's not your fault. None of this is your fault."

"Yeah, it is," Drew agonized. "When I talked to him to let them know that we'd gotten back here, he asked about the airstrip we used. I didn't give him details, but he knew that was us. That means he knew whoever saw him was with us."

Walker stood with a shaking Julie in his arms, staring dumbly at Drew who was showing uncharacteristic shock. As a former Seal, Walker had been in a million different situations, trained to know how to react—or not react—to them all, but right now, he was clueless. The one thing he did know was he wanted to wrap Julie in his arms, chase her shivers away, promise to make it better, and then go after the fuckin' man who had terrorized her.

Mace looked toward Drew and said softly, "Give your phone to Tate." Shifting to look at the other men, he said, "Tate, Clay, Josh…get everything you can on this man. His contacts. His calls. Tap into his emails. And get his movements. I want to know everything about him ASAP. The rest of you…take what they give you and run with it." He walked closer to Walker and Julie, his eyes once again warm.

"Walker, you make the call on what you need to do." Turning to Drew, he said, "You need to be involved, but I need your shit together. Babs, I want you working this, too."

The Keepers left the room, Babs' hand resting lightly on Drew's back as they walked away. Walker turned toward Julie, but she spoke before he had a chance.

"Go. I'll be fine. I was shaken up and admit the memories came flying back, but I'm fine. You go and do what you need to do."

Agony shot through him as he warred with wanting to go into the compound and search out everything he could about Joseph while wanting to make sure Julie was comforted.

Helena stepped up, placing her hand on Walker, and said, "You go. Marge, Sylvie, and I will stay here with Julie."

He leaned forward and placed his lips over Julie's, feeling them quiver while trying to pour all of his emotions into the kiss. Her arm slipped around his waist, pulling him tighter, and for a few seconds, he lost himself in the taste and feel of her. Reality slipped in, and he pulled back with regret but kissed the top of her head before he turned and followed Mace and the others out the door.

As soon as they got downstairs, Tate and Josh moved directly to their computer stations while the others quickly settled around the main conference table, their tablets in front of them.

Mace began, "Drew, first off, none of this is your fault. So get that out of your mind so you can work the mission. Tell us what you know about Joseph, and we'll compare that to what Tate and Josh pull up."

Scrubbing his hand over his face, Drew took in a deep breath, let it out slowly, and said, "Joseph Martinez. I met him on one of my missions about five years ago on a CIA Special Op where we were working with a Mexican task force of police and military ferreting out some of the cartels' hideouts. Some of them are buried so fuckin' deep in the jungles and even in caves that the Mexicans have a hard time finding them even though they know the terrain. Our planes were equipped with sensors that were able to pinpoint some of their locations. He was at the end of his career, getting ready to retire. Not overly friendly, but then nobody was there to make friends, just do our job. He was professional and never gave me any reason to think there was any duplicity at all."

"Did you ever have a chance to talk to him privately?" Mace asked.

Nodding, Drew replied, "One night, some of us were at a small bar, nobody drinking heavily, just a chance to unwind. Most of the others left after a while, and it ended up being Joseph and me still at the table finishing our beer. He asked me some about how I got into flying. Nothing too invasive. I talked about growing up in the south and flying crop dusters as a teenager. The beer loosened him up some, and he talked about getting ready to retire. I remember he wasn't too happy about it because he felt like he was being pushed out due to his age."

Tate, his fingers flying over the keyboard, called out, "So far, all that checks out. He did thirty years in the military and retired three years ago. Divorced years before that. Two kids, now grown. His military pension would've been shit, which may have been one of the reasons he hated to retire."

Continuing, Drew said, "We rarely stayed in contact but met up to have drinks two other times I happened to be in Mexico on Special Ops missions. He never asked about my job, and I never spoke of it. I hadn't actually talked to him for about two years before this trip. As soon as we got the mission to go down and get Julie and the girls in Mexico, he was the first person I thought of to call to see if he could use any contacts to make sure we had a bird there."

Josh turned around from his computer station and faced the group. "His bank account is not one of somebody who was in the military only on a military pension. Large deposits made monthly for the past couple of years have given him quite a nest egg."

Walker, finally pushing thoughts of Julie's safety to the side while he focused on the information they were gathering, asked, "And no one in the Mexican government thinks to look at this?"

Shaking his head, Josh replied, "There's too much drug money floating around going into the pockets of all kinds of people for the banks to care or look into. Hell, probably a lot of their high-ranking officials are on the cartels' payrolls as well."

Looking at Drew, Walker asked, "When we got there, he didn't have the right size helicopter. Do you think that was on purpose to divide us up?"

Drew shot his haunted gaze over to Walker and shook his head. "Right now, I couldn't begin to tell you what he was doing. But I don't think so. After the earthquake, what he said to us about the military and police seizing all resources to get in help people was probably true."

Clay piped up, saying, "According to what I've looked at coming through all the Mexican official channels, that's right. Even people's private jets and helicopters were being commandeered to get supplies to the affected areas."

Walker asked, "What about the airstrip we landed at outside of Mérida? You cracked a joke about it being a strip for the cartels, and he said beggars can't be choosers."

"At the time, I just figured he was giving us a place to land that he knew of, and we weren't exactly picky where we landed as long as we could get to the girls."

"And the airstrip outside of Cancún?" Walker wondered aloud. "How the hell did he happen to be there when we were?"

Shaking his head, Drew said, "I've been thinking about that, but can't come up with anything other than that was just dumb fuckin' luck. It was one of the airstrips that he had mentioned to me when we were first going down to Mexico and needed a place to land that wasn't official. He said that he could get a bird to the one closest to Mérida, so that's why I chose that one when we went in the first time. Coming back to get you the second time, I chose the one closest to Cancún since you were on that side of the Yucatán."

Mace asked, "You didn't speak to him again after that first day you saw him in Mérida?"

"No, boss, not until the mission was complete. I expected him to be there when we returned, but he was nowhere to be found. I assumed he got called up for duty, so I got the girls in my plane and headed to Cancún, leaving the bird there in the hangar. I tried calling a couple of times, and I left some messages letting him know that I had left the bird. After I got back with Julie and Walker, he'd gotten my message and got back with me." Leaning back heavily in his seat, a dejected air about them, he looked over at Walker and said, "Fuckin' hell, man. I told him what happened to us at the airstrip. Fuckin' led him straight to Julie."

Shaking his head, he said, "That's not on you, Drew. That's on him, not you."

Josh called out, "Check the screen," drawing everyone's attention to the screen on the wall. "Using facial recognition, I ascertained that he only has one passport, and it's in the name that's on his birth certificate… Joseph Martinez, so he's not even attempting to disguise who he is."

Walker stared at the photograph of the man that he

had seen when he and Drew landed in Mexico. Staring at the screen, he committed that image to memory, the idea that he would be trying to harm Julie sending another wave of anger through him.

After a few more taps on the keyboard, Josh said, "He's here."

Walker jolted, leaning forward in his chair, his forearms resting on the table and his hands clenched together.

"Here?" Walker and Mace growled at the same time.

Josh stared first at Mace and then shifted his gaze over to Walker. "He flew into Jacksonville International three days ago."

"That's the closest international Airport to where Julie lives," Walker stated, his head feeling light from all the information coming in.

"Get on his trail," Mace ordered to the Keepers at their computer stations. "I want to know where the fuck he's been every second for the past three days."

Walker's body began to vibrate with anger, mixed with an unfamiliar emotion he could only label as fear. Holding Mace's gaze, he said, "I want him. He's mine."

35

Julie hated the way the women hovered over her as though she was going to fall apart. After a hot cup of tea as they all sat at the comfortable dining table, she finally said, "You all are being so nice, but I can tell you're walking on eggshells. Honestly, I'm not going to fall apart." Nibbling on her bottom lip, she admitted, "I realize this means that somebody is out there, probably looking for me because of what I witnessed. But with Walker taking care of me and all of the Keepers, I feel very safe."

"You are," Sylvie promised. "You're much braver than I was when David witnessed a murder."

Gasping, she looked at Sylvie and sputtered, "David witnessed a murder?"

Wincing, Sylvie said, "I'm sorry. I thought maybe Walker had told you. It was a year ago, and he was at my office where I used to work. He actually saw a man get murdered in the building across the street. I was a total basket case, but Mace came to our rescue." Shrugging her delicate shoulders, she added, "He made sure we were safe, and they worked on the investigation. We fell in love in the meantime, and he adopted David when we got married."

Eyes wide, she shook her head in shock. Glancing over at Helena, she said, "I hope you're gonna tell me that you and Rank were childhood sweethearts."

Helena threw her head back and laughed, then said, "Oh, no. I literally landed right on top of Rank in the middle of one of his investigations. He was furious, and I was mortified. But then, when someone came after me, Rank was right there offering his protection."

Sylvie smiled gently and added, "I sometimes think we're destined to end up with men like Keepers. Maybe that's why we see good things for you and Walker."

"How about a walk?" Julie suggested, finding herself wanting to get back outside to enjoy the beautiful day.

The others quickly agreed, and Sylvie led them down the lane, giving more of a history of Mace's ownership of the land. Just like at the top of the lighthouse, Julie lifted her face toward the sun, enjoying the warmth mixed with a gentle breeze blowing off the ocean. It reminded her of a summer day growing up in Pennsylvania, so much more temperate than Florida. She had never minded the seasons, even the cold, snowy winters. But when the job in Florida opened up, she had jumped on it, ready to try new things and go to new places. Now, the fresh air, green vista, and the ever-present roar of the waves crashing on the rocks nearby brought her a sense of peace in the middle of turmoil.

After making a long track around the property, they ended up on the grassy knoll behind the lighthouse and settled into the Adirondack chairs facing the ocean.

"This is glorious," she said. "It's like it's magical...here I am with everything swirling around me, and I feel such calm."

"I can't deny it," Sylvie said with Helena agreeing. "This place does have its own magic."

"Hey! I wondered where you'd gotten to," Babs called out as she walked from the house and joined them in the chairs.

Leaning forward, Julie stared at Babs and asked, "How's it going in there?"

First shooting Sylvie a look, Babs then turned to Julie and replied, "I can't respond to what they're doing directly, but they're working on it." Shaking her head, she said, "Drew is really kicking himself for even having made contact with Joseph at all."

"It's not his fault," Julie insisted. "He shouldn't take that on."

Snorting, Babs said, "Yeah, try telling that to a stubborn alpha male."

Julie sighed, her mind cast back to the middle of the previous night when the man was at her sliding glass door. *Jeez, that wasn't even twenty-four hours ago!* Thinking about him made her heart race faster, but she tried to imagine if that could've been the same man she had seen in Mexico. Having not seen his face at her apartment, she closed her eyes and tried to remember his body shape. Shaking her head in frustration, she sighed once again.

"Julie? What are you thinking about?" Helena asked

Jerking her eyes open, she blushed and said, "I was just thinking about the man who tried to get into my house and wondered if he was the person I had seen in Mexico."

Patting her arm, Helena said, "Don't worry. Walker and the others will take care of it."

Sitting up straighter, she said, "But I have to worry about it. If it was the same man, then that means he's identified who I am as the person who saw him kill somebody else. And if it was the same man, that means he's coming after me." Looking toward Babs, she said, "I have no idea about police matters and laws, but just because I say I saw him kill somebody in Mexico doesn't mean anything's going to happen to him here. We need to be able to get him on something in this country, and that would be trying to come after me."

Now it was Babs who leaned forward, shaking her head so hard that her hair was flying back and forth. "Girl, I don't know what you're thinking, but you better get yourself off that path. Whatever the Keepers are working on downstairs, you need to stay out of it."

"No, you're wrong," she insisted. "There's nothing that ties him to the man trying to get into my apartment. And there were no fingerprints so it's just my word that somebody was trying to get in. But if we can get him to come after me and catch him in the act, then we don't have to worry about him heading back down to Mexico and getting lost or getting away with murder. He'd have to answer to our justice system."

Helena stayed quiet, but her eyes were wide as she looked around at the others. Babs opened her mouth, but Sylvie got there first. Waving her hands back and forth, Sylvie said, "I know you're upset, Julie, and none of us blame you. But you've got to let Mace and Walker and the others handle this."

She sucked in her lips, thinking for a way to explain her thoughts so that they would make sense. Finally, she said, "I'm not trying to keep them from doing their job. I'm just saying that if this man is in the States and he's the one that was trying to get into my place, he's probably not going to stop. I don't want to be looking over my shoulder for the rest of my life. If there's some way that we could lure him, then he'd be caught red-handed in a crime here in the States." Looking at the others, she said, "I know I wouldn't be in any danger because everyone here would be after him. But don't you see, it would be a way to capture him."

Julie swung her head between the two women as Sylvie and Babs shared a look. Shrugging, Babs tossed out, "I'll go talk to the men and let them know your idea." Pressing her hands down on the wide arms of the Adirondack chair, Babs pushed herself upward. Walking back toward the house, she called over her shoulder, "Personally, it wouldn't bother me if they put a bullet right through him just like he did to that other guy."

Helena lifted her hand to her throat, watching Babs walk away. Sylvie shot a sympathetic look toward Julie, and said, "Don't get your hopes up. I can't imagine that the Keepers would ever agree to put you in harm's way just to get this man."

While the other Keepers were working, Walker found himself at loose ends, unable to concentrate, which only served to make him angrier. The sound of the chair next to him shifting caused him to look over, seeing Drew settle his large frame into the seat. Staring at his ravaged face, he almost did not recognize his friend.

Seeing Drew's mouth working as though he were trying to decide what to say, Walker jumped in first. "I know what you're going to say, man. I also know that nothing I tell you is going to make a difference right now. You feel guilty, but there's no reason. We've all made contacts in our years with military and CIA missions. You had no reason to look into this man considering the only thing you ever needed him for was a good place to land your plane. What he did, and what we think he wants to do, is on him. Not you. On him."

Drew gave a curt nod, but Walker was not finished. "Right now, I can't focus worth shit because all I can think of is if he'd gotten into Julie's apartment. So I'm relying on you, as well as the others, to help us figure out a way to get this piece of shit. I just got my head out of my ass about her realizing she's the one for me, and no way am I gonna let a fuck like him take her from me."

Drew's jaw tightened, and he clapped Walker on the

shoulder, his fingers flexing. "I'll do anything, man. Anything."

They were interrupted as Tate, at his station, began to curse in frustration. "I can't tell exactly where Joseph is right now. I got him on security cameras throughout the airport and getting into a taxi. The taxi records have him dropped off at a busy intersection in Jacksonville. I've got no other record of him in any hotels or using any other transportation. I figure he was picked up by a cartel contact."

Bray moved to the table and sat near Mace, across from Walker and Drew. "I hate to bring this up because I want to get this fucker as much as the next person, but even if we find him, there's nothing to get him on. He didn't enter the States illegally. We've got nothing to tie him to the attempted break-in at Julie's, and the murder she witnessed was in another country. The best we can do is turn him over to our contacts in the government and have him deported through back channels." Lifting his palms up while giving a little shrug, he added, "Of course, we can eliminate him ourselves, which none of us would have a problem doing." Staring across the table, he said, "I figure Walker and Drew would want in on that action, but I just wanted to bring this up so that we can be clear on our objective."

Before anyone had a chance to speak, a signal sounded letting them know someone was coming down the elevator. The doors opened, and Babs strolled back in, walking straight to the table. Walker watched her progress, the expression on her face unreadable.

Knowing she had just been with Julie, he sat up straighter, his entire body alert.

Babs made it to the table, slid a chair back, and planted her ass in it, her eyes skirting around the other Keepers who, like Walker, also had their attention riveted on her.

Unable to hold back, Walker asked, "Is Julie okay?"

Babs sucked in her lips for a second then plunged ahead. "Julie's a smart woman. She's already noodled that no evidence at her apartment is linked to the crime she witnessed in Mexico. She's also realized that she's the only witness to the murder in Mexico, so Joseph will get away."

The room was quiet, but Walker could not help but interrupt. "We know this, and as you say, Julie's smart, so I'm not surprised she realizes this, too. But then she doesn't know what we might do to mete out our own sense of justice….unless…"

"Fuckin' hell, Walker! What kind of idiot do you take me for? Of course, I wouldn't say anything like that to Julie!"

The air in his lungs rushed out in relief, not wanting Julie to know the extent of how far he would go to keep her safe. Scrubbing his hand over his face, he said, "Sorry, Babs… I just…well, I just want this taken care of."

Lifting an eyebrow, Babs tilted her head to the side, and said, "Well, to that point, Julie has a suggestion." Before anyone had a chance to say anything, she rushed, "Julie knows that Joseph is in this country and is the person that was at her apartment. She also knows that she's at risk because he wants to get her. So, in order to be able to get him while attempting a crime here in the States, she proposes using herself as bait."

Not a sound was heard in the cavernous compound as Babs' words sunk in. Then, all at once, the uproar of protestations began, Walker's being the loudest.

36

Mace once again called for quiet, which all the Keepers obeyed with the exception of Walker who had jumped to his feet, fists on his hips, staring down at Babs, protest still on his lips.

Throwing her hands up in front of her in a defensive posture, Babs said, "Hey, I'm just the messenger. We all tried to talk her out of it, but she's determined."

"Walker," Mace said, pouring a lot of meaning into his name.

Swinging his gaze from Babs to Mace, he was unable to keep the incredulity from his voice as he asked, "You cannot be seriously considering this."

Mace tilted his head to the side and replied, "And you cannot seriously be thinking that I would do anything to put one of our women in danger."

Walker knew his boss was right about that, and he jerked when a hand landed on his shoulder. Rank had walked up next to him and said, "Take it easy, man. Nobody wants anything to happen to Julie, but let's think this through. We all want Joseph to go down."

Walker sat back down, his heart still pounding erratically, but turned his attention to Mace.

"I've been talking to José Munoz, head of the Mexican Federal Crimes Unit. He knows about Joseph Martinez and was very interested in what Julie witnessed at the airstrip. He knows as well as we do that her word against a retired Mexican military veteran would not go over well, and without any other evidence, Joseph would not be convicted of that execution. But he also admitted that Joseph is a person of interest in their fight against the cartels. He's not at the top of the chain by any stretch of the imagination, more like a middleman, but they would love to get their hands on him. They don't care how we get him as long as we hand him over to them."

Walker's training had him focus carefully on not only Mace's explanation but where he knew the conversation was leading to. Outwardly stoic, his blood ran cold at the thought of LSI using Julie as bait.

Mace continued, "I propose that Drew call Joseph. He left a message on Drew's phone saying that he was in the States and wanted to touch base. He did this after trying to get into Julie's apartment, and I think we all agree that it was most likely him who was at her place. Let's have a plan in place, then have Drew call Joseph back. If it looks like he's digging for information about Julie, then let's see if we can lure him in."

"How the fuck would we do that?" Rank asked. "Drew would need to act like he knew where Julie was and create a place for her to be that Joseph would figure he can get to her."

Walker, his emotions in turmoil, blurted, "Boston. The Museum of Fine Arts in Boston."

Silence once again filled the cavernous room as all eyes turned toward him. Shaking his head in disbelief that he had actually spoken aloud, he sighed heavily. "I can't fuckin' believe I'm even considering this fuckin' plan," he bit out. "But I don't want her looking over her shoulder forever wondering who's coming up on her. I want this guy." He pinned the others in the room with his stare before landing on—and holding—Mace's eyes. "Full disclosure from me...I don't give a fuck if we hand him over to the Mexican government or he ends up having a fatal accident while here in the States. I want him eliminated."

Mace did not speak for a moment, then lifted his chin in acknowledgment. "Why the museum?"

"Just something Julie mentioned to me the other day before all this happened. She said the Museum of Fine Arts in Boston was having a special exhibit on Mayan artifacts. If we're looking for a place for her to be that's well lit, public, and easy for us to monitor, not to mention that it makes sense she would be there, that's the only place I can think of." Swinging his gaze back to Drew, he said, "But that's only if Joseph even mentions her. I'm not sending this guy after her, swinging her ass out there, if he's got nothing to do with it."

"Jesus, this sucks," Drew groaned, leaning back heavily in his seat. Looking up at Walker, he asked, "I'll make the call, but I gotta know…do you trust me with this shit?"

Without skipping a beat, Walker replied, "I trust everyone in this room with my life, and now with Julie's." As the words left his mouth, he knew he spoke the truth but wished the sick feeling in his stomach did not churn so hard.

"I can go with her."

All eyes now swung toward Babs, who continued to blurt, "I know y'all will be there as well but more in the background. I could go with her as a girlfriend just hanging out at the museum."

Drew startled, his brows lifting. "You don't have to do this, Babs," he said, lowering his voice. "You just helped…I mean…oh, hell, Babs…"

"Aww, Flyboy, I didn't know you cared," she joked.

Drew grimaced, adding, "You know I do…we all do."

The air left her lungs in a rush as she looked at him, uncertainty moving through her eyes. Opening her mouth to reply, Mace got there first.

"I decide who does what in LSI. Right now, we don't even have a mission to plan so let's take care of the business we need to."

Walker turned his attention to Mace, whose thoughts were passing through his intelligent eyes. Finally, he looked toward Walker and said, "Let's go talk to Julie."

In the time he had been around her, Walker was already learning the signs of Julie when she was nervous, and now, sitting on the sofa next to him focusing on Mace, she was nervous. Already regretting he had opened his mouth, he could not help but respect her for standing fast. Mace had laid it out for her, gently, that even without her assistance, they could possibly get their hands on Joseph before he left the country and quietly turn him over to the head of the Mexican agents in charge of investigating the cartels and curbing the drug business in Mexico. Mace had also let her know that LSI was not in favor of using her as bait to draw him out, keeping him in the country longer in hopes of capturing him.

"I understand what you're saying to me, Mr. Hanover—"

"Mace. You're part of the Lighthouse family now, and you call me Mace."

She offered a slight smile, her fingers linked with Walker's flexing. "Okay, Mace. I do understand what you're telling me, but I know he could be getting ready to leave right now. If that happens, we'll have no idea when he might come back. I know we can't know for certain that he was the one who tried to get into my apartment, but with everything you've told me, it seems like he's here for me. I still want to try to keep him here long enough and thinking he can get to me so that you can definitely get him first."

Walker's grip tightened, and she shifted while twisting her head around to look at him. Her voice a whisper, she asked, "Are you mad at me?"

Grimacing, he battled the desire to pull her into his arms and say, *"This is madness, and I refuse for you to do this!"* But he knew she was right…this was their chance to capture him.

He shifted their hold, pulling his hand away from hers so that he could wrap his arm around her shoulders, then moved his other hand in to link fingers with her again. With her now ensconced in his embrace, he shook his head and said, "No, babe. I'm not mad at you. Just concerned."

She gifted him with her full smile and said, "Don't be, Walker. I know you'll keep me safe."

With those words, his heart swelled, and he knew, no matter what, he would make those words come true. Shooting his gaze to the side toward Mace, he nodded. "Okay. Let's do this."

Hating to leave her side, he bent and kissed her lips before standing and walking out of the room with the others.

Once back inside the secure compound with Tate and Josh ready at their computers, Drew lifted his gaze to Walker and sighed. He pulled out his phone, made sure he had it on speaker, and dialed.

After the initial greetings, Drew said, "I was surprised to get your message and find out you were in the States. Where are you?"

"I flew into Miami," Joseph lied. "I have some relatives that I decided to visit."

"I was in Florida when I got back from Mexico," Drew said. "If I'd known you were coming, I could have made plans to stick around."

"What a shame we missed each other. By the way, how did everything turn out for you? The woman you flew out? She is well, I hope," Joseph said.

"Oh, yeah. Once we got away from that crazy-ass airstrip near Cancún, everything was fine. I know she was shaken up, but she must be doing okay. She keeps up with a friend of mine. In fact, funny that you mentioned her because I think she's up here visiting now."

"Oh?" Joseph asked. "Where are you these days?"

Chuckling, Drew said, "You wouldn't believe it, but she's visiting my friend and they're getting ready to go to a Mayan artifact exhibit in Boston tomorrow. Crazy, isn't it? You'd think she would have had enough of seeing all the Mayan pieces when she was in Mexico. But she convinced my girlfriend that it'd be a really cool thing to see. Museums aren't my thing. You wouldn't get me caught near one, but my girlfriend likes it."

Joseph said, "She must be doing well to be traveling again and ready to see more Mayan art."

"Why all the interest in her?" Drew asked, drawing Walker's wide-eyed look of surprise at his question.

"My country needs all the tourism we can get," Joseph replied smoothly. "I hated to think of anyone leaving with a bad impression." Pausing for just a few seconds, he continued, "It's been good to catch up with you, Drew. I'll be going back to Mexico in a couple of days, and perhaps we can see each other some other time."

Saying goodbye, Drew disconnected. No one in the

room spoke until Tate confirmed, "The connection is dead."

And so is Joseph, Walker thought, his hands clasped in fists.

37

The only light in Walker's bedroom was coming from the full moon reflecting onto the couple lying in his bed. The tension from the previous hours spent at the lighthouse in going over and over their plans had taken its toll on Julie, and he wanted to do nothing more than ease her worries, reminding her how good it was between them.

They had undressed slowly, as though they had all the time in the world. He had lowered her gently onto her back on his bed, determined to worship her body until she wanted him as much as he wanted her.

With her naked body stretched out next to his, they kissed for long moments, tongues gently exploring, breathing each other in. A little sigh of pleasure slipped from her lips and his arms tightened around her. Her fingers soothed up and down his back, occasionally stopping in their path to dig her fingernails into his muscles as she rubbed her body against his.

Kissing the corner of her mouth, he moved his lips over her jaw and down to the pulse point at the base of her neck. She leaned her head back giving him full access, and he nuzzled the soft, quivering flesh as he continued trailing kisses down her chest. With one hand cupping her breast, his lips latched over the other nipple, slowly drawing it into his mouth, his tongue teasing the beaded tip.

Her hands moved from his back, up over his neck, into his hair where she clutched him to her breast. His hand slid over her tummy, fingering lightly as it reached the tickle spots, before continuing its path downward. Her legs spread for him as she moaned, the sound vibrating against his lips still at her breast. Her hips undulated as he gently fingered her folds, his thumb circling her clit. Her body stirred to life, her desire evident in every little shift.

Leaving her breast, his lips trailed back up over her jaw before he held his face just above hers, their eyes meeting. She reached up, fingering the stubble across his jaw. Neither spoke, but emotions passed between them.

With his fingers sliding in and out of her sex, he watched as her eyes hooded with lust, her teeth digging into her bottom lip just before she sucked in a quick breath, a heated blush rising from her chest toward her face as she fell apart. Slowly withdrawing his fingers, he brought them to his mouth, sucking on them deeply. He leaned over, kissing her once again, allowing her to taste herself on his tongue.

Her chest heaved in desire and she whispered, "Please."

His lips curved, and he shifted his body, placing his hips between her open thighs as she wrapped her arms around his back, holding him close.

His cock nudged at her sex, and she tilted her hips upward to ease the entrance into her passage. Sliding into her, inch by inch, her eyes never left his even as she gasped. In the silence of the night, he continued to thrust, slowly at first and then with more vigor as their emotions collided with the physical need pounding between them.

Wanting her to come again, he shifted his hips so that he could slide his hand between them, fingering her clit as his cock moved deep inside. Her entire body quivered as her sex clutched his cock, and with a moan, his orgasm pulsed from his body into hers. Shuddering, he forced his eyes to stay open so that he could watch every nuance of their shared orgasm on her face. Her beauty stunned and humbled him as she lifted her hands and cupped his face.

He continued to thrust gently as her orgasm milked him, and when he thought his arms could hold him no longer, he fell to the side so as not to crush her, his chest heaving in powerful gasps.

Entangled, they lay as their bodies cooled from their shared passion. Keeping his eyes on her, he brushed her damp tendrils from her forehead before leaning forward and placing a gentle kiss there.

Terrified of ruining what they just experienced, he

bit back the words that had been longing to come forth. Words of care and concern. Words of heart and emotion. Words of love.

Instead of words, he tried to show her with his actions. Keeping his arms wrapped tightly around her, he kissed her gently, providing a safe harbor as she fell asleep.

Hours later, Julie woke, wrapped in the warmth and protection of Walker's arms, memories of their lovemaking bringing a smile to her face. She had wanted to declare her love for him, but fear had kept her quiet. Fear he might not feel the same. Fear that it might not be the right time. Fear of what those words would mean to their future and the decisions that would have to be made.

Staring at his face, illuminated by the moonlight, she smiled softly. She knew what her heart felt, and the fear slid away.

"I love you, Walker," she whispered, emboldened by his sleeping state, allowing the words to come easily. "I don't know what that means for us, but I want to be with you. Maybe that's crazy…we've only known each other for such a short time. A short, crazy time. I don't even know if you feel the same or if you want to be with me. But if you do, I'm here." Moving just a whisper away from his lips, she repeated, "I love you."

Closing her eyes, she settled once more, allowing

sleep to ease over her. She never saw his eyes open. She never saw them roam over her face. She did not see his lips curved into a gentle smile. Nor did she hear him whisper into the night, "I love you, too."

38

Julie and Babs walked toward the massive, white granite museum, the neoclassical architecture of the columns giving the building a stately and elegant appearance. East and West wings surrounded them, creating a courtyard as they climbed the steps to the front door. Once inside, they moved to the reception desk where they paid the entrance fee and received maps of the various exhibits.

Julie felt Babs' eyes on her and glanced to the side. "Before you ask...yes, I'm nervous."

Babs linked her arm through Julie's, and they walked across the massive, multi-storied entrance hall toward the first exhibit room. "Just remember that we're two friends deciding to enjoy a day at the museum."

Julie nodded, having been drilled for the past twenty-four hours in what was going to happen. After the Keepers had gone back to their secret lair, as she called it, they had come back upstairs and met with her. Walker had begun the explanation, telling her that when Drew made the call to Joseph, the conversation had quickly come to the point where Joseph had asked about the woman Drew had rescued and hoped all was well. Knowing Joseph had asked about her sent a shiver down her spine, but she was more determined than ever to help.

She had wondered how Drew was able to set things up, but Walker would only tell her that Drew was the consummate professional who managed to drop enough hints that Joseph would've been able to find out where and when she was going to be without it seeming as though Drew was setting him up.

Now, she was in the beautiful museum filled with exhibits of paintings, sculptures, antiquities, and yet, could not focus on the exquisite works of art.

Babs gave a slight tug on her arm and said, "Stop looking around like you're looking for someone. Remember, we're just strolling through the museum, enjoying our afternoon."

"I hope I don't see him," she admitted. "I'm not sure I can hide the emotions on my face."

"Don't worry about him. You know the plan…we're under constant surveillance. The Keepers are stationed everywhere."

Her forehead crinkled, and she whispered, "I don't see how you can have that many big, handsome men hanging around a museum and not look suspicious."

Babs snorted and replied, "I know you're right about

them being handsome, but because I work with them every day, I guess I'm immune."

Coming to a stop, she turned and said, "Immune? How could you be immune to that?"

"You forget that I'm around them all the time. You should smell them when they come out of the gym. That's one of those times I definitely don't think about them being attractive."

Julie tried to stifle her giggle, not wanting to make too much noise in the quiet museum. Sobering, she cast a slanted gaze toward Babs and asked, "Does that immunity go for Drew as well?"

Wincing, Babs quipped, "No, I notice. I just don't let myself go down that particular rabbit hole. No sense in wanting something you can never have."

About to retort, Julie's words halted in her throat as Babs stopped one of the guards moving past a large group of tourists that were gathered around a guide. In a loud voice, she asked, "Can you tell us where the Mayan exhibit is?"

The guard smiled widely at the two of them, then promptly pointed them in the right direction. Thanking him, they turned and moved toward the wide staircase heading to the second floor of the right wing.

"I have to admit," Julie said as they walked up the staircase, "there are a lot more people here than I thought."

"When I knew we were coming, I looked up some information on this museum," Babs said. "It has one of the most comprehensive art collections in America. The left wing was added less than ten years ago."

"When I was reading about the Mayan artifacts exhibit, I saw where the new renovation brought in work from South and Central America," Julie said as they rounded the top of the staircase and made their way toward the exhibit.

As they stepped through the entryway, Julie smiled at the works of art displayed. There were decorative pieces of pottery with detailed scenes painted on them. Another case contained gold and jade stonework. A large portrait mask that would have been of an important figure, possibly a ruler, was displayed in the next case. She forced herself to stand in front of each display, pretending to read the information about the object while being terrified that Joseph was suddenly going to appear next to her.

As though reading her mind, Babs whispered, "You're doing great. If it makes you feel better, I can tell you that Blake is in the room with us, and Bray is just on the other side of the doorway."

She wished that Walker could be with her or that he would be near, but Mace had insisted that he and Drew stay out of sight. They were the two that Joseph would recognize and give away their presence.

The next display definitely captured her attention as it was an intricately carved incense burner top. The details included the rendering of a human head with wide, circular ear flares and a large headdress. It was so similar to the many carvings she saw on the pyramids and temples. It had only been a couple of weeks, but right now Mexico seemed very far away. Closing her eyes for an instant, she tried to remember the feelings she had when she saw the wonderful Mayan cities, but her eyes jerked open at the memory of seeing Joseph with the gun in his hand. Swallowing deeply, she allowed Babs to lead her around as she forced her thoughts back to the task at hand. More cases of painted vases decorated with Mayan gods, dishes, and jewelry were displayed.

In the farthest case was a U-shaped yoke to be worn around the waist of the ballplayers. She instantly remembered Hernando leading her and the girls around the ball courts at the various cities. A slight smile curved her lips at that memory, and she vowed that one day she would be able to think of her trip to Mexico and remember the many wonderful things that she had experienced.

She heard a soft whisper and glanced to the side, seeing Babs speaking into her hidden radio. Tate had set her up with an undetectable earpiece and microphone. Looking at her, Babs then said, "No one has spotted him. Let's keep moving around."

As they made their way into the jewelry exhibit, a large group of high school students was pushing by them, causing both women to be jostled apart. Julie felt a sudden onslaught of panic, breathing easier when Babs grabbed her hand and pulled them back together. "I can't believe how crowded the museum is today," she complained. "All these people make it hard for me to see who's coming up on us."

Shaking her head, Babs said, "No, it's really better. Joseph would feel more secure in making a move when there are lots of people around. It's the best way to draw him out."

"That's what I'm afraid of," she muttered.

Babs grinned and assured, "Don't worry."

They walked past the exhibits of Egyptian beaded, broad collar necklaces and breastplates, ancient Greek golden earrings, inlaid Persian earrings, and fifth-century Korean necklaces. Vowing to come back to the museum at a time when she could relax and appreciate the exhibits, Julie was glad when Babs said, "I'm hungry. Let's hit the museum cafeteria before it gets too crowded."

Making their way to the basement, they discovered that other people had the same idea. The teenagers had not made it down yet, but a large group of Japanese tourists was placing their orders, their guides trying to handle the money exchange. There was even a crowd near the soda dispensers.

"Why don't we just get something to drink?" Julie suggested, looking at the long line near the food.

"Agreed!" Babs responded.

After standing in line, they paid for two sodas and proceeded to a table, sliding into the plastic seats, placing their order number where it could be seen. A young female server, a tired smile on her face, walked over with a tray containing their sodas.

"Is it like this every day?" Julie asked.

"I've only been working here for a few months as part of my work-study scholarship," the server replied. "I was told that the last weeks of summer are the busiest, and I have to admit it's true. We've been swamped for the past three weeks. I make it back to the counter and the next order is ready for me to deliver."

Handing her a generous tip, they looked at each other and grinned, glad to be sitting after walking around the museum for the past two hours. Glancing around surreptitiously, Julie whispered, "Are we still under surveillance?"

Babs laughed and nodded. "The only place we're not is in the ladies' room, but even there, we'll stick together."

Taking a sip of her soda, Babs scrunched her face and gave her head a shake. "I didn't order a diet drink. Did I get yours by mistake?"

"No, I ordered two regular sodas."

Taking another sip, Babs said, "Ugh. It must be flat."

Julie slurped some of hers through the straw and said, "Mine is fine. It's not flat at all."

Taking another large sip, Babs made another face before pushing it away. "Damn, I thought I could drink it because I'm thirsty, but that's nasty."

Scooting her drink to the other side of the table, Julie said, "Here. Have some of mine. I don't need to drink the whole thing anyway."

"Thanks," Babs said and reached her hand across the table for the cup. Her hand began to shake, then flopped palm up on the table.

Julie watched Babs' face go slack, her mouth falling open before she slumped forward. "Babs! Babs! Oh, my God! Babs!" She had no idea which Keeper would be close, but she screamed, "Help!"

Almost instantly Rank appeared at her side, gently

lowering Babs to the floor as he radioed for assistance. Bray rushed into the cafeteria, making his way to them. Julie scrambled to the side so that they could see to Babs, who was lying unconscious on the floor. *He was here! That drink must've been meant for me!* She stared in horror as her fears for Babs intensified.

39

Mace had assigned Walker and Drew to the outside surveillance, not wanting to take a chance that Joseph would recognize either of them. For the last several hours they had monitored the women's progress as they moved through the museum, coordinating the movements of the Keepers inside.

At the first sound of a scream, Walker's heart jolted, and he jumped up from his seat in the back of their van. Thinking Joseph had gotten to Julie, he barely registered as Rank's voice announced that Babs was down. He and Drew rushed from the van, parked on the side of the building, both intent on seeing firsthand what had happened. Almost immediately Bray's voice came across the radio, calling for an ambulance for Babs to get to the cafeteria. Tate was still in the van, and Walker knew that he would take care of the emergency call.

Just as Drew was bolting toward the front door of the museum, Walker called out, "I'm going to the back cafeteria entrance. If that's where he was, that's where he's coming out."

Drew hesitated for a second and Walker saw the anguish on his friend's face. "Go. Go to Babs."

They separated, and Walker ran around the building, calling out his position so the other Keepers would know where he was. Rounding the corner, the back of the museum extended for two city blocks. A bread delivery truck was near a back entrance, and as he neared, a man came running out, jerking a white coat off his body, tossing it to the side.

Not close, he still was able to recognize Joseph's grey, military haircut and stocky build. His feet pounded the pavement as he raced forward. Joseph, obviously hearing the approaching, running footsteps, turned and looked behind him before running in the opposite direction.

Radioing his pursuit, he continued pounding the pavement, each step eating up more distance between him and Joseph. The race was on, and Walker knew he was going to win. He was younger. More fit. Faster. And fuckin' pissed.

Aware of his surroundings, he noticed when Mace darted around the other end of the building, cutting off any chance that Joseph would be able to get away. Joseph stumbled slightly just as Walker kicked in an extra spurt of speed. Seeing the older man reach toward his pocket for a possible weapon, Walker leaped into the air, tackling him to the ground.

The force knocked the wind out of Joseph's lungs,

and Walker took advantage with his fists landing against Joseph's jaw.

Blake came up from behind, having come through the museum cafeteria. Walker reared back, ready to throw another punch, when Mace ordered, "Stand down."

His chest heaving, Walker felt the rage flow through every fiber of his being and held the position of raised fist for a moment, until Mace's words slowly penetrated the red filling his vision.

Hands zip-tied behind his back, Joseph was hauled to his feet by Mace and Blake. Blood was coming from his mouth and nose, but he grinned nonetheless.

"You have nothing on me. No proof. Nothing that will stick," Joseph said, then spit saliva and blood at Walker's feet.

A white van came driving around from the side, parking next to them. The door opened and Mace shoved Joseph inside. Moving to the back door, Walker growled, "Don't think you're getting off so easy, old man. Where you're going, you'll get what's coming to you."

"You can't get away with this!" Joseph argued.

In the driver's seat, Tate turned around and grinned. "Clay took care of us. Video cameras wiped. Security cameras wiped. Traffic cameras wiped."

Walker looked down at Joseph's stunned face and said, "It's like we weren't even here, asshole."

Blake climbed into the van, and Mace moved around to the side. Stopping before he climbed in as well, he turned to Walker and said, "We've got him. Just got radio notice that the ambulance has arrived for Babs, but according to Bray, she'll be fine. You go see to your girl."

Without hesitation, he turned and ran toward the back cafeteria door that Joseph had run out of. Pushing his way through surprised food service workers, he weaved his way between counters and ovens until he raced into the large cafeteria.

The paramedics were loading Babs onto a gurney, Drew hovering nearby, his face full of anguish. Rank had his arm around Julie but loosened his hold as soon as he saw Walker running toward them. She looked over, a trail of tears on her cheeks, and threw open her arms in time for their bodies to slam together, his arms circled tightly around her.

With his lips pressed against the top of her head, he mumbled against her hair, "It's okay. It's okay. You're okay. I've got you now."

She leaned her head back and looked up, her eyes searching his face. "There must've been something in the drink. I think it was supposed to be for me, but I never saw him—"

"Shhh," he hushed, cupping the back of her head with his large hand. "It's okay. We got him."

Eyes wide, she gasped. "You got him?"

"He must have followed you to the cafeteria and made his way over to the drinks. When the server was distracted, he easily poured something in your drink."

"Where is he?" she asked, her voice tinged with panic.

His jaw hardened, but he forced his voice to be easy.

"You don't have to worry about anything, Julie. Where Joseph's going, there will be no escape."

She sighed heavily in relief, pressing her cheek against his steady heartbeat once again. He sucked in a ragged breath, letting it out slowly, reveling in the feeling of her safely tucked in his arms. *Yeah, where Joseph's going, there's no coming back.*

"I want to go to the hospital with Babs," she said, twisting her head to look toward the door where paramedics rolled Babs out.

"Absolutely, babe. I'll take you anywhere you want to go."

That evening, with Joseph in a private holding cell, the Keepers met. While the mood was somewhat upbeat with Babs' positive prognosis and the capture of Joseph, Mace was furious that he had not anticipated Joseph attempting poison instead of a full, frontal attack.

"Boss, everything about an executioner for a cartel suggested he would go with a weapon," Rank said, quickly echoed with affirmatives from the others.

Walker thought Mace's jaw would crack with tension as he argued back, "We're the best because we expect the unexpected. We're lucky that because he was in a hurry, he dumped too much poison into the drink, giving it a bitter taste. If he had been more adept at poisoning, we may have lost one or both women, and that's unacceptable."

As usual, Mace set aside his ire and focused on the

results of their capture. "I've spoken with José, and he'll meet Drew and Walker for the transfer. Assigned to one of the harshest work camps, Joseph will spend the rest of his life in his unofficial incarceration. Cruel to some, but that's not our worry. The man's a killer, and as far as I'm concerned, he'll get what's coming to him."

"Amen to that," Walker bit out.

"Thank God for Drew's actions," Bray said. "I hesitated, not knowing what Babs had swallowed, but Drew just grabbed her head, stuck his fingers down her throat to make her gag, and she threw everything up. Maybe not the best technique in medical practice, but it was effective."

"When she recuperates, LSI is sending her on a cruise," Mace announced. "I think she deserves a vacation."

"How's Julie?" Tate asked, drawing everybody's attention to Walker.

Expelling the breath from his lungs, he thought back to his heart pounding fear when he heard her screaming over the radio. "She's good. Shaky, of course, but she's a real trooper. She's thrilled that Joseph was caught but feels guilty that Babs ended up getting the poison that was meant for her."

The others shook their heads, murmuring that it was not her fault.

"I know that, and intellectually, she knows that, too. I think once she sees Babs up and talking again, she'll feel better."

The meeting continued for a few more minutes before Mace dismissed them to finish the reports. As everyone dispersed from the conference table, Walker made his way over to Mace, saying, "I know you're kicking yourself because we didn't anticipate Joseph using poison, but Mace, we got him. And I just wanted to thank you for kicking my butt in the direction of realizing that Julie's the woman I want to be with. I have no idea where our relationship will go from here, but at least I know what my feelings are for her."

The tension visibly relaxed in Mace's shoulders as he smiled. "Good to hear, Walker." Mace cast his gaze to the side, where Sylvie sat at her desk. As though she knew she was being observed, she lifted her gaze toward her husband and smiled.

Walker remembered all the times that Julie had looked at him with the same affection in her eyes, smiling. Vowing to do what he could to keep the smile on her face, he finished his report quickly and headed out of the compound, anxious to see her again.

Early the next morning, Walker watched from the copilot seat as Drew's small plane landed at a secure, discrete airstrip in southern Florida.

They taxied to a hanger where another private jet sat waiting. He alighted from the aircraft and walked toward the man standing nearby. Tall, muscular but lean, his black hair trimmed short and eyes hidden behind reflective, aviator sunglasses. Sticking out his hand, he already knew the man's identity, but questioned anyway, "José Munoz?"

José nodded, a smile firmly on his face, and clasped Walker's hand in a firm shake as he slid his sunglasses off with his other hand.

"I cannot tell you how glad I am I that you are bringing me a present," José said, his smile widening at his own joke. "It's something that I have wanted for a long time."

Looking over his shoulder as Drew alighted from the aircraft, a handcuffed Joseph in tow, he met José's grin with one of his own. "I hope you have something special planned for your present."

José's smile faltered, and he replied, "My country has a cancer on its very soul, and I am dedicated to cutting it out even if I have to do it piece by piece." Nodding toward the approaching Joseph, he continued, "He is not as high level as I would like to get my hands on, but because of his background, he rose quickly through the ranks in the last several years. It's been rumored that he was considered by the New Generation Cartel to be one of their most vigorous interrogators and executioners. Getting my hands on him will go a long way in cutting out more of the cancer."

"I wish you the best," Walker said, both impressed with the man standing in front of him and awed at his dedication. "A good friend was recently touring your country. She loved the beauty and the history. I was only able to spend a short amount of time there, but through her eyes, I was also able to experience some of it myself."

Shaking his head with an air of sadness, José said, "Mexico is beautiful and is rich with history. There is so much to offer the world, and yet, men like this piece of trash you captured make my country a feared place for others to visit." Sucking in a quick breath, he added, "It may seem to some that my job is futile, but eradicating this threat is what I'll do to my last breath."

With renewed respect for the job José was committed to doing, Walker said nothing as Drew approached, his hand tightly around Joseph's upper arm, hands handcuffed behind his back.

Joseph's face had several new bruises, and he held his body stiffly as though his ribs were injured.

José stared at Joseph for a moment and then said, "It looks as though your visit to the United States was a little hard on you."

Joseph glared, but Drew chuckled, saying, "I don't understand it. He just kept running into my fist."

José kept his gaze firmly on Joseph, and said, "I see recognition in your eyes. You know who I am. You know to fear me."

Joseph sneered, "Who doesn't know the head of the Mexican Federal Crimes Unit? But you've got nothing on me. This sham of an arrest will not stand up in court."

Walker watched the exchange with interest, seeing José's lips slowly curve into a smile.

"You see, Joseph, that's where you are mistaken," José began. "This is not an official arrest. In fact, this is not an official anything. Where I am taking you, there will be no coming back. I have the right to assign you to a labor camp...a particularly *difficult* labor camp."

Joseph's eyes widened in fear, but José simply

continued to smile then turned toward Walker. "One of the great things about my position is that the government has afforded me certain *liberties* in cleaning up the cartels." Turning, he waved his hand, signaling two armed men over. They took possession of Joseph and marched him to the Mexican plane.

Thrusting his hand forward again, he said, "Give Mace my best, and assure him that Joseph will have many years of hard labor in front of him."

Walker and Drew shook hands with José and watched as he began walking toward his plane as well. Stopping, he turned and called back, "I hope you will give my country a chance again and come visit. Mexico would welcome you with its hospitality." With a final wave, he climbed the steps into the private jet, and Walker watched as it rolled down the runway, lifting into the air.

Shifting his gaze over to Drew, his grin spread wider as he asked, "He kept running into your fist?"

Maintaining a straight face, Drew nodded. "Yeah, it was the damnedest thing. I'd hold my fist up, and Joseph would just keep running right into it." Shaking his head, he repeated, "Damnedest thing."

Slapping his friend on the shoulder, the two men walked toward their plane, both ready to get back to Maine.

40

Three days. Three days of hanging out with some of the Keepers at the lighthouse and double dating with Rank and Helena. Three days of walks along the rocky shores and hiking through the thick forests. Three days of dining out in restaurants and cooking together in his kitchen. Three days of snuggling on the couch watching TV, learning about each other, laughing together, and sharing.

Three days of checking on Babs who had come home from the hospital and was excitedly getting ready to leave on her LSI-gifted cruise. Babs was surprised at first, but Mace told her that anyone who was seriously injured in the line of duty got a vacation. Considering she knew their schedules, she knew he was telling the truth, so she agreed joyfully.

And three nights of making love, discovering each other's bodies, soft touches, energetic sex, and whispers in the night.

For Julie, it had been three days and three nights of bliss, and with each passing hour that brought her closer to the end of her vacation, she felt her heart tugging a little more. It had been so easy to whisper her vows of love the other night when he was sleeping. But in the light of day, she found the words halting in her throat once again.

Now, they had driven sixty miles to Acadia National Park, another place that Walker wanted to show her. They had crossed the bridge to Mount Desert Island and driven around the Park Loop Road. Everywhere she looked, the beauty of Maine took her breath away. Cliffs leading down to the crystal blue water. Rocky shores. The road winding through a forest of thick, green trees. Several times he stopped the car and they got out to walk to one of the scenic overlooks.

She stood at the railing staring out over the forest leading right down to the edge of the ocean, the sun warm on her face and the breeze gently blowing her hair. Deeply inhaling the clean fresh air, she felt the cares of the world drift away.

"Walker, it's absolutely beautiful. It's the most breathtaking sight I've ever seen."

He stood behind her, his arms surrounding either side of her, his hands resting next to hers on the rail. Whispering in her ear, he agreed, "Yes. Absolutely the most breathtaking sight I've ever seen."

She twisted her head around, catching him staring at her. She blushed as she said, "I was talking about the ocean."

His lips curved into a smile, and he replied, "And I was talking about you."

Staying within his embrace, she twisted around so that her back was leaning against the rail and her front was pressed against his. She slid her hands from his forearms up to his shoulders before looping them behind his neck, pulling them even closer. Standing on her tiptoes, she touched her lips to his, feeling the strength in his body and the tenderness of his kiss.

Gathering her courage, she said, "This place makes me want to not go back to hot, humid Florida."

A flash moved through his eyes, but she was unable to interpret it. Hesitating, she chewed on the side of her lip as she pondered how much more to confess.

He leaned down, taking her lips in his own with another kiss. Lifting his head, he held her gaze and asked, "What would it take to get you to stay?"

She had always been honest with him since the moment they met and decided that even if he rejected her, she would rather he know her feelings. Keeping her fingers tightly around the back of his neck, she said, "I would just need for the man I love to feel the same way about me."

Another flash moved through his eyes, but this time she could tell it was a twinkle that matched the smile spreading across his handsome face. She held her breath, waiting to see what he would say, and he did not make her wait long.

"I kept waiting for the right time to say this," he admitted, "and I guess this is it. Julie, I love you. I think I started falling in love with you the first time you went all *mama bear* on me, making sure the girls were taken care of in Mexico. I think I fell more in love with you when you put up with everything, never complaining. When you offered yourself to me on the top of the pyramid in the evening sun, I thought I'd died and gone to heaven, and not just because it was every man's dream come true, but because to me, you were *my* dream come true."

Joy moved through every part of her body, but she worried her bottom lip again, hoping to keep the tears at bay. Swallowing deeply, she whispered, "What now?"

Pulling her tighter, he said, "Could you be happy here in Maine?"

Her spirits soared, and she answered, "I can be happy anywhere with you."

"My job is here, Julie. I need to be here."

She held his gaze and said, "I know that, sweetie. But I can work in any school." She sighed, and added, "I would have to put some things in place first, though. I need to see if there any jobs around here that I can apply for. The school year is almost ready to start so I doubt that I can find something right away. But if the cost of living isn't too high here, then I can take something even temporary. I would have to go back to Florida and put in my notice." Sucking in a quick breath, she added, "Am I crazy? Is this too soon?"

"Only you can answer that, babe. Only you can decide if the time is right and this is what you want to do. For me? It's absolutely right, but I know you're the one who's having to uproot your life."

"I'll have a lot to put in place. I admit it feels scary…

finding a new job, moving to a new state, all for a man that I haven't known very long. Some people would even say that it isn't very smart, but being with you makes me happy. Like the parts of my life that didn't seem to fit before, when I'm with you, they fit."

"I want you with me, however we can make that work," he vowed. Lifting his hands to cup her face, he kissed her lightly once more before pulling her in tightly, tucking her head under his chin. "I won't rush you. You take all the time you need, but just know that I'm here, waiting for you, loving you."

They turned their bodies slightly, staying entwined in each other's arms, and watched as the waves continued to crash against the rocks, the gulls dove into the sea, and the sun moved across the blue sky, warming the couple below.

---

4 months later

Walker shook the snow from his boots as he got to the front door of his apartment. His hands were full with the tree that had been tied to the top of his SUV. Throwing open the door, he stepped inside, propping the tree up against the wall while he shucked off his coat and gloves and toed off his boots.

The gas logs in the fireplace were lit, emitting warmth as well as a warm glow about the room.

Hearing a giggle, he grinned as he stepped further into the living room. Julie was sitting on the sofa with her laptop propped on the coffee table. He leaned his shoulder against the entrance to the room with one wool-socked foot crossed over the other and admired the view.

"I think that's wonderful, Tiffany! If you're going to Tufts University in Boston, I can definitely come visit you easily." She looked up, caught sight of Walker standing there and grinned. Turning back to her computer screen to finish her Skype, she added, "There's a great museum there, and last summer they had an exhibit of Mayan artifacts. Maybe it will still be there this next summer when you arrive on campus."

He rolled his eyes as he moved from the doorway, heading into the kitchen. Pulling a beer from the refrigerator, he twisted off the top, taking a long swig. As he closed the refrigerator door, his gaze snagged on a few of the photographs held in place with magnets. Pictures from his time in Florida when he went down to help her get things packed up. Pictures from Thanksgiving, spent at his parents' house, with all his relatives excited to see him bring home a girl. A weekend spent in Pennsylvania meeting her family. And, front and center, the picture of them at the Tulum ruins

Finishing his beer, he walked back to the front door to get the tree. He could not help but listen as she continued her conversation.

"I miss you girls so much, but I do like my new school. It's much bigger than your school, but I find that all students have most of the same problems, and I feel like I have a lot that I can offer them. Plus, it was amazing that there was a counselor going on maternity leave right after school started, and I was able to take her position. She's also just announced that she's not coming back, so I get to keep the job for the rest of the year."

Hefting the tree up in his arms, he carried it into the living room, and she said, "Walker is back with the Christmas tree, so I have to go now. Please give Jackie and Andrea my love, tell your parents I said hello, and we'll talk again soon."

She closed her laptop and scrambled up from the sofa to help hold the base for the tree as he settled it into the stand.

"Babe, you didn't have to stop your conversation on my account." Looking down, he admired her ass as she was bent over, shimmying out from under the tree. She sat back on her heels, looked up at him, and smiled.

"We were finished talking anyway, and I wouldn't miss this for anything. Our first tree and our first Christmas together."

"Did I hear that Tiffany has decided which college she wants to go to?" he asked, holding out his hand to assist her up.

Nodding as she stood, she enthused, "Yes. She's decided to go to Tufts in Boston." Stepping closer, she slid her arms around his waist and slanted her eyes up toward him. "I told her that there was a lovely Mayan exhibit there."

He palmed her ass and said, "I heard. Very funny."

Lifting on her toes, she planted a kiss on the underside of his jaw, then said, "Let's decorate the tree to celebrate our first Christmas together as a couple."

It took almost an hour for them to hang the lights and all the decorations on the large tree. Standing back, he wrapped his arms around her as they admired their handiwork. Taking her hand, he led her next to the tree and said, "Stand there and admire it, and I'll get a picture of you."

He took several pictures with his phone, some as she made a goofy face and others as she smiled beautifully. Finally, he said, "Okay, now for the last one. Look at the special ornament tied with the red ribbon, right to the side of you."

Julie turned, her eyes searching the tree, before landing on the red ribbon he indicated. Bending closer to see what it was, she gasped, her hand flying to her mouth. Turning back to him, her eyes dropped as he smiled up at her, kneeling on bent knee.

"Take the ring from the tree, babe."

Her fingers shook as she did what he asked and then turned back to him. He took the ring from her hand, then slid it onto her finger. "I know what a sacrifice it was for you to uproot your entire life and move here to be with me. I want to spend the rest of my life proving to you that you made the right decision. From the moment I first fell in love with you, I knew that I wanted you to be my wife. Will you do me that honor?"

She dropped to her knees, tears falling freely, and cried, "Yes. Yes. Yes. A thousand times yes!"

She threw her arms around his neck, her lips immediately finding his. He pulled her tightly to him. She moaned into his mouth, and that little sound was all it took for him to burn for her.

Angling his head, he took the kiss deeper, reveling in the feel of her in his arms. He mumbled against her lips, saying, "You want to take this to the bedroom?"

She shook her head and mumbled in return, "No way."

Leaning back in surprise, he watched as the firelight reflected in her eyes and her smile widened.

"I want to make love right here in the living room in front of the fireplace and next to our first Christmas tree."

His heart warmed at her words as they kneeled together, their hands peeling off each other's clothes.

Later, still lying on the rug in front of the fireplace, their arms around each other, legs tangled, breathing beginning to slow, he vowed to celebrate every Christmas exactly the same way. And prayed that they would have a lifetime of Christmases together.

The End

Don't miss the next Baytown Boys
Baytown Boys (small town, military romantic suspense)
Coming Home
Just One More Chance
Clues of the Heart
Finding Peace
Picking Up the Pieces
Sunset Flames

Waiting for Sunrise
Hear My Heart
Guarding Your Heart
Don't miss other Maryann Jordan books!

Heroes at Heart (Romance)
Zander
Rafe
Cael
Jaxon
Asher (Coming 2019)
Zeke (coming 2019)

Lighthouse Security Investigations
Mace
Rank
Walker (coming 2019)

Saints Protection & Investigations
(an elite group, assigned to the cases no one else wants…or can solve)
Serial Love
Healing Love
Revealing Love
Seeing Love
Honor Love
Sacrifice Love
Protecting Love
Remember Love
Discover Love
Surviving Love

Celebrating Love

Follow the exciting spin-off series:
Alvarez Security (military romantic suspense)
Gabe
Tony
Vinny
Jobe

Letters From Home (military romance)
Class of Love
Freedom of Love
Bond of Love

The Love's Series (detectives)
Love's Taming
Love's Tempting
Love's Trusting

The Fairfield Series (small town detectives)
Emma's Home
Laurie's Time
Carol's Image
Fireworks Over Fairfield

Please take the time to leave a review of this book. Feel free to contact me, especially if you enjoyed my book. I love to hear from readers!
Facebook
Email
Website